## "Cut the crap, Blair.
## I know why you're here."

She shook her head in frustration; this was not going the way she'd planned. "Lucas—"

"I'll make this simple for you," he said, not concealing his anger. "If you're here to ask for my help, the answer is no."

"That's unfair," she cried. "You haven't even heard what I have to say."

"I'm not interested."

"My brother's innocent. He didn't murder that girl."

"Sounds like the D.A. has an airtight case."

"I know you can poke holes in everything he has."

Lucas's eyebrows shot up. "Really? So you need a cutthroat attorney? That's what you called me, isn't it? A cutthroat attorney putting criminals back on the streets for big bucks and personal gain."

Her cheeks grew hotter and she gripped her hands together. "Yes, I said that," she admitted. "And at the time I meant it. I had my reasons for feeling that way...."

Blair realized her hopes were dwindling fast. "Blake and I are twins," she said. "We're closer than most siblings." She took a deep shuddering breath. "I can't let him be convicted of a crime he didn't commit. *Please* help me."

Dear Reader,

I would like to take this opportunity to thank you for your many letters and e-mail messages concerning *The Truth About Jane Doe* and *Deep in the Heart of Texas*. I'm so pleased you enjoyed the books.

*Straight from the Heart* is a story about Lucas Culver, Jacob's brother in *Deep in the Heart of Texas* (published in August 2000). He was a strong character in that book and my editor and I felt he would make a great hero. So my job began: finding the perfect woman for Lucas.

Lucas is an outgoing, well-liked defense attorney who truly believes that everyone is innocent until proven guilty. I had to find a woman who was his complete opposite so I'd have something to write about! The heroine is Blair Logan, a courageous, straitlaced assistant district attorney; she's dedicated her life to putting criminals behind bars. How these two people come together in a quest for love and truth—that's what this book is about. I hope it will keep you turning the pages.

From my heart to yours, I give you Lucas and Blair's story. Enjoy.

Sincerely,

*Linda Warren*

Thanks again for the many letters. I love hearing from you. I can be reached at P.O. Box 5182, Bryan TX 77805 or you can e-mail me at LW1508@aol.com.

# Straight from the Heart
## Linda Warren

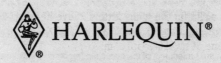

# HARLEQUIN®

TORONTO • NEW YORK • LONDON
AMSTERDAM • PARIS • SYDNEY • HAMBURG
STOCKHOLM • ATHENS • TOKYO • MILAN • MADRID
PRAGUE • WARSAW • BUDAPEST • AUCKLAND

ISBN 0-373-70991-9

STRAIGHT FROM THE HEART

I dedicate this book to my parents.

When I think of my dad, I remember his big heart, his wonderful sense of humor and his belief that I could do anything. He's the reason I had enough courage to try my hand at writing. Ever since I can remember, I have loved to read. Whenever my dad saw me reading, he'd say, "Girl, you always got your head in a book." One day, just to get my attention, he added, "You should be reading those encyclopedias I spent so much money on, then you'd be learning something." After that, when he saw me reading, I'd say before he could, "No, Daddy, I haven't read those encyclopedias yet." It became a standing joke between us. Then one day, out of the blue, he said, "Girl, you've read so many books, why don't you write one?" That's how the dream began.

Sadly, before my dream could become a reality, my dad passed away. But when a senior editor at Harlequin called to say she wanted to buy my first book, I could almost hear his voice. And I said, before he could, "No, Daddy, I haven't read those encyclopedias yet, but I've learned something. Hard work pays off. Just like you taught me."

So I dedicate this book to my father, James Siegert.

And to my mother, Mary Siegert. When I think of my mother, words fail me. She was the center of our family, always there for her children, and since I was the only girl, we had a close relationship. When Alzheimer's took her mind, it was the biggest heartbreak of my life. She passed away while I was writing this book. She is at peace now and she is with my dad and she remembers. Momma, I love you—always.

And to the other mother in my life, my mother-in-law, Faye White, who breaks the stereotypes about mothers-in-law. Thanks for the love and support.

And a special thanks to Gil Schultz, the investigator, and Laurie Siegert, my lawyer niece, who answered all my questions with patience and understanding.

Any errors you find are definitely mine.

# CHAPTER ONE

BLAIR LOGAN HELD her breath as the jurors filed into the jury box. She studied their faces, trying to gauge their state of mind. Their solemn expressions told her nothing. *Look at me,* she begged. *Let me know you're on my side.* But the jurors' attention was focused on the judge. That wasn't bad and it wasn't good. She folded her hands in her lap and waited.

"Madam Foreperson, have you reached a unanimous verdict?" the judge's voice rang out.

The foreperson stood. "Yes, we have, Your Honor," she answered and handed a piece of paper to the bailiff. The bailiff took it to the judge, who read it quickly and handed it back.

"Will the defendant please rise," the judge said.

Hector Raye, along with his attorney, Lucas Culver, got to their feet.

"What is your verdict, Madam Foreperson?" the judge asked.

"On the count of the indictment—murder in the first degree. We find the defendant guilty."

Yes, yes, yes, ran jubilantly through Blair's mind, but nothing showed on her face. She didn't even blink at the rumble of noise and voices behind her. She was good at hiding her emotions.

"Quiet," the judge ordered and banged his gavel. "So be it. Sentencing will be in two weeks. The jury is dismissed." The gavel banged again.

Blair got to her feet and put papers into her briefcase with methodical movements. Outwardly she was cool and reserved, as always. Inside she was ecstatic. She had finally beaten Lucas Culver. She was determined that he wouldn't beat her again. She felt like jumping up on the table and doing a dance of victory, but she would celebrate later.

As the guards came to escort Hector back to his cell, he suddenly jerked free and began to fight them. It didn't take the guards long to restrain him.

"I'll get you, bitch," he screamed at Blair. "I'll get you."

Blair's jubilance vanished in a wave of nausea and she had to take several deep breaths. She knew she had to get out of the courtroom and fast.

Lucas was taken aback at Hector's outburst. He did his best to believe in his innocence, but he'd never liked the boy. He'd taken over the case from a colleague who had become ill. It was a bad situation, but he didn't regret his decision to help Jim Tenney. The case was known as an open and shut, and there was very little he could do to throw doubt on Hector's guilt. The loss didn't sit too well with him, though. But in light of Hector's behavior, he was thinking that maybe it wasn't a bad verdict.

He'd looked at Blair during the disturbance, and her creamy white skin had paled. Of course, it was hard to tell with Blair, since she always wore that cool facade, but he knew Hector had gotten to her.

He picked up his briefcase and turned at the same time as Blair. They came face-to-face. She had dark hair, almost black, pulled back in a knot at the nape of her neck, giving her a stern, businesslike appearance, but he was mesmerized by her eyes. They were the most gorgeous blue he'd ever seen, clear and bright like a summer sky, and they seemed to look right through him. She had made it very plain on more than one occasion that he was not on her list of favorite people.

"Congratulations, Counselor," he said, his lips curving into a slight smile.

"That's one criminal you won't be putting back on the street," she replied sharply, unmoved by his smile.

Lucas sighed. "Why do you always feel that it's my goal to put criminals back on the street?"

"Because it's what you do—represent vermin."

"Have you forgotten that everyone's entitled to a fair trial—even people like Hector Raye?"

"You live with your ethics and I'll live with mine." With that, she whirled around and headed for the door.

Someone was going to shake Blair Logan one of these days, and it just might be him, Lucas decided.

Blair was receiving congratulations from her assistants when Lucas emerged from the courtroom. Out of the corner of her eye she saw him hugging a blond woman. Jennifer Walker, Judge Barrett's clerk. Lucas must be dating her, Blair thought idly. She'd heard the rumors about Lucas. He changed women the way most men changed their shirts. And the women didn't seem to mind. Lucas was known for the affable breakups and lasting friendships with his lady friends. Well, they were welcome to him. His dark good looks and charming smile did nothing for her.

Why did he make her so angry? *Because he's an arrogant man,* she told herself. And arrogant men seemed to have that effect on her.

All thought of Lucas left her as she spotted her brother, Blake, standing to one side. Being twins, they had the same dark hair and blue eyes, but they were different in so many other ways. Blake had been the wild one, always in trouble. She'd been the quiet, studious one, always striving for excellence.

She walked over to Blake and he smiled at her with an

impish grin that didn't quite reach his eyes. Something was obviously bothering him, but she had no idea what.

"Hi." She smiled, and stood on tiptoe to kiss his cheek. Blake was six feet tall and she was only five foot four. "What are you doing here?"

Blake lived in London and he was home for a brief visit. She hadn't expected him in the courtroom today; she assumed he'd be spending time with their parents.

He grinned again and rocked back on his heels. "I just came to watch my baby sister in the courtroom." Having lived in London on and off for sixteen years, his voice now had an attractive English intonation that still surprised her whenever she heard it.

Adjusting her purse strap, she said, "We're the same age, Blake. We're both thirty-two."

"But I'm three minutes older."

"Big deal."

"It is," he said. "I'm older and male and…" His voice trailed off, and she knew exactly what was on his mind.

"Blake—"

He interrupted her. "When they told Dad he had a son, he probably thought all his prayers had been answered. Little did he know I'd be nothing like him."

Growing up as Sam Logan's son hadn't been easy for Blake. In fact, it had almost been a nightmare, with Blake rebelling every chance he got. In his teens, he was uncontrollable, and their parents sent him away to boarding school in England, hoping a change of environment would help him. It was the first time Blair and Blake had been separated, but the miles hadn't diminished the bond between them.

They'd always been close, but Blair was the stronger one, protecting and shielding her brother from their father's wrath whenever Blake did something stupid. That happened plenty of times. Blake seemed bent on a course to upset their father and Blair was generally caught in the middle. For someone she considered mild and loving, Blake sometimes had an obstinate side she didn't understand.

Blair glanced at him now. "I thought you'd gotten over all that."

He shrugged offhandedly. "I have, but seeing you in the courtroom today, I couldn't help thinking how proud Dad must be of you and how disappointed he must be in me."

"Oh, Blake, I—"

"Evan wants to see you." The district attorney's secretary came up to her, cutting her off in midsentence.

"Tell him I'm on my way," Blair answered, knowing Evan wanted to talk about the trial. For once, it was good news.

Blair quickly kissed Blake's cheek again. "I've got to run. We'll talk tonight after dinner."

As she hurried down the corridor to the underground tunnels that connected many of Houston's downtown buildings, Blair thought about Blake and wished he'd come home to the States to live. Maybe that would mend the rift between father and son, but she knew it was only wishful thinking. Since Blake's rebellious youth and his decision not to go to law school, things hadn't been the same in their family, and she didn't think they ever would be again.

Blake worked as a journalist, but he spent a lot of his time at a school for delinquent youths in London, helping and teaching troubled teenagers. It wasn't the future Sam wanted for Blake, but Blake was good with kids and he seemed determined to steer them away from drugs, drinking and rebellion. Blair decided not to think about her father's reaction. She'd concentrate on spending quality time together as a family.

It was a short walk from the criminal-courts building to the district attorney's office, a walk that gave her a chance to clear her head. She tapped on the district attorney's door and entered when she heard Evan's "Come in." Evan Holt was of medium height and almost completely bald. He stood in the middle of his domain with a golf club in his hands. He was an avid golfer and had a small putting green in his office. He studied the ball in front of him, then glanced at the cup some distance away.

"I'll be right with you, Blair," he said, and swung the club. When the ball rolled in, he turned to Blair with a triumphant smile. "Well, you did it. You beat Culver."

"Yes," she answered. Evan was reputed to know everything that went on in the courthouse...sometimes even before it happened.

Evan moved around his desk and sat down. "You did a great job. Though I must say, clients like Raye aren't usually Culver's style. When Jim Tenney was handling the case, I figured we'd be able to put ol' Hector away for a long time, but when Culver took over, I was worried he'd use some of his theatrics to get Raye off." Evan picked up a pencil. "Never understood why Culver took the case at all."

"I heard that Tenney's an old friend, and when he had to have emergency heart surgery, Lucas stepped in to help him out." Blair repeated the rumors, although she was reluctant to give the man that much credit.

Evan rested back in his chair. "You don't like Culver, do you?"

Blair shrugged in a nonchalant manner. "I don't know much about him. All I know is I don't care for lawyers like him."

"Your father's a lawyer like him."

Blair's eyes narrowed. "What are you getting at, Evan?" She knew he had something else on his mind besides the Raye trial. She'd worked for Evan for six years and she was well acquainted with his tactics. He'd skirt an issue before getting to the point.

Evan leaned forward. "I was thinking about the Easton case and your father's involvement."

There was not a flicker of emotion or movement on Blair's face, even though the name Easton sent chills down her spine. She stared Evan straight in the eye. "My father was his attorney, that's all."

Her father was a well-known defense attorney in Houston, in Texas and beyond. As his daughter, she was expected to follow in his footsteps—as was Blake. After Blake's defection, as her father called it, Sam Logan focused all his efforts on his daughter. He wanted her to work for his firm, but she couldn't because she and her father had different points of view on the law. He defended criminals and it was her goal to keep them behind bars.

This caused more than a few arguments—with Sam insisting that her perspective was oversimplified. She knew her judgment and reasoning was colored by the past, but that didn't make her wrong. It only made her more strong-minded, more—

"I heard there was a disturbance in the courtroom." Evan's words broke in.

"Yes." Blair forced her thoughts back to the present. "Raye wasn't pleased with the verdict."

"Are you okay?"

"Yes." She looked at him with guarded eyes. "Why wouldn't I be?"

"You don't have to be so tough, Blair. I'm well aware of what happened to you."

"It was a long time ago, and like you said, I'm tough. I can deal with it."

"Blair…"

She stopped him. "If that's all, I've got a mound of paperwork waiting for me."

Evan watched her for a moment, then said, "No, that's not all. I brought Todd Easton up for a reason."

God, she knew that. Evan never did anything without a

reason. She waited, wishing that name didn't make her feel so afraid.

"I wanted to inform you of something that's about to break," he said slowly. "Bonnie Davis's family has hired a detective to find the second boy involved in her rape and murder, through new DNA testing. We're hoping to make an arrest."

Blair's eyes widened. "But the police never could identify him."

"Yeah. I was newly elected then, and I really wanted to find him. Skin from two different people was found under Bonnie's fingernails. That really bothered me, but I never could link another boy to the murder. I always wondered why your father didn't pursue it. It could've helped Easton."

"I'm not privy to my father's cases, and I really don't like to talk about Todd Easton."

"I'm sorry," Evan said quickly. "I didn't mean to upset you."

"It doesn't," she said, and they both knew she was lying. She drew a deep breath. "But I would like to prosecute this guy when they catch him."

Evan shook his head. "I don't think so, Blair. You're too closely involved."

"Maybe," she admitted. "But I hope you put him away for a long time."

"I intend to."

"I'd better go," Blair said, backing toward the door. "I've got a lot to do."

Evan stood. "Great job today."

"Thanks."

Blair closed the door, leaning against it as if she needed the support. Why did Evan have to mention the past? Why did he have to bring up Todd Easton? Ever since Raye's outburst, she'd been trying to keep the memories at bay, but now they seemed to come rushing back.

She was sixteen years old and looking forward to spring break. She was going to Cancún, Mexico, with her friend and her friend's family. Her father had just finished a difficult case. A business acquaintance of his had a son who was accused of murdering and raping a fifteen-year-old girl, Bonnie Davis. It was a certainty that Sam Logan would get the boy off, but Todd Easton was found guilty. The Easton family was very upset, especially Todd. It had been a long, hard trial and her father, mother and Blake went on a cruise to get away from the reporters and the Eastons. They wanted her to go, too, but she'd already made other plans.

Everyone had said that Sam Logan was losing his magic touch. It was one of the few cases she remembered her father ever losing; at sixteen, though, she didn't really think about such things. She was just eager to leave on her trip. Her family had left that morning, and Blair was waiting for her ride. She'd heard a noise downstairs, grabbed her suitcase and hurried to the front door. As she reached the bottom step, she saw the housekeeper tied up. Before she could move, Todd appeared from a doorway holding a gun. His eyes had a glazed, wild look, and his face was red. He asked her where her father was. She told him he wasn't home, that he'd gone on a cruise. Todd had laughed cruelly and said that was just as well, because he knew of a better way to get even with Sam Logan. He was leering at her and she knew what he had in mind. She dropped the suitcase and ran up the stairs—but he was faster. He caught her at the top, began to hit her with the butt of the gun... Over and over he drove the gun into her face, her stomach, her chest. Then he started to tear at her clothes. She didn't have much strength left, but she started to fight. Her efforts stilled at the sound of sirens. Todd didn't hear them. He was too engrossed in hurting her.

The police burst into the house. They'd been on Todd's trail since he'd broken out of prison. Although she was floating in and out of consciousness, she heard them yell at Todd to drop the gun. The next thing she heard was gunfire and Todd fell on top of her...dead.

She woke up in a hospital. She had a concussion, a cracked skull, broken jaw, a fractured arm and several broken ribs. Her parents and Blake immediately flew home from their cruise. It was weeks before she was able to leave the hospital and by then she was scared of her own shadow, of everything around her. Her mother wanted her to see a psychiatrist, but she refused. She could handle it by herself, she'd insisted. But the trip back to health was long and arduous, and at times she didn't want to go on. She forced herself to face life and not give up. She'd refused to let Todd Easton destroy her emotionally. And she made it. Yes, she'd made it. She had gotten her degree and was practicing law, putting criminals like Todd Easton away.

She knew that sometimes she went overboard, like today with Lucas. Lucas had a way of getting to her with his handsome face and devil-may-care smile. He was a lot like her father, same charisma, same magnetism. Maybe that was why she resented him and his representation of criminals. But today...today she'd finally triumphed over Lucas. Yes! She'd beaten him and his fancy tricks in the courtroom. And that felt good—really good.

Pushing away from the wall, she headed for her office. She wasn't going to think about the past, her father or anything that would ruin her mood. She wanted to enjoy this moment. She entered her office, kicked off her heels and slipped out of her navy-blue suit jacket. She undid the first three buttons on her white silk blouse. Next she took the pins out of her hair and shook it free to her shoulders.

To alleviate the tension, she started to dance, something she loved to do—ever since she was a child and had taken ballet lessons. It always lifted her spirits. She whirled gracefully around the room singing, ''I won. I won. Whoa-oh-oh. And it feels so-o-o-o good. So-o-o-o good. Oh, oh, oh, yeah.''

LUCAS HURRIED out of the courthouse. He had just enough time to stop by his office before his date with Jennifer. He'd been dating her for a month and she wanted to make dinner for him tonight. That bespoke an intimacy he wasn't ready for. He didn't know if he ever would be. His brother, Jacob, had been after him to settle down. After all, he was now forty-two, but he just could never take that final step. When he got married, he wanted a strong, passionate marriage like his brother's. But the odds of that happening were getting slimmer and slimmer. He was too much like his father, he'd concluded, and he knew the feelings he had about his father were the reason he was still single.

His father had been a policeman who worked long hours—or so they'd believed until they discovered he'd been spending a lot of those hours with other women. The secret came to light when his mistress shot him with his own gun after he decided to end the affair. The news devastated his mother, and she died one week later from a massive heart attack. He'd been only fifteen years old, but he'd never forgotten the hurt, pain and disillusionment in his mother's eyes. He was never going to hurt a woman like that—never. Until he found a woman he could stay faithful to, he planned to remain single.

For some reason he thought of Blair Logan. She was different from the other women he'd met—mainly because she hated his guts. But she'd enjoyed beating him today. Blair would never let her emotions show, but it was no secret that she'd been gunning for him for a long time. He was sure this victory was a big deal for her. That should annoy the hell out of him, but it didn't. In his younger days, he would have been angry at the loss. *Younger days!* Good Lord, now he was thinking in terms of younger days. What the hell was wrong with him?

Lately he'd been feeling a restlessness, a dissatisfaction with everything in his life, and he found himself questioning everything he'd ever done. He was displeased with both his personal and his professional life. He'd worked for Harris and Harris for the past fifteen years and he'd never had any complaints until now. Clive and George Harris were brothers, and now their sons were also attorneys who'd joined the firm. Lucas knew that in the near future he'd probably be working for them and he didn't like that. He was the reason quite a few clients chose Harris and Harris, and everyone knew it. Lucas's salary was raised every year in appreciation, but now he wanted more. He wanted his name on the door. He wanted everything that came with his years of experience and he wasn't willing to settle for less.

Then again, he'd made enough money and invested it wisely. He could retire and move to Austin to be near Jacob and the family. Hell! He shook his head in frustration. He'd spent all his adult life practicing law and he had no intention of giving it up so easily. The restlessness was getting to him, that was all; so was losing this case. He should have never taken it in the first place. Clive and George had advised against it, but he couldn't let Jim down. Jacob had taught him always to stand by your friends and he had, and he refused to have regrets about that. He just wished he'd felt more confident of Hector's innocence. That restlessness again. Good thing he'd scheduled a vacation. He needed one to make some decisions about his life.

"Hey, Culver," a voice called.

Lucas turned and saw Roger Collins, an old friend of his brother's, coming toward him. Roger was in his forties, a police detective who'd worked a lot of cases during his career—some Lucas had been involved with.

They shook hands. "How you doing, Lucas?"

"Fine." Lucas smiled.

"How's Jacob?"

"In love and happy."

"If anyone deserves happiness, it's Jacob," Roger said solemnly.

"I'll second that."

"How many kids does he have now?"

"Five," Lucas said. "They had another girl a few months back."

"That's great...just great."

"Yeah."

Roger changed the subject. "Well, I heard Blair stuck it to you today."

"I wouldn't call it that," Lucas responded mildly.

"You just hate to lose."

"Yes, it's one of those annoying flaws of mine."

"I also heard Raye wasn't pleased with the verdict." Roger looked at him carefully.

"No, he wasn't. He caused an ugly scene."

"Is Blair okay?"

Lucas's eyes narrowed. "Why wouldn't she be?"

"Evidently you haven't heard what happened to her some years back."

"I don't guess I have."

"It was sixteen years ago, so you were probably away at law school." Roger went on to tell him about Blair and the attack by Todd Easton.

"You know, I vaguely remember reading something about that incident—mainly because it was Sam Logan's daughter. Hell, I *knew* she was Sam's daughter, but I never connected it to the attack."

"She's had a rough time. I hope this hasn't upset her."

Lucas grinned. "Sounds like you're pretty fond of Blair."

Roger grinned back. "You could say that, but Blair doesn't let anyone get too close to her. I keep trying, though. Think I'll check on her." He glanced at his watch.

"Damn, I have to be in court in five minutes. I'll catch her later. I've got to run. Tell Jacob I said hi." With that, he dashed into the courthouse.

Lucas stared after him with a puzzled expression. He now understood Blair Logan a little better. No wonder she was so cold and detached. He'd never dreamed she'd had this kind of trauma in her past and was a little surprised he hadn't heard anything about it before. He hoped Raye hadn't caused her any more stress. Still, it was none of his business, he told himself, walking resolutely toward his vehicle.

He threw his briefcase into his Ford Expedition and got into the driver's seat. But he didn't start the engine. He kept thinking about Blair. Maybe he should reassure her that Hector was just talk and she had nothing to worry about. No, he told himself again. She wouldn't thank him for his concern.

Concern? *Was* he concerned for Blair? Yes, he was, he had to admit. He'd always thought Blair was strong enough to handle anything. Could he be wrong? Could her strength only be a facade to hide her fear and pain?

Without a second thought, he climbed out of the car and headed to the district attorney's office. He had to tell her that Hector wasn't a threat to her.

*And Blair Logan was going to eat him alive.*

IT DIDN'T TAKE Lucas long to find Blair's office. The door was open a crack. He pushed it a fraction to see if she was inside. He stared in disbelief. Blair, a Blair he'd never seen before, was dancing around the room singing under her breath. Her dark hair was loose around her shoulders, her eyes sparkled and her face was enraptured. God, she was beautiful. So feminine, so enticing...

She held her arms out and her hips swayed gracefully. She'd had ballet lessons, he decided. It showed in every seductive line of her body.

"It feels so-o-o-o good. Oh, oh, oh, yeah," she sang. She whirled around and came to a complete stop when she saw Lucas.

"OhmyGod," she murmured. She quickly gathered her hair and twisted it into a knot. She reached for a large clasp that lay on her desk and fastened it to her hair, but several strands lingered around her face.

She inhaled deeply and demanded, "What are *you* doing here?"

She'd immediately collected her wits, her cool businesswoman demeanor back in place, but Lucas didn't seem to notice. His eyes were on the opening of her blouse. Several buttons had come undone and her lacy bra was showing. Blair wore lacy things. He'd never have figured that.

"Your blouse is open," he told her, and her cheeks turned a delicate pink.

She nervously buttoned her blouse to the top.

She was mortified that he'd seen her doing a victory dance, and she was desperately striving for some measure of respectability. But she feared she'd lost every ounce of that. Oh God, how had she let this happen? And of all men…Lucas Culver.

"If you're through leering," she said coolly. "You can tell me why you're here."

Lucas realized he had a silly grin on his face, but for the life of him he couldn't stop smiling. "You know," he replied, "it went right out of my head."

"Then you can leave."

His grin broadened. "You really enjoyed beating me today, didn't you?"

He had guessed why she was making a fool of herself. Of course he would! How did she get out of this?

"A victory is always a…pleasure," she answered, and the words sounded phony even to her own ears.

Lucas stepped closer, although the desk was between

them. "If I'd known it would make you so effervescent, I'd have let you beat me a long time ago."

"You didn't *let* me anything," she flared. "I beat you fair and square."

Lucas held up his hands. "Okay, I concede."

They stared at each other and Blair felt his dark eyes touching her in a way she usually hated when other men did it. But Lucas was making her feel warm and bubbly...and angry.

"What do you want, Lucas?" she asked abruptly. "And stop staring at me like that. I don't like it."

"It's hard not to," he said wickedly. "Especially after seeing...so much."

"Get out of my office," she said, her confidence beginning to shred.

Her words had no effect on him. "Don't be so rigid, Blair. I'm only teasing you."

She decided to take another approach. "I'm not used to being teased, so can we just forget about this?"

He lifted an eyebrow. "I don't think so."

"Okay," she snapped. "Have your fun, but you'd better enjoy it because you'll never, ever get another glimpse—"

"Of you being human," he finished for her.

She bit her lip, not knowing what else to say, wishing he'd do the decent thing and leave.

He saw her nervousness and relented. "Okay, Blair, I'll forget about it."

"Fine," she said ungraciously.

"I only came by to reassure you that you had nothing to worry about from Raye. He just has a big mouth."

She glanced apprehensively at him. Surely he didn't know. It had happened so long ago and ever since, her family and friends had been very protective of her feelings. The attack wasn't a topic for idle conversation. She didn't want anyone's pity. "Why do you think I'd be worried?"

He watched her for a moment and he could see she

didn't want him to know about the past. So he gave in to her wishes. "He was my client and I feel responsible for his behavior."

She breathed a sigh of relief. This she could handle. "You don't have to be. I can take care of myself."

"I'm sure you can, but I had to make the effort."

"Well, you wasted your time." That came out wrong, but she couldn't take it back.

His eyes gleamed. "Believe me, I didn't waste my time."

"You said you were going to forget it," she reminded him.

"*Forget* was the wrong word," he said with a devilish grin.

"You're very good with words. So don't tell me that."

"I promise no one will hear about your secret passion from me, but I can't wipe it from my memory. I have a feeling I'll remember it late at night when—"

She cut him off. "Goodbye, Lucas, and next time you plan on coming into my office, would you please have the decency to knock?"

She had to get rid of him. The tension was so thick she had trouble breathing. It was sexual tension and Lucas was very good at creating it. She hated his easy flirting, which created a fear deep inside her. Over the years she had forced herself to date, to come to grips with her terror, but it hadn't worked. Men in any kind of sexual context—the very thought of sex—stirred a revulsion in her that she couldn't control. She was beginning to wonder if she ever would.

With his hand on the doorknob, he said, "You have a thing about intimacy, don't you, Blair? I was only going to say late at night when I feel…" He stopped, then added, "Hell, you were right. I did have something risqué in mind."

Lucas grinned all the way down the hall. Roger was the

wrong man for Blair. She needed someone to unlock all
those emotions she had hidden away. Someone with passion and ardor. He suddenly stopped walking. He was
thinking about himself. No, he was already involved with
Jennifer. He didn't need…but he enjoyed sparring with
Blair—maybe too much, maybe not enough. She made his
blood rush, kept him on his toes. "No," he muttered
aloud. "No way." It wouldn't be the first time he'd fooled
himself about a woman.

AS THE DOOR CLOSED on Lucas, Blair picked up a paperweight and threw it. It bounced off the wall and landed on
the carpet with a thud. *Arrogant bastard,* she thought, and
immediately checked the door to made sure it was locked.
She leaned against it and sank to the floor, drawing her
knees up to her chin. How was she going to live this
down? Lucas had seen her in a state she'd never allowed
any man to see. And the way he'd gazed at her—as though
she was an attractive woman he *liked* looking at. She could
still feel those dark eyes heating her skin, her blood. Oh,
no. *Don't even think it.*

She gulped in some air and did the only thing she could.
She started to laugh. After a moment, she sobered, wiping
tears from her eyes. Despite the turmoil of this day, she
could still laugh. That was good. Maybe Lucas *was* good
for her. No, no, no, she told herself. She wasn't going to
be like every other woman in the courthouse—bowled over
by his charm. She intended to avoid Lucas Culver. Like
the plague.

## CHAPTER TWO

LUCAS DROVE to his office to check his messages and finalize his plans for a long vacation with Jacob and the family. He couldn't believe how much he missed the kids and he couldn't believe how much he enjoyed being an uncle. It would be nice to have his own kids, but he didn't see that in his future.

As he let himself in the side door of his office, Blair's face flashed into his mind. A Blair with her blue eyes dreamy and her dark hair mussed. He shook his head, smiling. He had a feeling that picture was going to haunt him for days.

He sat at his desk dealing with messages, when his secretary, Joan, stepped into the office. At sixty, Joan was a stoic, unflappable woman, an invaluable asset. Her hair was blond with streaks of gray that didn't bother her. She had a husband, three kids and a grandchild, yet she managed to handle all his affairs with effortless ease. She was better than a wife, or so his friends told him. She kept his life organized but didn't nag or complain. At the moment, though, she seemed flushed and out of breath.

He lifted an eyebrow. "What is it, Joan?"

She leaned over and whispered, "Sam Logan is here to see you."

Lucas frowned, thinking he'd heard her wrong. "What did you say?"

"Sam Logan. He wants to see you," she whispered again.

"Why are you whispering? He can't hear us."

"I know…but I've heard all these stories about him and I've never met him. He's very impressive in person."

Lucas had heard the stories, too. Logan was overpowering in a courtroom. In college Lucas had wanted to be like him—a winning lawyer with the respect of his peers. These days Lucas just wanted to be himself.

Why the hell was Sam Logan calling on him?

Had Blair told him what had happened in her office? No, she wasn't that kind of woman.

"What should I tell him?" Joan asked.

"Have you cleared my schedule for a couple of weeks?"

Joan's eyes widened in shock. "Of course, but…surely you're going to see him."

"He doesn't have an appointment, does he?"

"No," Joan said slowly. "But it's Sam Logan."

"So what?"

Joan planted her hands on her hips. "Lucas Culver, what are you trying to pull? You know you're going to see him, so why are you giving me a hard time?"

"I've just never seen you so flustered before." He smiled mischievously. "If it'll make you happy, send the man in."

"Really, Lucas, sometimes…" Her voice trailed away as she left the room.

Lucas got to his feet and fastened a button on his dark gray suit. What a day, he thought. Sam's daughter had just beaten him in court and he'd seen that same daughter in a state of undress. What next?

Sam Logan entered the office. He was solidly built, about five foot ten and weighed maybe one hundred and eighty pounds, Lucas surmised. He had dark hair, almost black, that was beginning to turn gray, and blunt masculine features. Nothing out of the ordinary, but there was something about Sam Logan that drew one's attention. An unmistakable aura of power and strength...

Lucas stayed behind his desk instead of joining him at the door. He felt as if he could now meet Sam Logan on equal ground.

Sam walked over, and they shook hands. "Thanks for seeing me on such short notice," he said, and sat in one of the leather wingback chairs. He was dressed in a tailored navy-blue suit, a pinstriped shirt and navy tie—impeccable in dress and manner.

Lucas glanced at his watch as he took his seat. "I have a few minutes between appointments," he answered. "What can I do for you?"

Sam placed his fingers together in a thoughtful gesture. "I know we've never met, but I've watched your career over the years. You've become a great lawyer and I admire your work."

Praise was the last thing he'd expected from Sam Logan, and he had to resist the urge to shift uncomfortably in his chair. But Sam wasn't going to make him feel like a bumbling lawyer without any experience. A smile touched his face. "I find that ironic since your daughter just beat me in court."

Sam dismissed the comment with a wave of his hand. "Any A.D.A. could have won that case."

For some reason, Lucas didn't like the way that sounded. Sam Logan made it seem as if he didn't have any confidence in Blair. "Don't underestimate your daughter," he said more sharply than he'd intended.

Sam raised a dark eyebrow. "I don't," he answered. "Blair's getting very good in a courtroom, but you and I both know that your heart wasn't in the Raye case."

*Was that obvious to everyone?* Lucas wondered. *Was he losing his edge?*

"However, I don't want to talk about that case," Sam said. "I want to talk about the future."

That caught Lucas's interest. What the hell did his future have to do with Sam Logan?

"You see, I'm thinking about retiring," Sam went on, studying the end of his fingertips. "My associates, Derek Johnson, Frank Mann and Theo Barker, are also getting on in years. I have other attorneys, but they're not measuring up. I need new blood, someone who can control a courtroom and maintain the prestige that is synonymous with my firm." He raised his eyes to Lucas. "You're the best I've seen in a long time. I'd like you to consider working for my company."

"You're offering me a job?" Lucas asked with deceptive calm; he knew there had to be more to this than a job offer. But what?

Sam nodded. "Yes, you can come in as a senior partner with a salary commensurate with that status."

Few things in life shocked Lucas, but this one threw him right into orbit. Logan and Associates offering a senior partnership to a new attorney was unheard of. Like the old saying went—it had to be earned. Sam Logan had the best defense team in the state and no one entered that prized sanctum without paying some dues. So what was Sam Logan up to?

Lucas met his gaze. "How will your top guns feel about this?" It was well known that Sam called his best attorneys "top guns."

Sam suppressed a smile. "You've heard about that?"

"Hasn't everyone?" Lucas quipped. "And I'm not too eager to get involved with office politics."

"I am head of Logan and Associates and I make all hiring decisions. Anyone who has a problem with that can leave." Sam spoke quietly but with force, and Lucas didn't miss the fire in his voice.

Before he could respond, Sam continued. "To be honest with you, my top guns, including me, have begun to lose some firepower. We need someone younger—someone like you.''

Lucas didn't blink. There were more than forty attorneys in Sam's office and some of them were very good. ''I'm happy with my job at Harris and Harris.''

''I've checked into your job status,'' Sam returned. ''You've gone as far as you can go here. Even though you bring in most of the money, Clive and George are not going to promote you over their sons.''

''You seem to know a lot about me.''

Sam stood up. ''I do my homework. You deserve prestige and everything that comes with it. Logan and Associates can give you that.''

Lucas also stood, thinking this day had turned pretty darn interesting. A job offer from Sam Logan... It didn't make sense, and he still wasn't buying a word out of Sam's mouth. There was something else going on; Lucas knew it.

Sensing Lucas's hesitation, Sam reached inside his jacket and pulled out a card and gold pen. ''My wife's giving a dinner party tonight for our son, who's home from London. Some of my business associates will be there. Why don't you come and meet them? Maybe it'll put your mind at rest.'' He scribbled something on the back of the card. ''This is my address. Dinner's at eight.''

Lucas took the card and stared at the prestigious River Oaks address. A dinner party? Oh yeah, this was more than interesting. It was getting bizarre. He wondered if Blair would be there and how she'd react to him sitting down to dinner with her family. She'd probably throw knives and forks at him. Oh yes, this was bizarre.

''I know you're having doubts,'' Sam said. ''But I don't make offers lightly. Give this some serious thought. It could only help your career.''

Lucas's dark eyes caught his. ''Why are you so concerned about my career?''

"I'm not," Sam admitted frankly. "I'm concerned about my firm and its future. The bottom line is numbers, and I believe you have the talent to bring in big numbers."

*Now* they were getting somewhere. It all came down to money. Was that what all this was about? Lucas didn't think so, but for the moment he had to go with what Sam was telling him.

"Think about it," Sam added. "Come to the party, meet the team and then make your decision."

Lucas fingered the card. "I have other plans."

"Break them."

"It isn't that easy."

"Yes, it is, Lucas," Sam said. "If you want to play with my team, you'd better straighten out your priorities."

"I don't like being pressured," Lucas said tersely.

Sam ignored the warning. "If you want to play in the big leagues, get used to the pressure."

Lucas was about to tell him what he could do with his job offer, when Sam walked to the door.

"Think about it, that's all I ask," Sam said. "Dinner's at eight."

FROWNING, Lucas sat staring into space. Sam Logan was manipulating him—but why? Why would a man he'd admired for years suddenly turn up at his office, offering him the job of a lifetime? All he knew was that Sam's offer had made him very curious. He wouldn't be able to concentrate on anything else until he figured out what was behind this generous deal.

Could it have something to do with Blair? No, he didn't think so.

Joan walked in with a piece of paper in her hand. "Well, well, well," she said smugly. "A job offer from Sam Logan. Are you feeling very pleased with yourself?"

Lucas glanced up. "Are you psychic? Or were you listening at the door?"

She smiled. "A little of both."

"There's some ulterior motive here, and I'm going to find out what."

"Has it occurred to you that maybe this is just what it seems to be—a great offer for a great attorney?"

"If I was naive, I'd believe that," he said. "But I haven't been naive since I was fifteen years old."

"What are you going to do?" Joan asked.

Lucas picked up the card on his desk. "I don't know, but I'm thinking of showing up at the Logan house for dinner."

"Oh," Joan said quickly, handing him the piece of paper. "Jennifer called and said she has to work late. She said to meet her at her apartment at eight-thirty, and she wants you to pick up some wine from that little shop she likes. I wrote the address down and the type of wine."

He took the paper with an exasperated sigh. Jennifer was giving him orders. Why did that upset him? Because he didn't like bossy women who wanted to control him. Oh hell, was he having a bad day or what? He wasn't usually this touchy. Jennifer was trying to take their relationship to another level and he could feel himself backing off— as always.

"Thanks, Joan," he said offhandedly.

"Lucas…"

He stopped her. "Don't worry. I'll let you know how it turns out."

She bit her lip, then murmured, "You know, Lucas, I never thought I'd have to stroke your ego, but you're an exceptional attorney. I'm sure Sam Logan recognizes that. So don't do anything stupid."

Lucas grinned. "Have I ever done anything stupid?"

Before she could answer, Lucas held up his hand. "Don't answer that. I'd probably have to take the fifth."

She laughed, shaking her head. "I'd better get home. I've got a family waiting."

After Joan left, he sat thinking about this strange turn of events. He had to make a decision. Did he go to River Oaks or did he spend the evening with a beautiful woman—even if she *was* just a bit controlling? Blair flashed into his mind again, not the Blair in the courtroom but the seductive, dancing Blair. What was she like in her home, with her family?

He ran both hands through his dark hair. Why couldn't he get her out of his head? She was just another woman, he told himself, but he had a hard time believing that.

*Dammit, Blair, what are you doing to me?*

He crumpled Sam's card and threw it into the trash. He wasn't going to get mixed up with the Logan family. He had enough problems of his own.

SAM LOGAN CHARGED into his office and sat in his high-tech office chair, lightly drumming his fingers on the padded arms.

Derek Johnson, Theodore Barker and Frank Mann followed him inside. Frank quietly closed the door. Frank was short, bald and stocky and always had a ready smile. "How'd it go?" he asked.

"What did Culver say?" Derek put in just as quickly. Derek was of medium height, with reddish-blond hair, and was known for both his temper and his finesse in a courtroom.

Sam shrugged. "Hard to tell with Lucas. He knows all the tricks—doesn't let anything show on his face—but I have a feeling he's not planning to accept the offer."

"That bastard," Derek growled. "Doesn't he know when something's being handed to him on a silver platter?"

"That's just it," Sam told him. "Lucas is doing very well where he is. He doesn't need us, but we sure as hell need him."

"That's not true," Derek answered. "I told you from the start that I could handle things. I—"

"Shut up, Derek." Theo spoke up. Theo was tallest of the three men, with a thatch of curly brown hair and blue-green eyes. "You're not Perry Mason, even though you think you are. If Sam doesn't think you can handle it, then—"

Frank interrupted. "Okay, let's just calm down and let Sam tell us what happened."

Sam watched his three top attorneys, his gaze hooded. He folded his hands across his desk and began to speak in a slow forceful manner. "I am still head of Logan and Associates, and I make all hiring decisions without asking your permission. I'm only consulting you as a courtesy. If anyone has a problem with that, you'd better say so now so you can pack your things and get out."

"Wait a minute, Sam." Derek put up a hand. "I was only voicing my opinion…what I think is best for the firm."

Sam's mouth twisted wryly. "You know, Derek, I don't remember ever asking you to take the responsibility for my firm." He put a heavy emphasis on the word *my*.

Derek didn't say another word.

"We either do this together, or I do it alone," Sam added. "Your choice."

"I'm with you, Sam," Frank immediately said.

"Me, too," Theo stated.

All eyes swung to Derek. "I was just questioning whether Culver's the best choice, that's all."

Sam eyed Derek, his expression calculating. "If you have any problems with Lucas, we'd better get them out of the way now, because if we're lucky enough to have him join us, I won't tolerate any dissension among my staff."

Derek glanced down at the desk, clearly struggling.

Sam got up and walked to the window, looking out at

the glass skyscrapers of downtown Houston and the busy streets below.

Silence ensued.

Theo broke the stalemate. "Hell, Derek, why don't you just admit it? You're afraid Culver might outshine you in a courtroom. But this isn't about you and your gigantic ego. It's about the future of the firm."

"I know," Derek admitted grudgingly. "I'm behind Sam all the way."

"That's good to hear." Sam turned from the window. "I just hope things don't come to a head before I get Lucas on board." There was a pause, then he added, "Damn bad luck to have Blake pay us this surprise visit."

"You need to get him back to London, Sam," Theo suggested quietly.

"I will, but first I'll let him spend some time with his mother and sister."

"We don't have the valuable commodity of time," Derek said.

"I'm well aware of that," Sam muttered.

"Have you heard anything else?" Frank asked.

"Not a word," Sam muttered. "Holt's keeping a lid on everything until he's ready to pounce."

"Hell, Sam," Frank said. "Your daughter works at the D.A.'s office. Surely you can get some information out of her."

Sam's eyes turned a steel blue. "I will not drag my daughter into this. Do you understand me?"

Frank's brown eyes narrowed. "My God, you haven't told her, have you?"

Sam looked away. "No. I need to have all my i's dotted and my t's crossed before I tell her. Besides, I won't compromise her job." His face was grim. "Everything depends on tonight."

"What's happening tonight?" Theo asked.

"I invited Lucas to the dinner party," Sam answered.

"If he shows, I know we have a chance of convincing him to accept the offer. If not…"

Sam let the words hang, and each knew exactly what he meant.

Finally Frank asked, "Will Blair be there?"

"Of course," Sam snapped.

"I don't think you've thought this through," Frank said slowly. "After the day Lucas and Blair just had in court, do you think it's wise to expect them to sit down to a friendly dinner? You know how she is about defense attorneys."

"Dammit," Sam clenched his fists. "This is all happening too fast. I haven't had time to think about Blair and her feelings."

The three men shared a secret glance.

"Well." Sam slapped a hand on the desk. "Blair's a mature adult woman and I know she can handle it."

Theo gave a gruff laugh. "I don't mean any disrespect, Sam. But do you actually know your daughter? She's been trying to beat Culver for two years. It's common knowledge around the courthouse—and so is her dislike of the man."

"I know," Sam said tightly.

"Again, I don't mean any disrespect," Theo continued, "but are you sure Culver *is* the right man for the job? After all, Blair did beat him today."

"Have you ever seen him in a courtroom?"

"Not lately," Theo murmured.

"Today was just a fluke. Raye was guilty, and everyone knew it, even Lucas, and though he wouldn't admit it, he didn't give this case his best."

"Why do you say that?" Theo wanted to know.

"Because Lucas has this chemistry, especially with female jurors. You have to see it to believe it, but he can razzle-dazzle a jury better than anyone I've ever seen. I need that type of charisma on my side. Someone who can beat the odds and win.''

''Why didn't he do that with the Raye case?'' Derek asked.

Sam shot him a piercing glance. ''Because he didn't choose the jury. Tenney did, and Lucas didn't get to establish that intimacy with them. Besides, Raye was guilty as hell.''

He paused, then asked, ''Are you questioning my judgment?''

''No, of course not,'' Derek was quick to say.

''I've researched this, and I know Lucas Culver inside and out. He's the best, and we need him.''

''What about Blair?'' Frank asked again.

''Blair will understand…in time.''

''Why don't you just tell her the truth?''

''I can't—not yet.''

''I hope you know what you're doing,'' Derek put in.

''I do. Everything depends on Lucas.''

BLAIR RUSHED from her office. She was running behind, and her mother hated it when she arrived late. She had just enough time for a shower and a change of clothes. Her mother also hated it when she wore business suits to her dinner parties. She was considering what to wear, when Lucas's smile entered her mind—the smile that had lingered on his lips as he watched her dance…his dark eyes touching her in ways that… No, don't think about him, she warned herself. Any decent man would have apologized profusely for intruding on such a private moment, but not Lucas. Oh no, he had to capitalize on it for his own pleasure. She *wouldn't* think about him. She wouldn't.

She had the whole evening ahead of her, an evening with her brother and family, and she refused to let thoughts of Lucas ruin it. If she hurried, she might have a few minutes alone with Blake before dinner. She missed their long talks and—

Blair came to a complete stop. Her briefcase dropped to the pavement and her purse slid from her shoulder. All she could do was stare at her car in growing horror. Across the windshield was scrawled in red lipstick, *I'll get you, bitch.*

Her body started to tremble, and fear was on the verge of consuming her—a fear from the past, a blinding, helpless fear. *No, no, no,* she told herself. She would not allow Hector Raye to do this to her. He wasn't going to manipulate her with threats. Summoning all her strength, she forced the fear away. She had survived worse than Raye, and she would survive this.

She retrieved her purse and found her cell phone. She dialed Roger Collins's number, and he was at her side in less than ten minutes; in another five, he had the situation under control.

Evan Holt was notified and the police were taking prints from the car, prior to beginning their investigation. Blair just wanted to go home.

"Are you okay?" Roger asked for the third time.

"I'm fine," she answered with a stiff smile.

"It has to be Raye's gang trying to scare you," Roger said, gesturing at the ugly words.

"I know, but I don't scare easily," she said with more bravado than she felt. Glancing at her watch, she asked, "How much longer do you think it'll be? I have to be at my parents' for dinner."

Roger spoke to a policeman, then turned back to her. "I'm sorry, Blair, but this is going to take a while. We don't want to miss anything."

"I really have to go."

Roger looked at the car and shrugged. "Tell you what, I'll drive you to your parents'."

"Thanks." She smiled slightly. "But I need to have my

own wheels. Could you drive me to a rental agency?'' She thought of Roger as a good friend, but she realized his feelings for her went much deeper and she didn't want to encourage him. But right now, it was hard not to let him take over and protect her.

''I don't think you should be alone. You never know who's waiting out there. I'd feel better if—''

She stopped him. ''I'm not alone.'' She opened her purse and showed him the small handgun. She'd had it for years, and Roger had actually given her shooting lessons.

''I'd forgotten about the gun,'' he said. ''Still—''

''No.'' She stopped him again. ''I'm not letting Hector Raye and his gang frighten me with threats.''

Roger shook his head. ''I'm just worried about you, that's all.''

''I know.'' She shifted her purse strap higher on her shoulder in a nervous gesture. ''You're a very good friend.''

''Blair, I could be—''

''Are you driving me to the rental agency?'' she interrupted, knowing what he was about to say and not wanting to deal with another emotional upheaval. Not at that moment, anyway. She'd have to talk to Roger in the near future about his feelings for her, and she wasn't looking forward to it.

''Your wish is my command,'' he answered.

''Great,'' she said with a sigh, and they started toward his car.

''I think I'll give Lucas a call and let him know what his client's up to,'' Roger said.

Blair grabbed Roger's arm. ''No, please don't call Lucas.''

Roger frowned. ''Why not? He should know what Raye's doing.''

Blair took a deep breath and tried to explain. ''I just can't deal with Lucas Culver anymore today.'' The words sounded stupid to her own ears, but she was hardly going to tell Roger that she *couldn't* face Lucas.

Roger's frown deepened. ''If that's the way you want it.''

''It is,'' she told him, hoping he'd leave it at that. He did, and Blair was grateful. If she never had to see Lucas Culver again, it would be too soon.

# CHAPTER THREE

WITHIN MINUTES she was in a rental car and on the way to her apartment. She'd told Roger she wasn't afraid; now all she had to do was to convince herself of that. She purposely kept the horrid message out of her mind as she showered, dressed and headed to River Oaks. She had learned that trick years ago and it had saved her so many times.

She drove up to the big gates and saw that Horace was on duty. Horace was the groundskeeper and handyman who had worked for her father for years. Tonight he was manning the gate, which meant there were other guests besides family. She waved and drove through. Usually a code had to be punched in for the gate to open. Her family had moved here after the attack, and an up-to-date security system had been installed for their safety. The large two-story chateau-style house had been a haven during the healing years, and it was always a pleasure to come home—even though she knew there was still tension between her father and brother. How long could her father keep blaming Blake for not becoming a lawyer?

She drove to the garages and used her remote control to open the door for her parking spot. Since she was more than fashionably late, she planned to sneak in through the kitchen so her mother wouldn't see her. She felt as though she was fourteen again and trying to put something over on her mom. Greta, the housekeeper, met her at the kitchen door. Greta wore her black uniform with the white frilly apron, which confirmed that tonight was a formal occasion.

"Miss Blair, what are you doing coming in through the back door?" Greta chided.

Blair held a finger to her lips to silence her.

"I see you, Blair," Ava Logan called from the kitchen. "So you can stop trying to sneak past me."

Blair smiled at her mother, knowing it was useless even to try to fool her. She hadn't been able to do it in thirty-two years and she wasn't going to do it now. She gave her mother a hug and a kiss as Ava meticulously placed hors d'oeuvres on a silver tray. Hors d'oeuvres she had made herself, Blair knew. Her mother was a gourmet cook and either supervised or did most of the cooking.

At sixty-two, Ava Logan possessed a timeless beauty. Her hair, a golden blond that now came out of a bottle, hung in a pageboy around her dainty features and emphasized her light-brown eyes. She wore a peach silk dress, presently covered by a white apron. Blair was always amazed at her mother's ability to remain cool and collected in times of stress. Her mother's calm had been invaluable to her after the attack. Her father thought *he* was the backbone of the family, but it was her mother with her gentle ways and dedication to family that held them together.

"I had a busy day at the courthouse," Blair said in her own defense. She didn't plan to tell her parents about the message on her windshield. It would only worry them and they'd worried enough about her. Besides, tonight was a night for fun.

"Yes, I heard." Her mother glanced at her. "Congratulations, darling."

Before Ava turned away, Blair caught a glimmer of something unexpected in her eyes. Apprehension? But why?

"Mom, is everything okay?" Blair asked tentatively.

Ava slowly removed her apron and placed it carefully

on the counter. "We have a houseful of guests, good food and wine, so what could be wrong?"

Her mother's words sounded forced.

"I don't know. You tell me, because you're acting strangely."

"It's nothing." Ava dismissed her daughter's concern with a shake of her head. "It's just that your father has to turn every party into a business meeting. I was hoping we could have only family tonight."

That didn't ring true, because she knew her mother enjoyed parties and cooking and everything connected to them. And she was used to her father springing extra guests on her. So what was going on? It was increasingly clear that her mother was nervous about *something*.

"Who's here?" Blair asked as a way to get some answers.

"The Johnsons, the Manns, the Barkers and Calvin, Natalie and Tiffany," her mother answered.

That didn't give Blair any clues. Her dad's business associates were frequent guests. Natalie was her father's sister, and Calvin her husband. Tiffany was their daughter. Calvin was also the firm's accountant, so their presence wasn't out of the ordinary. Besides, they were family.

"How's Tiffany doing?" Blair asked. Her cousin, a year younger than her, was going through a bad divorce.

"Still bitter."

"I'm sorry."

"So is Tiffany, but Nat felt that company might cheer her up."

Poor Tiff, Blair thought. After five years of marriage, she'd come home one day to find her husband in bed with another woman. Joel, Tiffany's husband, had seemed like a nice guy, but apparently he wasn't satisfied with just one woman. He had hurt Tiffany very badly.

Blair was thankful she'd never have to deal with a situation like that. Years ago, she'd decided she didn't care for men all that much, so the odds of her getting married were very slim. She knew she had a problem in that area, but it was *her* problem and *her* business.

Oh, God. She closed her eyes for a second. She didn't want to be a frigid old maid. She needed to get out more, resolve those emotions that were tied to the past. Suddenly she remembered Lucas and his charming smile and— She quickly opened her eyes. Why couldn't she stop thinking about him?

"You look beautiful," her mother was saying. "I'm glad you didn't wear one of those dreary suits."

Shaking Lucas from her mind, Blair glanced down at her dress. It was deep blue with a square neck and cap sleeves that showed off her neck and long slender arms. The hem came two inches above her knees and showed more leg than she liked, but in her rush, she'd grabbed the dress at random. She didn't want to be later than she absolutely had to.

"Darling, promise me something." Ava's concerned voice caught her attention.

"Sure," Blair answered immediately.

"Don't let your personal feelings get involved tonight. Be an adult and—"

"Hey, sis," her brother interrupted as he came into the kitchen. "You're finally home."

She hugged Blake, still thinking about Ava's odd request. She had no idea what her mother was talking about and she didn't have time to figure it out.

Ava wrapped an arm around each of them. "My two children both at home. I can't tell you how good that makes me feel."

"Me, too," Blair and Blake chorused, then laughed.

"I wish you'd stay home for good, Blake. London's so far away," Ava said plaintively.

"Now, Mom, don't start." Blake sighed. "You know that's not possible."

"But Blake," Blair started, then stopped as Blake raised a hand.

"No pressure, ladies. Besides, we have a family member who's desperately in need of our attention. Tiff can't stop talking about Joel and the divorce, and it's really more than I want to hear. She only drops that subject long enough to talk about—" Blake looked hesitantly at his mother, then at Blair.

"What?" Blair asked. He was hiding something from her; she'd sensed it earlier and now she was sure of it.

"Nothing." Blake shrugged and took her hand. "Let's join the guests."

Blair trailed behind him into the living room and Ava followed. "I've brought reinforcements," Blake announced, and glanced warily down the hall.

Everyone was acting strangely, Blair decided as she spoke to Meg Johnson, Nancy Mann and Beth Barker. She hugged her aunt and Tiffany.

"I guess Blake's tired of listening to me," Tiffany said.

"Never mind Blake." Blair smiled at her beautiful cousin, who had pale blond hair and green eyes. As a young teen, she used to envy Tiffany's hair because she'd heard that blondes had more fun. But now she was satisfied with her darker coloring.

"How're you doing?" Blair asked sympathetically, giving her cousin another hug.

"Terrible," Tiffany admitted, swirling wine around in her glass. "But I'm sure Blake's already told you that. You two used to tell each other everything, and I'm sure that hasn't changed."

"A little," Blair had to confess, and noticed that Blake kept looking toward the hallway leading to her father's study. Was he nervous about seeing their dad? Their father was obviously holed up in the study with his cronies.

"But I'm feeling much better since I met that gorgeous

hunk your father invited," Tiffany said, smoothing a hand over her slim hips. "Oh, yes, I'm feeling *much* better."

"For heaven's sake, Tiff," Natalie spoke up. "Remember your manners." Natalie's dark hair was now almost completely gray, but her blue eyes were as vivid as ever. Blair had always been told that she resembled her father's sister, and she knew she had the Logan hair and eyes, but she had her mother's dainty features.

"Mother, I'm entitled to some fun," Tiffany reminded her.

"Just be careful. This man's a complete stranger and we know nothing about him."

Voices in the hall put an end to the conversation. Blair wondered who Tiffany was talking about. All the men gathered in her father's study were married. Had he invited someone else? Her mother hadn't said.

"Remember your promise," Ava whispered as the men entered the living room.

Blair's eyes swung from her father, to Derek Johnson, to Frank Mann, to Theo Barker, to Uncle Calvin—and settled on the sixth man. He was dressed stylishly in a dark brown suit, light brown shirt and darker tie. He was smiling devilishly at her, and everything in Blair exploded with a rage she hadn't felt in a long time. How dare he! How dare he come into her home! *What was Lucas Culver doing here?*

She hadn't even realized she'd spoken the words aloud until her father put an arm around her shoulder and answered, "I invited him, sweetie."

"You *invited* him?" Blair repeated in an incredulous tone. "You invited Lucas Culver to dinner?"

Blair's reaction didn't surprise Lucas. He'd expected it. He not only saw her anger, he felt it. There was pure fire coming from those beautiful blue eyes and it was aimed directly at him. He'd seen Blair out of her element earlier, but this Blair was completely different. She was woman—

all woman—from the dark hair hanging around her shoulders to the high heels. Her blue dress magnified her eyes and clung to her curves—curves that drew his eyes like a magnet.

He'd always considered Blair a petite person, but her legs were long and shapely and had his full attention. He was losing it, he told himself. The woman was furious at him, and he was mentally undressing her. Yep, he was losing it.

"Now, Blair, be reasonable," Sam was imploring.

"Reasonable?" Blair pushed out of his arms and stared at her mother. "You knew," she cried, then pinned her gaze on Blake. "And so did you."

Ava and Blake had the grace to look ashamed, but it didn't mollify Blair in the least. "No one thought to tell me. No one considered *my* feelings."

"Blair, darling, don't make a scene," her mother begged.

"Okay, Mother," Blair snapped. "I'll leave, so you can get on with your party." Having said that, she turned and stormed out of the room.

Voices followed her. "Jeez, what's got her so riled up?" Tiffany said.

"I told you, Sam. I told you," her mother declared.

Blake caught her in the kitchen. "Sis, don't leave, please."

"Why is my kitchen all of a sudden Grand Central Station?" Greta asked, putting the finishing touches on spinach salads.

"We'll be out of your way in a sec," Blake told her.

"Elsa and I will be in the dining room," Greta said as she and the maid loaded salads onto a tray. "So talk all you want."

When they left, Blake pleaded, "Try to understand."

"All I understand is that you let me walk in there without any warning," she said angrily. "In the old days you'd never have done that to me."

"Blair, it was a business meeting—an important business meeting. And frankly, we didn't know how to tell you. You have such a short fuse these days."

"Now it's my fault," she choked out, taking a long breath. "I hadn't even realized it, but I came here tonight hoping Dad was going to say, 'Great job, Blair. I'm proud of you.' Instead, he invites Lucas to dinner. That's like a slap in my face."

"I'm sure it wasn't intended that way," Lucas said from the doorway. He knew he was taking his life in his hands, but somehow he had to make this right.

Blair quickly turned around, unable to look at Lucas. She didn't want to talk to him—not now, not ever.

"Mr. Culver, I don't think this—"

Lucas stopped him. "It's all right, Blake. I just want to explain." Lucas motioned for Blake to leave the room.

Blake hesitated.

Blair couldn't see him, but she knew from Blake's silence that he was deciding whether or not to leave. *Don't you dare,* she was thinking, but the sound of his receding footsteps told her that hope was in vain.

"I'm sorry if my presence upsets you," Lucas started, wishing he could ease her hurt, which surprised him since this was business and he shouldn't care about her feelings. But he did.

Blair counted to ten and turned around again, staring down at her hands instead of at Lucas. "I find that hard to believe," she said sarcastically.

Lucas noticed she wasn't looking at him and realized he had some apologizing to do. He'd embarrassed her in her office today, and it was clearly still on her mind.

"Well, I am," he told her. "And I'm also sorry for not knocking on your door today. As you said, common courtesy dictates that I should have."

Common courtesy and Lucas Culver. The thought made her want to laugh. Courtesy had nothing to do with Lucas. He'd been through so many women he should be in *The Guinness Book of Records*. She frowned; why was she thinking that? This wasn't about Lucas and his women; it had to do with respect and dignity, and everyone in her family was conspiring to deprive her of those—even Lucas, with whom she had no personal relationship. But his voice sounded sincere and she was so tired after this horrendous day and she just wanted to go home.

Slowly she raised her eyes. Lucas could see that the storm in their blue depths had calmed.

"What are you doing here?" she asked point-blank.

"Your father invited me."

"Why?"

"He's offered me a position in his firm and he wanted me to meet his associates."

"What?" She blinked in confusion. "Let me get this straight. I beat you in court so my father offers you a job."

"The offer didn't have anything to do with the trial."

"Really?" She raised a dark eyebrow. "I have a habit of forgetting that my life is very unimportant to my father. If you mentioned the trial to him, I know exactly what he said. Any A.D.A. could have won that case. Raye was guilty. Enough said."

Lucas suspected that Blair had probably been striving all her life for Sam Logan's approval, and today she thought she'd finally achieved it. Now he'd turned it upside down for her. God, he shouldn't have come. He should be in Jennifer's apartment, enjoying something a whole lot better than this hollow feeling.

He told Jennifer he had an unexpected business meeting. She'd been annoyed at first, but he'd promised to make it up to her. If he was completely honest with himself, though, he'd have to admit that Blair was the main reason he was here tonight. He was curious about Sam's offer, but seeing Blair somewhere other than the courtroom was the big selling point. Now he'd hurt her, and that was the last thing he'd wanted to do. He had to resolve this.

"It doesn't matter what your father said or didn't say," he told her. "You don't need his approval."

"You don't know anything about me," Blair muttered, and bit down on her lip to keep more words from tumbling out.

"I know what it's like to seek approval from someone you love. I used to do everything I could to gain my brother's approval. Then I grew up and realized it was always there. I just chose not to see that."

"You don't know anything about my relationship with my father," she said tersely. "Any more than you know about me."

"No, I don't," Lucas conceded. "And I regret my decision to come here tonight."

"Then why did you?"

"Curiosity got the best of me."

She frowned. "Curiosity?"

*Curiosity about you, Blair.*

"Yeah." He rubbed the bridge of his nose. "I wanted to find out why Sam was offering me a job. It's not like I campaigned for it."

"Did you find out?" she asked quietly.

"No, I'm still in the dark."

Besides his desire to see Blair in a different context, he had decided to accept Sam's invitation because he couldn't stand not knowing. He had to find out the truth, but he wasn't any closer to that than before he got here. Derek, Frank and Theo were all enthusiastically backing Sam in saying that they needed new blood. Even Calvin, the accountant, had shown him some impressive figures and encouraged him to join the Logan team. They were feeding him a line of crap, and Lucas knew crap when he heard it. But why were they pursuing him? He still hadn't figured that out, and now he didn't really care.

Blair took a step toward him. "I'll tell you why, Lucas," she said cryptically. "It's because you're a cutthroat attorney like he is. You don't care about the law or about human consequences—just the big bucks. That's what my father admires. So congratulations, you're in the big leagues."

He was trying to be conciliatory, to apologize for a bad error in judgment, but her words angered him, and suddenly he'd had enough. As she started to walk past him, he grabbed her arm. "Someday, Blair, someday I'm—"

He stopped as he saw fear flash into her eyes. Was she afraid of him? That possibility took him aback. They stared at each other for a long, silent moment, and then Lucas saw the pulse in her neck beating erratically. Other feelings started to surface and all he could think about was touching it with his lips and...

Blair tried to say something, but for once, words stuck in her throat. His hand was still closed around her arm, his fingers warm and firm. She felt the heat as it rushed up her arm to various parts of her body, and she was experiencing all sorts of emotions that were threatening to overwhelm her. Emotions she'd only read about—and all because of a touch. How many other women had felt this way about Lucas? she wondered. She was well aware that it should be irrelevant to her, and yet the thought infuriated her.

She looked at his hand. "Let go of my arm," she said coolly.

He saw the desperation in her eyes but didn't relent. "I don't think so," he said just as coolly. "I'm not through. I'm tired of justifying my career to you—a career that I'm good at—and I'm also tired of having my apologies thrown back in my face."

Blair didn't answer. She couldn't. She was too consumed with the new reactions that were tripping through her body.

When she remained silent, Lucas went on, "I'm not sure why your father invited me tonight. In hindsight, I see that I shouldn't have accepted, but I'm sure he thought you were mature enough to handle it."

Mature enough! The words jarred her already shaky composure and she felt like screaming. She was mature enough to handle the sexual banter between Lucas and her earlier that day. She was mature enough to handle Hector Raye's threat on her life. She was mature enough to handle Lucas in her home. Or was she? No, she wasn't *that* mature, answered a tiny voice inside her head.

Her head started to throb, and she touched her forehead to still the pain. She knew she was acting irrational, and she also knew she had to get away from him to sort through her emotions, regain her sanity.

Blair jerked her arm free, eyes blazing. "Hindsight is always twenty-twenty and I really don't care why you're here or why my father invited you, because I'm leaving."

Lucas stepped in front of her. The woman just didn't know when to quit and she certainly didn't know how to accept an apology. "You don't have to leave. I'm going." He turned toward the door. "Tell your father thanks but no thanks for the job offer. Never mind, I'll tell him on my way out."

At the door, he looked back at her. She was rubbing her arm where he'd held her. Had he hurt her? God, she made him crazy and he was acting so out of character. The sooner he distanced himself from the Logan family, the better off he'd be.

"Are you all right?" he couldn't help asking.

The gentleness in his voice made her answer more abruptly than she'd intended. "I don't need your concern."

Instant anger surged through him, and just as quickly it

cooled. He was beginning to see that Blair had a sponta-
neous defense mechanism—her sharp tongue. It was just
as Roger had said; she never let anyone get close to her.
Well, she didn't have to worry about him.

His dark eyes swept over her. "Don't worry, Blair, you
won't get it again." Without glancing back, he disappeared
through the door.

Blair stood there trembling from so many emotions—
new, alien emotions that she'd denied for a very long time.
How did she deal with all of this? she asked herself as she
unconsciously rubbed her arm. She didn't know. She only
knew that she was hurt and confused...and afraid. Not of
Lucas but the feelings he engendered, feelings she didn't
*want* to experience.

*Stay out of my life, Lucas Culver.*

*Please stay out of my life.*


EVAN HOLT SAT at his desk studying the latest putter he'd
purchased.

Carl Wright, his chief prosecutor, entered his office, followed by two detectives.

"Anything new?" Evan asked the lead detective, Mike
Wilson.

"Logan was over at Lucas Culver's office this afternoon
and Culver had dinner with him tonight," Mike answered.

"Dammit." Evan slammed the putter onto his desk and
got to his feet.

"What do you think that means?" Carl asked.

"He's trying to recruit Culver—that's the only explanation."

"Why? He's got his own team."

"Sam knows we can handle Johnson, Mann and Barker,
but Culver—that's a whole different situation."

"What do you mean?"

"Culver has a way of controlling a jury, and this case
is all going to come down to the jury."

"Don't be so sure," Mike said, placing a folder on his desk. "The DNA is a perfect match."

Evan quickly leafed through the papers and a smile spread across his face. "This will be the nail in Sam Logan's coffin, and even Culver won't be able to save him. Logan should've tied up these loose ends sixteen years ago. Now I'm going to."

"What about Blair?" Carl asked.

Evan closed the folder and sat in his chair. "Are you ready to make the arrest?" he asked Mike.

"As soon as you give me the word."

"I want the element of surprise, so do it first thing in the morning."

"Yes, sir," Mike said, and left the room with the other detective.

"What about Blair?" Carl asked again.

"I hope Sam has the good sense to tell her before this breaks. If he doesn't, I'll let her know before it hits the press."

"I don't like hurting Blair," Carl admitted.

"Well, you'd better put those feelings where I won't see them," Evan told him. "This case will be the hardest you've ever tried and you can't let emotions sway your thinking."

"I won't, Evan. You know that."

"I do, but having Blair in our office makes it difficult. She'll have to choose between her job and her family. I guess we'll see whether she hates defense attorneys as much as she claims."

# CHAPTER FOUR

BLAIR HAD a restless night. So many things were crowding in on her that she couldn't sleep. She'd apologized to everyone at the party and said she had a headache and quickly left. She could see that her father was upset with her and her mother was worried. Blake begged her to stay, but she couldn't. She had to leave.

Raye's threat had her running scared, and her fear was making her act irrational. She'd been rude to her family and Lucas, and she hoped an apology would suffice. If that wasn't good enough for Lucas, she didn't really care.

*Stop it,* she said to herself. *Stop blaming Lucas for everything.* Her father had invited him, so he had a right to be there. And she'd told her father several times that she didn't want to work in his firm. She was happy keeping criminals behind bars. So what was the problem? *Lucas,* she muttered aloud. He had such an odd effect on her and she wanted—

"What? What?" she shouted into the darkness. When she didn't get an answer, she grabbed her pillow and headed into the living room to curl up on the sofa. What *did* she want from Lucas? He was always so pleasant, and that irritated her. He was always smiling, and that irritated her, too. He was very good-looking and that irritated the hell out of her. No man had any business being that handsome and charming. Was that it? Was she *attracted* to Lucas?

*No!* She sat up and tried to dismiss the possibility, but

she couldn't. Maybe she *was* attracted to Lucas—and maybe that was why she was always pouncing on him. Maybe that was why he made her so angry. No. She shook her head vehemently. It couldn't be.

She lay down and tried to come to grips with her contradictory reactions. She didn't know how to do that, but she owed Lucas an apology for her behavior—of that she was sure. He'd been nothing but pleasant, and she had literally come unglued. That wasn't Lucas's fault; that was hers.

All these years, she'd been trying to bridge the gap between her father and her brother—not understanding that there was also a gap between her father and *her*. That had become clear tonight when she'd reacted so violently to Lucas's presence. He was right; she *had* been waiting for Sam Logan's approval.

She groaned into her pillow, thinking this was a little too much soul-searching. Life was becoming too complicated, too fast, and all she wanted to do was sleep.

She heard a noise outside the living room window and immediately sat up, her heart in her throat. Then she relaxed as she realized it was only the wind. She lived in a gated apartment complex, so there was no way anyone could get in without her knowing it. Still, she felt uneasy. She went into the bedroom and got her purse. Pulling out the small pistol, she carried it into the living room. She placed it on the end table within easy reach. If anyone had told her years ago that a gun would make her feel more secure, she would have laughed. But the gun gave her the extra bit of reassurance she needed to face her fears. No one was going to attack her again.

As she drifted off to sleep, her last thoughts were of Lucas. Tomorrow she'd apologize for her rudeness. Knowing Lucas, he'd accept and they'd go back to battling it out in court. Polite adversaries—that was all they could ever be.

LUCAS WOKE UP with a frown on his face—and the urge to strangle Blair Logan still on his mind. He was finished with apologizing to that woman and he was certainly finished with making excuses to her. As far as he was concerned, Blair could go to hell.

Running both hands over his face, he stumbled out of bed in his black briefs and headed for the kitchen. The strong smell of coffee pulled him forward. Thank God he used a cleaning service. He paid the woman extra to make his coffee. The coffeepot had a timer and coffee was ready at precisely six o'clock every morning. He wasn't human until he'd had his first cup.

He poured a mug full, letting the aroma tantalize his nostrils. He picked up the mug and returned to the bedroom. Sitting on the bed, leaning against the headboard, he sipped at the black magic. Oh, yeah… After a moment, he tipped his head back, feeling his brain slowly come alive. Now he could face the day.

But the day wasn't on his mind; last night was—and Blair. After leaving her family's home, he'd driven around for a while, then planned to see Jennifer. He had thought he'd salvage something of the night. But he kept seeing Blair's wounded face. He had hurt her, unintentionally, but still he'd been the cause of her pain. He didn't like that. It left a bitter taste in his mouth and he had no desire to be with Jennifer or any other woman. So he drove home, determined to put the evening and Blair behind him.

But his first thoughts this morning were of her. "Damn you, Blair Logan, stay out of my head," he shouted to the room. He got up, coffee in hand, and walked into the bathroom. He set the mug on the vanity as he stared at himself in the mirror. His dark hair was tousled across his forehead and he had a growth of dark beard. He drew one hand over the stubble and did a double take. He raked his hair back to look more closely at his temples. Gray hair! His hair was turning gray. Damn, when did that happen?

The absurdity of it hit him and he started to laugh. What the hell did he care if he had gray hair? But he *was* getting older, and he wasn't any closer to settling down than he'd been ten years ago. That was what bothered him. He didn't want to spend the rest of his life alone.

He left the bathroom, opened a drawer and pulled out a tank top and jogging shorts. He slipped into them, then hurried toward the front door. He ran two miles every morning, and he was going to run until all his frustrations were gone. Then he'd call Jennifer, apologize again, and tonight he'd deal with the rest of his frustrations. Assuming Jennifer was willing to help, of course… That was his plan, anyway.

And Blair? Well, Blair had her own problems and he didn't want any part of them. It would probably take a team of psychiatrists to sort out her issues with her father. He stopped with his hand on the doorknob. Hell, that was one thing he and Blair had in common—he had issues with his father, too. They actually had something to talk about. He shook his head, ridding himself of *that* idea. He wasn't talking to Blair. He wasn't doing *anything* with Blair except forget he'd ever met her.

*Dammit, Blair, stay out of my head.*

WHEN BLAIR GOT to her office, she knew something was wrong. People were rushing through the corridors, phones were ringing and everyone was ignoring her.

"April." She interrupted Evan's secretary. "What's going on?"

"I can't talk now. I've got a million things to do," she said nervously as she hurried off.

Must be some major new case, Blair thought, entering her office. She'd find out later. She put her heavy briefcase on the desk and sat down to study her calendar. Her parents hadn't called this morning; neither had Blake. That was strange. She'd expected them to phone just to find out how she was. Especially Blake—she'd expected to find him on her doorstep. Maybe they were still upset with her for ruining the party and making a fool of herself. But most of all, she'd driven Lucas away. Her father wasn't going to forgive her so easily for that.

She sighed; she'd call Lucas later today and try to make amends. It didn't matter to her if he worked for Logan and Associates. She wasn't sure why it had bothered her so much last night. Well, actually, she did know. So many things had happened yesterday, and Lucas had been the final straw, so to speak. Today her head was clear, so she could deal with Raye, Lucas and anything else.

There was a tap at the door and April poked her head around. "Evan wants to see you immediately."

"I'll be right there," Blair responded, figuring that now she'd find out what was going on.

When she made her way to Evan's office, she discovered that the room was full—every A.D.A. seemed to be present and Blair knew that something important was taking place.

"Ah, Blair," Evan said when he saw her. "Come in."

She smiled at the other A.D.A.s, but everyone avoided looking at her. Evan nodded and they filed out of the room.

"Have a seat," Evan invited.

Blair sat down and glanced at the door. "Why's everyone so...tense?"

"How are you?" he asked, ignoring her question.

She knew he must be talking about the message on her windshield. "I'm okay. They're still checking out my car."

"I'll see that Roger stays on it. I won't have my A.D.A.s threatened."

"Thanks, Evan."

There was a moment's silence, then Evan asked, "Have you spoken to your father this morning?"

Blair gave him a puzzled look. "No. Why?"

Evan folded his hands across his desk. "I've got something to tell you and I'm not sure how to start."

Blair laughed slightly. "That's not true. You always know what you're going to say before you say it."

"This is a rather delicate situation."

That made Blair nervous. This "delicate" situation obviously involved her father. She had no idea what it could possibly be, so she waited, knowing Evan would find the words eventually.

"There's been a second arrest in the Bonnie Davis murder."

Blair watched Evan closely, unable to see exactly how her father was affected by this. Since he'd been Easton's attorney, he shouldn't have any dispute with a second arrest.

"That's great," she offered. "But I'm not sure how this concerns my father."

Evan shook his head. "You don't have an inkling, do you, Blair?"

"No," she replied tartly, tired of Evan's cat and mouse game. "So tell me."

"The private investigator the Davises hired did a very thorough job—better than the police ever managed. He found witnesses who'd seen the suspect with Easton and Davis. He found another witness who saw the suspect get into the car with Easton and Davis. And he got DNA evidence from the suspect that matches the skin under Bonnie's fingernails."

"Wow. Sounds like you're not going to have a problem convicting this guy."

"No, I don't think so."

Suddenly Blair felt a glimmer of excitement. There was a reason Evan was telling her all this. A reason he'd spoken to the other A.D.A.s before her. And that reason was probably why they seemed uncomfortable around her. Everyone wanted this high-profile case. She decided to get straight to the point. "Evan, have you decided to let me handle the case?"

She sat forward, on the edge of her seat, as she waited for his answer.

"No, Blair, you won't be handling this case."

She took a deep breath. "Well, then I don't understand what's going on."

"We made two arrests this morning."

"Two?" she echoed.

Evan's green eyes caught hers. "Sam Logan and Blake Logan."

Blair put a hand to her head in confusion. "I—I thought you said Sam Logan and Blake Logan."

"I did," came the chilling words.

She felt the color drain from her face. "What—what did you arrest them for?"

"I don't think you're following me."

"I guess not," she muttered, "because I'm completely lost."

"We arrested Blake for the rape and murder of Bonnie Davis and we arrested Sam for obstructing justice, withholding evidence and probably a lot of other things we haven't thought of yet."

A tortured sound escaped Blair and the world spun away, leaving her suspended, alone and afraid. For a moment she was consumed by the horror of it all, but her mind quickly rejected what Evan was saying.

"No," she moaned. "That's not true."

*There had to be a mistake.*

"I'm afraid it is."

"No, it isn't," she said again, refusing to even contemplate such a thing.

"The evidence doesn't lie. Haven't you always believed that?"

"Yes," she answered quietly.

*But there had to be a mistake.*

"The skin under Bonnie's nails matches Blake's DNA, and we have proof that Sam knew of his son's involvement all along. He paid Easton to keep quiet—that's why Easton never identified the other boy. Sam figured he'd get Easton off and both boys would be free and clear, but it didn't turn out that way."

For a moment nothing registered in her mind except the cream walls and the pictures of Evan's children hanging there. Two girls and a boy—laughing, happy. Then everything started to spin. Evan's concerned face, the pictures, the walls, they all spun around and around in her head until the truth exploded through the confusion with searing pain.

Blair still refused to accept it. "There *has* to be a mistake."

"No mistakes." Evan paused. "I'm just sorry Sam didn't tell you before this broke."

"Dad knew?" she whispered, the pain barely allowing her to speak.

Evan nodded. "Yeah, someone let something slip and Sam got wind of what was about to happen."

Blair remembered the conversation she'd had with Evan yesterday. "You thought it was me," she murmured.

"I didn't know if you'd heard Carl or one of the others talking."

"Everyone knows?"

"Just about, and in a way, I have to admire Sam for not telling you. It would've been highly unethical, considering your job. But Sam was getting all his affairs in order. He even tried to hire Lucas Culver, but Culver turned him down."

*Lucas? Lucas? Lucas?*

So many things suddenly became clear in her throbbing head. Her father's job offer. Lucas being invited to dinner. OhmyGod, what had she done? She'd been thinking about herself while her family was falling apart. OhmyGod, what had she done?

She swallowed and gathered the remnants of her sanity. "My brother did not rape or murder Bonnie Davis. I know him. He isn't capable of a crime like that. And my father would never withhold evidence. He's a tough lawyer, but he has ethics."

"Well…" Evan inclined his head. "We'll see what a jury thinks."

She got to her feet, anger curling through the shattered fragments of her heart. "How can you do this? They're my family!"

"I'm not doing it out of spite, Blair," he told her. "I'm doing it for justice—the same thing you've always fought for."

Blair closed her eyes as turbulent emotions threatened to overcome her. Her brother wasn't guilty and there was no way Evan could make her believe otherwise.

"Still want to prosecute this case?" Evan asked arrogantly.

Her eyes flew open, her blue eyes burning him like a laser. "That's cruel."

Evan picked up a pencil and tapped it on his desk. "It might be, but you and I both know you have a choice to make. You can't play both sides."

Her eyes continued to burn. "You'll have my written resignation in an hour."

He laid the pencil down slowly. "It didn't take you long to make that decision."

"This is my *family!*" she shouted. "Do you even understand what that means?"

"Your brother committed a horrible crime. Do you understand what *that* means?"

She covered her ears with her hands. "Stop saying that!"

"It's the truth, so you'd better start facing it because we're going to prosecute this to the fullest extent."

She removed her hands and tried to swallow the huge lump that had formed in her throat. After a moment, she asked, "Where are they?"

"In jail, of course," was the quick response. "But I'm sure Johnson will have your father out in no time. Blake, that's another matter. He's a flight risk. I don't know if I'm going to recommend bail."

The lump in her throat became so large she couldn't breathe. She struggled to maintain her poise. "He won't flee. I promise."

Evan twirled the pencil in his hand. "Are you asking me for a favor?"

"I'm asking you to be fair. That's all."

"I'll give it some thought."

"When can I see the evidence?"

Evan lifted an eyebrow. "Are you going to represent them?"

"No, but I want to see what we're up against."

Evan stared directly at her. "You're not going to see a thing," he said. "Blake's lawyer is the only one who'll be looking at the evidence. And I'd like to know who that is as soon as possible."

"I'm sure you would." She narrowed her eyes as something occurred to her. "How did you get Blake's DNA sample?"

"Don't worry, it's all legal. You won't find a loophole there." Evan got to his feet. "I'm sorry it had to end like this, Blair. You're a good attorney." He shrugged, then added, "Gwen will take over your caseload. Be sure to talk to her about Raye's sentencing."

Blair didn't say anything as she walked to the door. There was nothing left to say. Evan had made up his mind, and now she had to find a way to save her brother.

And her father.

LUCAS WAS SIGNING letters and finishing up some last-minute details. He had a hearing at the courthouse, then he was free for the rest of the day. He was looking forward to his evening with Jennifer. He'd gotten sidetracked by the Logan family, but he wasn't making *that* mistake again. He'd told Jennifer about the job offer and she understood. He'd sent roses to show he was sincere.

Lucas glanced up as Joan burst through the door gasping for breath.

He stood immediately. "What's wrong?"

"I…I…" She held a hand to her chest and took a gulp of air. "I…ran from my car… I had to tell you…what's happening…"

"What?"

Joan collapsed into a chair. "Sam Logan's been arrested."

There was a long pause, then Lucas smiled. "Did you have margaritas with lunch again?"

Joan shook her head. "I only did that once and it was my sixtieth birthday and you don't have to keep reminding me."

"Well, you're talking nonsense."

"I am not," she snapped. "Sam Logan's been arrested and so has his son, Blake."

The smile left Lucas's face. "What the hell for?"

Joan spoke in a rush. "Years ago Mr. Logan represented Todd Easton for the murder and rape of a young girl. Mr. Logan lost the case and Easton broke out of jail and beat up Sam's daughter for revenge. The police shot and killed Easton." She took another breath. "There were two sets of skin under the girl's nails, but they could never identify the other boy. Now they have. They say it's Blake Logan and that Sam paid Easton to keep quiet."

"Oh, God," Lucas said, sinking into his chair. None of this made sense. "I met Blake last night and he seemed like a nice guy—clean-cut and decent.'' He looked at Joan. "Are you *sure* about this?''

She raised her eyes to the ceiling, then got up and switched on the TV set in the corner. There, in living color, were Sam and Blake in handcuffs being escorted to jail. Reporters hovered around, throwing out questions that went unanswered. The TV reporter was giving an update of the events and it was pretty much as Joan had said.

"See?'' Joan muttered, switching off the set. "So do you think this had anything to do with Mr. Logan's job offer?''

The same thought had occurred to Lucas. "I'm not sure,'' he admitted. "Sam has a very good team. Why would he need me?''

"Lucas Culver.'' She sighed in annoyance. "You're better than all of them put together and Sam Logan knows it. If you ask me, you'll be getting a call from him.'' She grabbed her side. "God, I'm too old to be running. I think I'm having a heart attack.''

"Don't you dare have a heart attack,'' he called out as she walked into her own office.

"Such sympathy,'' she mumbled, closing the door.

Lucas sat there, stunned. But one thought kept invading his mind—Blair. How was she taking this? She and Blake were twins—this had to be hard for her. He straightened. Oh, God, Blair worked in the D.A.'s office. How in the hell was she handling that? Even as he asked the question, he knew the answer. He'd bet she'd already resigned. He didn't know Blair well, but he knew her loyalty was with her family.

He went over last night's events in his head. Did Blair know what was going to happen? Was that why she seemed nervous and edgy? Blair suppressed her emotions, so it was difficult to tell. But his heart ached for her and that threw him. The woman had done everything but scratch his eyes out, yet here he was feeling sorry for her.

*God, what a mess.*

*But it wasn't his mess.*

By the end of the week he'd be with Jacob, Miranda and the kids. He needed that peace and the serenity Jacob was always talking about. He sighed. The older he got, the more he was becoming like his big brother. Maybe that wasn't a bad thing, though.

As he signed the last letter, his thoughts returned to Blair. He told himself that he shouldn't waste his time; she wouldn't appreciate his concern. She'd already told him that. Then why in hell couldn't he stop thinking about her?

*Dammit, Blair.*

# CHAPTER FIVE

BLAIR TYPED her resignation, signed it and handed it to
Evan personally. She then cleared her personal belongings
out of the office and left. She went immediately to the jail,
hoping to see her father and Blake, where she was told
that her father had been released on his own recognizance
and Blake was still being processed. She asked to see him,
but they wouldn't let her. They said he could only see his
attorney. She started to lie and say she was his lawyer, but
they knew her and her position in the D.A.'s office. Unless
Evan specified otherwise, she knew she wasn't going to
get anywhere near him…at least not today.

Although she tried to keep her mind blank, she found it
impossible. The whole thing was too horrible to push
aside. She had to have some answers, and the only way to
get those was to talk to her father. She called his office,
but his secretary said he wasn't there, so she knew the
only other place he'd be was at home with her mother.

On the drive to River Oaks, she thought about that time
sixteen years ago. Her twin brother had been rebellious
and uncontrollable. He'd been drinking, doing drugs. But
in her heart she knew he had not committed this crime.
She knew him as well as she knew herself, and even on
drugs he could not have done such a terrible thing. There
had to be another reason his DNA matched the skin under
Bonnie Davis's fingernails.

*Evidence doesn't lie.* How many times had she pro-
claimed those words, believed them religiously and used

them to seal a case? Now she'd have to take a second look at what had been driving her all these years. Had it been justice or plain old revenge? No, she couldn't think about that now. She had to concentrate on Blake and on finding out the truth.

She punched in the code at the gate and it promptly swung open. She recognized the other cars in the driveway: Derek's, Frank's and Theo's. The partners were plotting strategy, planning how to handle the situation. She knew her father would not rest until Blake was free.

She drove to the garages and parked in her usual spot, then hurried through the kitchen, as she had yesterday. God, it seemed like forever since last night. So much had happened and so much was still to come.

Greta met her at the door. "Oh, Miss Blair, it's awful, just awful," she cried, wringing her hands.

"Where're my parents?" she asked.

"Your mother took a couple of aspirin and went upstairs to lie down, and your father's in his study with his lawyers."

"Thanks, Greta," she replied, and headed for her father's sanctum.

She could hear raised voices, but as soon as she opened the door everything became quiet—too quiet.

Sam was sitting on the leather sofa by the French windows. He looked haggard and old, and Blair's heart crumbled in agonizing pain. She'd never seen her father like this and for a moment she didn't know what to do. Then she did what her heart dictated—she ran to him and wrapped her arms around him.

"Blair, darling, I'm so sorry," he mumbled in her hair.

"It's all right, Daddy," she reassured him. "We'll sort this out."

"Blair." Derek spoke up. "I don't think it's wise for you to be here. After all, you do work for Holt."

Blair released her father and faced Derek. "Not any-more. I resigned."

"Oh, no," Sam choked out. "I never wanted that to happen. None of this should be happening."

Blair took her father's hand and held it tight. "Tell me what's going on."

His hand gripped hers just as tightly. "I'm so sorry you got hurt, but I was powerless to stop any of this."

"Don't worry about me."

"I do," he admitted. "You're my daughter and I handled last night badly. I wanted to convince Lucas to take this case. I didn't think about much else."

"Let's forget about last night," she told him. "I understand now why you did what you did. I'm just sorry I ruined the evening." She didn't want to think or talk about Lucas, but she knew that she would...later. Right now she had to have answers. "Tell me what happened back then—and tell me the truth. I don't need to be protected."

"It's not a pretty picture."

"I don't expect it to be, but I know Blake did not kill that girl."

Sam gripped her hand with both of his. "He was there, Blair. He was there."

She swallowed hard. "So? That doesn't make him guilty."

Sam shook his head sadly. "It makes everything a mess—a terrible mess."

"Why was Blake there?" she asked, needing to hear the story but wondering if she had enough strength to listen without breaking down.

"He met Todd and the Davis girl coming out of a party. There was a guy outside selling marijuana and crack co-caine. Todd and Blake bought some, then they drove to that secluded park to get high. The cocaine made Blake sick and he ran into the bushes and puked his guts out. He said that's when he heard the girl scream. By the time he

reached her, Todd had already raped and murdered her."
Sam paused for a moment. "Blake didn't know if she was
dead or not, so he checked her pulse. She reached up and
caught his arm, then she went limp. Blake ran down the
street to a pay phone and called 911 for help."

Sam stopped speaking, obviously having difficulty with
his emotions, as Blair was. "When Blake returned, Todd
was doing cocaine while the girl lay there dead. Blake told
him he'd called the cops and they had a fight. When they
heard the sirens, they both jumped into the car and drove
off." He took a breath. "Later, when Todd was arrested,
I didn't know Blake was involved. I didn't find out until
Todd almost killed you. That was when Blake told me
everything. He was so worried about you, and the guilt
was destroying him. I immediately sent him out of the
country, hoping I could resolve things, but..."

Sam rose and walked unsteadily to the windows, shoving his hands into his pockets.

Blair took a breath, desperately needing it for what she
had to say. "Evan says you knew about Blake's involvement all along and that you paid Todd to keep quiet."

Sam whirled around. "That's not true! During the trial
I *didn't* know Blake was involved and I never gave Todd
a dime. This is all Lloyd Easton's doing. He claims I paid
Todd and now he has Holt believing it."

Blair swallowed, hating to say what had to come next,
but she had no choice. "Evan isn't doing this on the word
of Todd's father. He has proof. You can count on it."

"My sources say Evan has witnesses that Todd came
out of my house with large sums of money, but that's just
not true. I never met Todd at the house and I certainly
never gave him money. Evan can't prove that I did."

Blair remained quiet, trying to deal with her father's
statement. She knew Sam Logan and his ethics. Even
though his only son was part of this mess, Sam wouldn't

do what Evan was insinuating. Blair didn't doubt his honesty or his integrity.

"I'm not lying to you, Blair," Sam said in a low voice. "I should have come forward with what Blake told me after you were beaten, but I couldn't. Todd was dead and you were struggling to survive. I didn't see any reason to cause my family any more pain, so I kept quiet about Blake. Now Holt's got me—and he's got Blake, too."

"We're not giving up, Sam," Theo said.

"I didn't say I was giving up," Sam said sharply. "I'm just stating the facts. Holt thinks he has everything all wrapped up, but this isn't over by a long shot. Holt might have me on a technicality, but Blake didn't commit a crime. He was just in the wrong place at the wrong time, and I know Lucas can make a jury believe that. I've got to see him and try to convince him to take Blake's case. It's our best chance."

At the mention of Lucas, Blair's head jerked up. Until that moment, she'd been sitting there in some sort of limbo, trying to understand what had happened all those years ago. Now she knew what she had to do.

"I'll talk to Lucas," she offered quietly.

Derek said, "I don't think—"

"I can handle this," she interrupted him, speaking to Sam. "Lucas responds much better to a woman. Especially when she's apologizing," she added with a wry grimace.

Sam didn't say anything.

"No offense, Blair," Derek put in. "Culver wasn't exactly bowled over by you last night. In fact, he was more than a little put out."

"And he's known for his honesty," Frank said. "When he finds out what we were trying to do, he won't be too thrilled."

"I can deal with Lucas," she stated.

Sam looked at her. "How can you be so sure?"

"Because Lucas has a soft spot for women."

"I thought it was the other way around," Theo said with a laugh.

"This isn't funny," Blair snapped.

Theo held up a hand. "Sorry."

"As I was saying," she went on, "it's common knowledge around the courthouse that Lucas has a hard time saying no to a pretty face. I hate to trade on that, but I will. Besides, I owe Lucas an apology."

There was silence for a moment.

"Go ahead, Blair," Sam said finally. "See what you can do."

She went to Sam and hugged him. "Thanks, Daddy."

"Honesty is a big thing with Lucas," he told her. "Try not to forget that. I wish I hadn't."

"I won't," she promised, then asked, "Has Mom called Uncle Howard?"

"Of course," Sam replied sarcastically. "He's the first one she calls whenever anything happens."

Blair heard the sarcasm, but she didn't comment. The relationship between her father and her uncle was tense. Howard was her mother's youngest brother and he remained an integral part of their lives, which Sam didn't like. Howard was a sheriff in the Austin area, and he and Sam had different points of view on the law.

However, her mother and Uncle Howard were close. Having no children of his own, Howard was also close to Blair and Blake; Sam didn't like that, either. But Blair loved Uncle Howard. He'd always been there for her, especially after the attack. He'd taken her to her grandparents' farm, where Howard and Ava were raised, and given her an opportunity to heal, away from all the distressing realities of her life. The farm was special to her and Uncle Howard knew that, and she'd always be grateful for his big heart.

She knew that he'd be here now, as soon as he could, to help them through this, and she couldn't dwell on the petty jealousy between her father and Howard. She had other things to worry about.

She turned to Derek. "How come you didn't get Blake out on bail?"

"Because Holt's dragging this out as long as he can."

"The flight risk," she sighed.

"He told you that?" Derek asked.

"Yes, but keep pressuring him. He hates pressure."

"He thrives on pressure."

"Yeah, but he doesn't *like* it," she replied. "So don't let up. With any luck, we might have Blake out by morning. Now I'd better try and find Lucas."

"Blair."

She turned back at her father's voice.

"I am proud of you. I don't think I told you that last night."

Blair bit her bottom lip to keep it from trembling. She had waited a long time to hear those words, and now that she had, it was just as Lucas had said. His approval had been there all along—in his support, his love and his patience. She'd just chosen not to see it.

She nodded and walked out of the room, seeing a lot of other things she'd chosen to block out. Like Lucas's kindness, his many attempts to be friendly, his integrity. He took more pro bono cases than anyone and he refused to be anything but honest in a courtroom. The judges all admired him for that. He might use charm and theatrics to get his point across, but the truth was always his bottom line. Now she was going to be as truthful and honest as she could because Lucas would recognize that and respond in kind. Lucas was about to see a different Blair Logan and she hoped he appreciated the transformation. He had to. Her life and her family's depended on it.

BLAIR WENT OVER to Lucas's office, but his secretary said he'd gone for the day—that he wouldn't be back until tomorrow. She asked for his home address, but the secretary refused to let her have it. Blair didn't give up that easily. She explained the situation and within minutes she had Lucas's address in her hand. She realized that as soon as she walked out the door, the secretary would phone him. That was fine. At least she'd get to talk to Lucas, which was her only goal at the moment.

Lucas lived in a house not far from downtown Houston. It was in Houston Heights, an older upscale neighborhood. Most of the houses had been remodeled to accommodate changes over the years. Lucas lived in a Tudor two-story with a manicured lawn. Not exactly what she'd expected. She'd thought he'd have what people used to call a "bachelor pad." A condo, perhaps, with sleek, modern furniture and lots of high-tech sound equipment. The houses here were more family-oriented.

She pulled into his driveway. His house was a multi-cream brick with a deep brown trim and English ivy trailing up the chimney. His garage door was open and a dark blue Expedition was parked inside.

Killing the engine, she sat for a second, trying to get her thoughts organized. Then she saw something that sent them in a completely different direction. There were three children's bicycles in the garage—all boys' bikes. Beside them was a pink tricycle and a stroller. Lucas had children! She'd never heard any mention of children. He was single—she knew that much—and she had never heard of him being married before. Could he have a secret woman and kids who lived here with him? No, if Lucas had kids, he would be married to their mother. She didn't know a lot about Lucas, but she knew that.

*Enough dawdling,* she told herself, and got out of the car. She had to talk to Lucas and it was now or never. Whoever the bikes belonged to was no business of hers. She walked up to the front door and pressed the bell before she lost her courage.

Lucas had just returned from one of his runs and was stripping out of his shorts and T-shirt when he heard the bell. "Damn," he muttered. Who the hell could that be? He wasn't expecting anyone, so it was probably Mrs. Bauer from next door. In her late seventies, she lived alone and often needed help with little chores like opening jars or getting things down from high shelves. He quickly pulled on his clothes and headed for the door, glancing at his watch as he went. He hoped this wouldn't take long; he'd promised Jennifer he wouldn't be late.

He jerked open the door without checking and received the shock of his life. Blair Logan stood on the threshold. It definitely wasn't Mrs. Bauer. Mrs. Bauer had never looked this good. Blair wore a purple suit and a cream silk blouse, her hair drawn back in usual stern style. Her skin was smooth and flawless, but her eyes were somber and troubled. Oh yes, Blair was here on a mission.

Staring at her, he reached certain conclusions about the events of the day before. He'd wondered about Sam's offer and hadn't come up with a good enough reason for it. Now he knew. Sam realized what was about to happen and was trying to cover all the bases. If Sam's top guns couldn't handle the case, he wanted someone younger, more aggressive, waiting in the wings. And Sam had done it all under false pretenses, which was what angered Lucas. If the man had been honest with him, Lucas would probably be at the courthouse this very minute fighting for Blake Logan.

Since Sam's tactics of last night had failed, mainly because of Blair, he'd sent her now to make amends. Lucas felt certain of that beyond a shadow of a doubt. But it wasn't going to do one bit of good.

Blair's breath lodged in her throat as Lucas continued to stare at her. She was staring back, of course; she couldn't help it. She'd never seen Lucas like this. His dark hair was tousled, falling across his forehead, and he had on a pair of skimpy shorts, a T-shirt and no shoes. In one glance she took in the long, muscled legs and arms lightly covered with dark hair. His stomach was flat and there wasn't an ounce of fat on him anywhere. She finally saw the sexual magnetism all the women at the courthouse talked about. She not only saw it, she *felt* it as her stomach constricted with an unfamiliar sensation of longing.

She immediately forced such reactions from her mind. She couldn't deal with this…this unwanted attraction right now. "May I speak with you, please?" she asked quickly.

She was clearly nervous, but Lucas figured Blair wasn't his problem and he wasn't planning to give her a chance to attack him again. There'd be no more attempts to pacify Blair. He frowned at his watch. "I've got a date in an hour. You should've called."

His secretary *hadn't* called him, Blair thought. She wondered why. But it didn't matter. "Lucas, I really need to talk to you," she pleaded. "It's important."

Lucas kept one hand on the door and one on the doorjamb. "Blair—"

Seeing that stubborn light in his eyes, she knew he had no intention of letting her in, so she ducked under his arm and into his house. From the entry, she walked into a large living area decorated in burgundy, blue and cream. There were wood beams on the ceiling, and a huge fireplace occupied one corner. The house had a sense of warmth and tradition, decorated in the style of bygone days. That surprised Blair. She didn't think this kind of ambience would appeal to Lucas. But then, what did she know about— Her thoughts stopped abruptly as she caught sight of the pictures hanging on one wall. Pictures of children. Dark-eyed children. A toy box against one wall and she noticed a high chair in the kitchen. There were definitely children in Lucas's life, but she didn't have the time or energy to concern herself with that.

Her legs felt wobbly so she sank down on the burgundy sofa.

"Why don't you make yourself at home?" Lucas quipped dryly.

"I'm sorry, but I need to talk to you."

"So you've mentioned."

She folded her hands in her lap. "First of all, I'd like to apologize for my behavior last night. I was very rude— to you, to my family."

He crossed his arms. "Really?"

God, she wished he'd put some clothes on. Her eyes kept straying to certain areas that were making her flustered.

"Yes, I was...having a bad day."

He raised an eyebrow. "When I saw you earlier, you seemed in high spirits—dancing around your office," he reminded her.

Her cheeks colored slightly. "It was after that."

"You mean after I ruined your evening."

"Lucas—"

He broke in. "Cut the crap, Blair. I know why you're here and it has nothing to do with an apology."

"But it does," she insisted.

"Do you think I live in a vacuum?"

"What?"

"I listen to the news," he informed her. "And I have a pretty good idea why you're here. Sam sent you."

She shook her head in frustration, this conversation was not going the way she'd planned.

"The generous job offer, the dinner, it's all clear now," Lucas said. "Somehow, Sam figures I'm the man who can keep his son out of prison, but instead of trusting me, he used underhanded tactics."

"My father's been under a lot of stress," she said defensively. "He didn't know whom he could trust. He had to be sure about you. He didn't mean to offend you."

"I'll make this simple for you," he said, not concealing his anger. "If you're here to ask for my help, the answer is no."

"That's unfair," she cried. "You haven't even heard what I have to say."

"I'm not interested."

"My brother's innocent. He didn't murder that girl."

"From the news, it seems that Holt has an airtight case."

"I know you can poke holes in everything Evan has."

Lucas's eyebrows shot up again. "Really? So you need a cutthroat attorney? That's what you called me, isn't it? A cutthroat attorney putting criminals back on the street for big bucks and personal gain."

Her cheeks grew hotter and she gripped her hands together. "Yes, I said that," she admitted. "And at the time I meant it. I had my reasons for feeling that way, but I don't think I need to go into that. It doesn't justify my attitude or my words. I'm having to take a new look at myself and my beliefs, and I'm not liking what I see."

Lucas was thrown for a second, but only a second. This amenable, conciliatory Blair was getting to him. God, he was such a sucker. He had a hard time saying no to women and Blair probably knew that about him. Oh yeah, she was pulling him in like a big old sappy fish. Or so she thought. His mother had always compared his temper to a tempest in a teacup. Right now, though, he was feeling more like Jacob, who rarely lost his temper—but when he did, it was a full-blown hurricane. Blair was playing him just as Sam had. He wasn't falling for it.

"Ever since I've known you, you've derided everything about me—my career, my clients—and you've impugned my motives," he told her. "But when the criminal's your brother, it's a different story, isn't it? Did you ever stop to think that the people I've represented had families who believed in them, too?"

"Lucas—"

He cut in. "Now that you need a favor, you can be sweet and apologetic. It's too late, Blair. I'm not taking anything else from you or your father. *Honesty* might be a word you need to look up in the dictionary."

Blair realized her hopes were dwindling fast, and she didn't know what to do. She stood up and brushed away a tear. "Blake and I are twins. We're closer than most siblings." She took a deep, shuddering breath. "I can't let him be convicted of a crime he didn't commit. *Please* help me."

Lucas stared into her watery eyes and felt himself weakening. No, she wasn't doing this to him, dammit! A few tears, and he was putty in her hands. No, that wasn't how it would be. Tonight he was going to Jennifer's. He refused to get involved with the Logan family.

"I'm sorry I can't help you," he said woodenly.

Blair bit her lip until she was afraid it might bleed. She didn't expect Lucas to be this hard. He'd always been so friendly and fun-loving, but now she was seeing the tough side of Lucas—the unrelenting side. But she had to keep trying.

She reached into her purse and took out her business card. On the back, she scribbled her home address and phone number, then laid it on the coffee table.

"That's my address and phone number," she said quietly. "If you change your mind, call me—anytime. I'll be awake."

Lucas swallowed at the pain in her voice. "I won't change my mind."

They stared at each other and Lucas found himself getting lost in the blue of her eyes. He wasn't giving in, though. But as she ran from the room, he didn't feel victorious. He felt like the biggest heel who'd ever lived.

# CHAPTER SIX

LUCAS TRIED to put Blair out of his mind as he dressed and went to Jennifer's, but all through dinner he kept seeing her blue eyes, her tears, and he knew his mother was right. His temper didn't last long, and now he was feeling the pangs of hurting someone…someone who…

He stopped, unable to complete that thought. He studied Jennifer's blond hair and lovely green eyes, watched her animated gestures. She was beautiful and charming, everything a man could want—but she wasn't… Oh, God. He shifted uncomfortably in his chair and Jennifer had to call his name several times to get his attention.

The evening wasn't going as he'd planned and now he had to hurt someone else. His feelings for Jennifer were superficial, and he couldn't keep letting her believe that they were more.

In that moment he made a decision. He only hoped it was the right one.

He told Jennifer how he felt. She wasn't too happy with him and he wasn't too happy with himself, either. He'd never been with one woman and unable to get another out of his head. It was a new experience for him, an experience he'd rather not repeat. It spoke too much of his father and he'd vowed to never be like him. Honesty was important to him—and to Jacob. But he carried it a little farther than Jacob did; sometimes he expected too much of people and he had to remember that everyone was human and fallible. He dealt with that fact every day. He shook his head slightly as he walked toward his car. It always amazed him how duplicitous people could be.

That was precisely what made Sam Logan's offer so objectionable. Sam had tried to use deceit to win him over. Apparently Sam had checked him out, but he must have done a lousy job because anyone who knew Lucas could have told him that was completely the wrong approach.

He wasn't ready to go home, so he drove on Interstate 10 for a while. On a whim, he turned off at the Port of Houston—Houston's gateway to the world. He parked in a secluded area and sat gazing at the water, the ships, watching the moonlight glitter on the surface. Much as he wanted to forget about the Logan family, he found he couldn't forget about Blair. She was in pain. He'd seen that same tortured look in his mother's eyes—a look of betrayal mixed with love and an inability to separate the two.

*Why should I give a damn?*

He ran both hands through his hair in an effort to clear his thoughts, but Blair was still there. He had a feeling she'd continue to be until…until he took the case. There, he'd said it. Now what? He couldn't work with people he couldn't trust. And Blair—he hadn't a clue about her real feelings. One day she hated him and the next she was begging for his help. She had apologized. He suspected she wasn't sincere, but then…she might have been. He found it difficult to believe anyone could change so quickly, and yet she'd gone from working for the D.A. to defending her brother in a matter of minutes. This had to be a real conflict for her, especially since she'd always seemed so dedicated to fighting for justice. Now she was forced to look at justice in a whole new light. She had to be dealing with a lot of raw emotion.

*Why should I give a damn?*

That question kept tormenting him, and he still didn't have an answer. As he watched the moonlight tempt the water with dazzling caresses, he knew what he had to do. He'd probably known when Blair walked out of his house in tears, but he had to justify his actions first.

He was taking the case, but he wasn't going to accept Sam's offer. He couldn't handle both at the same time, and he preferred to have his own people and his own space to prepare this case. Right now, he couldn't see Logan and Associates in his future.

He wasn't sure what lay ahead for him. He'd been feeling so restless lately that maybe a rigorous trial was what he needed, he told himself. The case had intrigued him since he'd heard it on the news. He was relying on something he'd relied on a lot in his career—pure gut instinct. Having met Blake, he was confident that the man couldn't have committed such a crime. Trusting that first impression, he was gambling that Blake Logan was innocent. But he had to hear that from Blake himself.

He took a deep breath and felt better, even excited. He was going to take the case and fight for Blake Logan—the way Blair wanted him to—but he planned to establish some ground rules before he went a step farther.

*Oh, Blair. Why should I give a damn?*

The answer to that question lay deep in his heart.

BLAIR SPENT the evening at her apartment, waiting, worrying, deliberating. She didn't know how to tell her father she'd failed. She considered lying—saying that Lucas was thinking it over—but then she remembered what Lucas had said about honesty. She picked up the phone and called, telling Sam exactly what had happened. He said it was what he'd expected and that he couldn't have done any better. He admitted he'd mishandled the whole thing from the beginning. He also said that Blake's arraignment was in the morning and that Derek would do everything he could to get Blake out on bail.

Blair paced the living room, jumping at every little

sound. She hadn't even thought about Raye's gang with everything that was going on, but now that it was dark, her old fear was back. The phone rang and she answered it immediately, hoping and praying she'd hear Lucas's voice. She didn't. It was Roger.

"Blair, are you okay?" he wanted to know.

"Yes," she said absently.

"I'm sorry about Blake and Sam. How're you holding up?"

"I'm hanging in there."

"Would you like some company?" She heard the eagerness in his voice.

"No, but thanks. I'd rather be alone." She hated to disappoint him, but just now she couldn't deal with his hopes or expectations. And casual conversation was simply beyond her.

"I understand, but if you need me, you know all you have to do is call."

"Thanks, Roger. I appreciate that."

"We didn't turn up a thing from the prints on your car."

"I didn't expect you would."

"We're still investigating—talking to members of Raye's gang. Someone might slip up."

"It doesn't matter," she said. "Compared with everything else, it seems rather minor."

"It's not, Blair. Not when your life's on the line."

She took a deep breath. "I've got to go. I'm expecting a call. Thanks for phoning."

"I'll talk to you tomorrow," he said, and hung up.

Blair couldn't think about Roger; she could only think about Lucas. She thought of all the things she could have said to convince him, but when she was around Lucas, the words came out all wrong. Was she attracted to him? She'd asked herself that question before, but now the possibility demanded an answer. No! She immediately denied that she felt any attraction. But she remembered Lucas's statement about honesty…and smiled wryly. Who was she trying to kid? When she looked at Lucas, her emotional scale went berserk. That was why she reacted so strongly to him. How would Lucas feel if he knew her emotions were all caught up in something she didn't understand? Romantic involvement was hard for her. She'd tried, but since the attack she had a difficult time tolerating a man's touch. With Lucas, it was so different, so… God, this honesty thing wasn't what it was cracked up to be.

She went into the bedroom and removed her clothes and slipped on a big T-shirt, then curled up on the sofa and stared at the phone, willing it to ring. Her stomach growled, and she recalled that she hadn't eaten a thing since her toast and coffee this morning. She didn't feel hungry, though; food was the last thing on her mind.

She drifted in and out of sleep, her attention always on the phone. When the buzzer rang, she immediately picked up the receiver, then realized it was the intercom. Frowning, she looked at the clock. One in the morning. Who would be visiting her this late? Maybe it was her father—maybe he had news about Blake. She ran to the intercom and pressed the button.

"Ms. Logan, I know it's late, but there's a Mr. Culver to see you," the security guard told her.

OhGod. OhGod. Lucas was here. That could mean only one thing. *Thank you. Thank you. Thank you,* her heart cried.

"Ms. Logan, did you hear me?" the guard asked impatiently.

"Yes. Please send Mr. Culver in."

She raced into the bedroom to change her clothes, but saw that she didn't have time. She didn't want to keep Lucas waiting. She dashed back into the living room just as the bell rang. She quickly turned off the alarm system and opened the door.

Lucas marched in, dressed in slacks and a knit shirt. His

hair was tousled and he had a growth of beard. Evidently he'd come here after his date—probably with Jennifer Walker.

"Okay, Blair, this is the deal," he said without preamble. "I'll take the case, but only if I have complete control. Neither Sam nor you, or any of his top guns, will interfere or question my decisions."

She smiled and said, "Hi." It sounded inane, but it was what came out of her mouth. She was so excited he was here, so grateful he'd agreed to take the case, and she didn't want him to be angry with her anymore.

Lucas's eyes narrowed on her face and he wondered if she'd been drinking. She wasn't acting like her usual grave self. Her dark hair was disheveled around her shoulders and her eyes were bright and she was smiling at him— which threw him because she *never* smiled at him. He stared at her body in the T-shirt. All the feelings and reactions he should have had at Jennifer's started to grip his body now, and he found himself smiling back.

"Hi," he answered.

Blair's knees felt weak and she hurriedly asked, "Would you like something to drink? Coffee? Something stronger?"

"No," he replied, getting lost in the brightness of her eyes. This was the way he wanted to see her—happy and excited. He vowed, in that moment, that he'd never make her cry again. He knew he was entering dangerous territory—where he cared more about her feelings than his own. "I just need to talk," he added quickly.

"Sure," she said, and sat on the sofa, curling her feet beneath her.

Lucas took the Queen Anne chair opposite her. Looking around, he took in the apartment. It was the way he'd expected it to be—tasteful and elegant—just like her. The apartment was almost completely white with birchwood undertones and silver and green touches. There was a pink blanket on the sofa and a white pillow with lace trim. He'd bet everything in her bedroom was pink and white and feminine. Okay, his thoughts were going places they shouldn't.

"Thank you," he heard her say, and he brought his eyes back to her. "I'm glad you changed your mind."

"Blair, I have to get something straight," he started, knowing he had to stick to business or risk getting completely sidetracked. "I can't work with people I can't trust."

"I'm sorry about all the scheming, but my father was trying very hard to hire you for my brother's sake. He really believes you're a good attorney. He believes you're the best."

"And you, Blair. How do you feel?"

Her eyes met his. "I'm ashamed of the way I treated you. I can't justify it, but there's a lot going on in my life that I have a hard time dealing with and I guess you were the perfect target for my frustrations." She drew a deep breath. "I'm trying to be honest here. I'm not good at sharing things about myself, but if you want honesty, I guess I should tell you about...my background."

He could see she was having trouble finding the words. "If it's about the attack, I already know."

Her eyes widened. "You do?"

"Yes, Roger told me."

"Oh."

"It wasn't your fault." He felt a need to remind her of that.

"I know, but Todd Easton is still hurting my family."

There was silence for a moment, and Blair decided that Lucas had to know everything—even if she didn't *want* him to. "There's something else I have to tell you."

"You don't have to tell me every little thing."

"I need to tell you this because I don't want you to hear

it from someone else. It might also help you understand why I acted so irrational last night.''

"Okay," he said slowly, disturbed by the way her eyes had filled with fear.

"I...ah..." She gulped in a quick breath and tried to get the words out. "Yesterday when I left my office, I found a message scribbled on my windshield."

"A message?" he echoed.

"Yeah, in red lipstick. It said, 'I'll get you, bitch.'"

"Oh my God, Blair, why didn't you say something?"

She shrugged. "I called Roger, and the police are investigating. I didn't see any reason to worry my family or anyone else. Roger thinks it's Raye's gang trying to scare me. If it is, the police will catch them."

"But your family needs to know. And you shouldn't be staying here by yourself."

"That's exactly the reaction I wanted to prevent. I can handle this on my own."

"I'll have a talk with Raye and squash this before it goes any further."

"Lucas—"

He held up a hand. "This is going to be stopped. I promise you."

For some reason, that made her feel so much better. Lucas was a man of his word and if anyone could still her fears, she knew he could. Where that feeling came from she wasn't sure.

Lucas was stunned by what she'd told him and he wanted to help, wanted to make her world safe, make her pain go away. But Roger was the one she called when she was in trouble. He didn't like that and he couldn't explain why. At least she had someone, he told himself, dismissing his uncharacteristic reaction.

His dark eyes held hers. "I'm sorry about last night," he murmured.

She shrugged again. "For what? It wasn't your fault."

"But I was Raye's attorney and you walk in and find me hobnobbing with your family. I'm surprised you handled it as well as you did."

"Let's just forget it. Okay?"

"No, we're not forgetting Raye."

"I meant the other stuff, like me calling you names and being extremely rude."

"Okay." He smiled. "I can forget that."

When he smiled, her heart did a crazy dance that left her breathless, and she was beginning to think that her attraction was a lot stronger than she was willing to admit.

"Thank you," she whispered, and Lucas lost a part of himself in those words. She was pulling him in and he didn't even want to resist, but he had to. They had a bigger problem.

"Let's talk about Blake," he said abruptly.

"His arraignment is in the morning," she told him.

"Who's set to handle it?"

"Derek, but you have to."

"Why?"

"Because Evan's going to try and keep Blake locked up until the trial and I can't see him wavering on that. Derek has a temper and he loses it easily. If that happens, we don't have any hope of a judge seeing our side."

Lucas leaned forward and rested his elbows on his knees. "Before I agree to anything, I have to talk to Blake. I know you told me he's innocent, but I have to hear that from him."

"Of course," she answered readily. "But you will take the case?"

"After I talk to Blake and after Sam agrees to my terms."

"Oh—Daddy." She clamped a hand to her cheek. "I need to call him. He's so worried."

"It's almost two in the morning," he pointed out.

"He's awake. Neither of my parents will sleep tonight."

She reached for the phone, which was on the sofa by her pillow, and he wondered if she'd been lying there waiting for his call. It made him feel more of a heel, but it didn't keep the doubts from lingering in his mind. He hoped he was making the right decision for all of them.

Blair quickly dialed the number and Sam picked up within seconds.

"Daddy," Blair said.

"Blair, is something wrong?"

"No, actually, things are a little better."

"Who is it, Sam?" She could hear her mother in the background.

"Blair," he whispered to Ava, then he spoke into the phone. "What are you talking about?"

"Lucas has agreed to take the case—on a couple of conditions."

"Blair, are you sure?"

"Yes, I'm sure."

There was a pause at the other end. Finally he asked, "What are the conditions?"

"That he talk to Blake first and hear his story, and that you let him have complete control."

"This is my son we're talking about. I can't stand back and do nothing."

"It's the only way Lucas will take the case."

"I don't know, Blair."

"This is for Blake," she reminded him. "I don't think we have much choice—unless you feel Derek can do the job."

There was another long pause. "Tell Lucas to meet me in my office at seven in the morning and we'll discuss it."

"Okay. And Daddy?"

"Hmm?"

"Try to get some rest. I feel we have a chance now."

"Me, too, sweetie. Me, too."

Lucas watched her face as she talked and he could see

how much she loved her family. He knew she tended to suppress her emotions. She didn't like to talk about what she was feeling; she'd told him that. It probably had to do with the attack she'd suffered all those years ago.

As she hung up, he said, "You're putting a lot of faith in me."

They stared at each other and neither spoke. Then she cleared her throat, "Just help my brother. That's all I'm asking and—"

"And what?"

"That you let me help."

"Blair." He sighed.

"Please, Lucas, I need to be involved. I won't interfere with any of your decisions. I can do research or gofer work. Anything."

He got to his feet, finding it hard to say no. "We'll see, and that's all I'm saying. Now, I've got to get some rest."

"Oh, Dad said to meet him at his office at seven."

"Great," he groaned and headed for the door. "Just what I need—about three hours' sleep."

"Lucas?" She followed him to the door and held out her hand. "Thank you."

His hand covered hers in a warm clasp and all of a sudden she felt breathless....

With her soft hand in his, Lucas acknowledged that he wanted a lot more from Blair than a handshake, and he wondered if she even realized it. Probably not. Blair's attention was totally on her family.

As he released her hand, he said, "Promise me something."

"What?" she asked, unable to keep her voice from shaking.

"That you'll tell your parents about the message on your windshield."

"Lucas." She tucked her hair behind one ear. "I can't. They have enough to worry about."

He gazed at her for a moment, then said, "You know, Blair, I have a feeling you can be very stubborn."

She grinned slightly. "I can," she admitted.

He grinned back. "Just be careful, and I'll talk to Raye."

"Thanks."

"See you tomorrow. Hell, it's already tomorrow. I'd better get going. Good night, Blair."

"'Night, Lucas."

Blair locked the door and turned on the security system. She grabbed her blanket and pillow, switched off the lights and crawled into bed. She placed her hand, the hand that Lucas had held, against her face. Yes, everything was going to be okay. With Lucas at the helm, Blake had a chance. If anyone had told her a couple of days ago that she'd be joining Lucas Culver in taking on the D.A.'s office, she would have laughed. She would have laughed her head off. But now—it gave her a very warm feeling. No matter what happened, she would never criticize Lucas again. As a matter of fact, she was thinking of doing a lot of other things with Lucas. She groaned and rolled over, hardly able to believe the direction her thoughts were taking. Lucas wasn't interested in her that way, and she didn't want him to be. Or did she?

LUCAS DROVE toward his house, then changed his mind and headed for the jail. He wasn't going to sleep anyway, so he might as well talk to Blake. He had to hear his story and he'd rather not wait until morning. He realized he might run into problems at this time of night, but he knew some of the guards and was hoping to find one of them on duty tonight.

Was he crazy for doing this? Was he crazy for getting involved with the Logans? But every time he asked himself that question, Blair's tearful blue eyes tortured him, and he knew he couldn't do anything else. He was disappointed that he'd have to cancel his vacation and he hoped Jacob would understand. Hell, Jacob always understood. It was the kids he worried about. He didn't like disappointing them, but he was sure Jacob and Miranda could explain the situation. He'd see if Jacob and Miranda could bring the kids for an afternoon. Jacob would be accommodating. Oh yes, he knew his big brother—and how he wished he could talk to him now. He'd call first thing in the morning.

He wondered how Blair would feel about his family. *Whoa, man!* What was he thinking? Sleep deprivation was making him punchy. Blair had nothing to do with his family and he needed to remember that.

## CHAPTER SEVEN

As Lucas had expected, there was opposition to his seeing Blake at this hour, but he knew the guard on duty. After a little straight talk—delivered with a degree of finesse—Lucas was escorted to Blake's cell. The jail was full, as usual. Some prisoners were sleeping; others were reading or smoking. A smell of smoke mixed with urine and something else he couldn't define filled his nostrils. He hated coming to this place. No matter how many times he came here, he still had that same creepy feeling—as if he was witnessing a part of society that was ugly and repulsive and despairing. He knew there was very little he could do about it, which always left him with a deep sense of hopelessness.

The guard stopped and inserted a key into a lock. Lucas saw Blake immediately. He was alone, sitting on the bottom bunk in a corner, his back to the wall, his head resting on his drawn-up knees. When he heard the jangling, he looked up and Lucas saw his desolate, empty gaze.

The guard opened the cell. "You have fifteen minutes, Counselor."

Lucas nodded and stepped inside as the door banged shut behind him. Blake scooted to the edge of the cot with an expectant look on his face. He wore prison orange and his rumpled appearance barely resembled the debonair young man Lucas had met the previous night.

"Mr. Culver, does this mean you're going to take my

case?'' he asked in his English-accented voice, which sounded strained and frayed.

''It all depends,'' Lucas said, sitting beside him on the cot. ''First, I have to hear your story.''

''Oh, God,'' he buried his face in his hands. ''It's horrible.''

''I still have to hear it.''

Blake glanced sideways at him. ''Didn't Dad tell you?''

''I haven't spoken with your dad. I've only talked to Blair.''

His expression shattered. ''How—how is she?''

''She's okay.''

''I'll bet she hates me,'' he muttered.

''No, she's actually fighting to save your life.''

Blake shook his head. ''That's Blair. No matter how much I hurt her, she always forgives me.'' He got up and walked to the edge of the cell, gripping the bars. ''When Todd almost killed her, I thought I—''

Lucas cut in. ''Let's start at the beginning. Can I trust you to tell me the truth?''

Blake looked soberly at him and nodded.

''How did you know Todd Easton?''

Blake turned back to the bars as he began to talk. ''We went to the same school and we were both always in trouble…. No matter what I did, nothing was good enough for Sam Logan. I dealt with it in a pretty stupid way—I started drinking, doing drugs, trying to forget I wasn't the son Dad wanted. Blair saved me so many times and I'd promise her I was going to quit and straighten up, but I never did. I never kept my promises. She never gave up on me, though, and look how I repaid her. I almost got her killed.''

Blake was eaten up with guilt; Lucas could see that. He could also see that Blair had always been the steadfast twin, always believing in her brother as she was now.

"Tell me about that night," Lucas invited, hoping to get his mind off Blair.

"I went to a party to buy drugs and so did Todd. Todd had a date, Bonnie Davis. She did drugs, too. We bought marijuana and crack, and then we went to that park to get high. I didn't want to go because I felt like a third wheel, but I didn't have much choice. Todd had the car. Dad refused to buy me one until I cleaned up my act." He leaned his forehead against the bars. "Todd and Bonnie were going at it pretty heavy in the back seat, so I got out and sat on one of the benches. I was smoking marijuana, drinking whiskey and doing crack all at the same time, trying to block out the mess I'd made of my life. I guess it was too much, because I got sick and ran into the bushes and threw up. I couldn't seem to stop. That was when I heard Bonnie scream. At first I thought they were playing, then the scream turned into an agonizing sound—as if she was in pain. When I got to her, she was lying on the ground with nothing but her blouse on and it was opened in the front. I pulled it together to cover her up and I reached over to check her pulse. As I did she caught my arm and then she went limp. I asked Todd what had happened and he said the bitch got what she deserved. I told him I thought she was dead and he laughed. I panicked. I didn't know what to do, but I knew if Bonnie wasn't dead she needed help. I remembered a pay phone down the street. I ran and called 911 and told them where Bonnie was." He paused for breath. "When I got back, Todd was sitting on a bench doing crack. I was so angry that I hit him, knocking him to the ground. We started to fight, then we heard the sirens and jumped in the car and fled. Todd dropped me off at my house and said that if I told anyone what happened, he'd say I helped him kill her. I went into the house and threw up again. I threw up for the next two days. When Todd was arrested, he called and said I'd better make sure my dad took his case. I didn't have to worry because Dad knew Lloyd Easton, Todd's father, and he talked Dad into doing it.'' He took another breath. ''When Todd was found guilty, I was stunned and I kept waiting for him to finger me. But he found a better way to get even. God, when I saw Blair in the hospital I was so filled with rage. She'd never hurt anyone and she lay there fighting for her life. Her face was so swollen she couldn't open her eyes. I hardly recognized her and I knew I couldn't keep the truth inside anymore. I told Mom and she told Dad. I thought Dad was going to be angry, but he wasn't. He was in a state of shock. He immediately got me out of the country and said he'd handle things.'' Blake turned to look at Lucas. ''Dad didn't know about my involvement until after Blair was beaten up. That's the truth, Mr. Culver, I wouldn't lie to you.''

''I hope not. I sincerely hope not,'' Lucas replied, trying to digest the information Blake had just given him. Through it all, he couldn't shake the image of Blair. He hadn't realized she'd been beaten so badly. And now Raye's gang was stalking her. She had to be terrified, yet she seemed to be coping. But he was going to make damn sure Hector stopped the harassment.

Lucas quickly returned his thoughts to Blake's story. ''How was Bonnie Davis murdered?''

''Todd strangled her.''

''I'll get all the information from the D.A.'s office, but the DNA evidence I've heard about concerns me. Do you have any idea how that was obtained?''

''I...I...'' Blake's skin turned a grayish white and Lucas could see he was worried about the DNA, too. Or was there something Blake wasn't telling him? Lucas decided not to press him right now, but he would later.

''I'll get all the evidence, then we'll go over it thoroughly. With any luck, I might be able to prove the DNA was illegally obtained.''

Blake remained quiet and that bothered Lucas. Blake

should be grasping for a way out of this. Again, he decided not to press him. Not yet, anyway.

Lucas rested his elbows on his knees and folded his hands. "I'm going to ask you some personal questions and I need you to tell me the truth. Anything you tell me is confidential."

"Okay."

"Did you have sex with Bonnie Davis?"

"No," was the answer. "She was Todd's girlfriend."

"Did you kill Bonnie Davis?"

"No."

"Did you see Todd Easton kill her?"

"Well, actually, no. I was in the bushes throwing up when it happened."

"You called 911?"

"Yes."

"If you had nothing to do with her death, why didn't you tell the police the truth?"

Blake ran both hands through his hair in a weary gesture. "Because I was stupid and scared," he admitted. "I didn't know what to do. My mind was so messed up. I didn't want my dad to find out about the drugs. During the trial, I wanted to call the police, but I never did. I was a coward—a yellow coward. I've hurt so many people with my behavior, people I love. I just want it to stop, and I'm ready to face the consequences of my selfishness."

Lucas rose to his feet. It was clear that guilt was driving Blake Logan. It was also clear that Blake wasn't a bad person. He'd made a lot of bad choices, selfish choices, and now he needed to rectify those wasted years. Lucas was good at reading people, which was the reason he was standing in this cell tonight. He had to know if Blake was innocent or a spoiled rich kid waiting for his father to save him. Lucas was convinced that Blake wasn't guilty of any crime—except the crime of teenage stupidity.

"The arraignment is in the morning, so try and get some rest," he told him.

"You believe me, don't you, Mr. Culver?" Blake asked in a desperate tone.

"Yes, I believe you," Lucas responded without hesitation.

Blake let out a deep sigh. "Thank you. Thank you."

"Don't talk to anyone unless an attorney is present, either me or someone from your father's office. Do you understand what I'm saying?"

"Yes, sir."

"I'll see you in the morning," Lucas said as the guard approached.

"Mr. Culver?"

Lucas turned back.

"If you can't arrange bail, don't worry about it. I'm getting what I deserve."

"Blake—"

"It's true," Blake cut in. "Look what happened to Blair and that girl. I can't live with the guilt anymore. It's time to face my punishment."

"You've already punished yourself more than the system ever could," Lucas said, knowing Blake had sentenced himself a long time ago. Lucas didn't have much time left, but he had to ask one more question. "Blake, what have you done with your life in the past sixteen years?"

Blake shrugged. "I finished school in London with a degree in journalism and a minor in sociology. My visa was up, but I wanted to stay. I'd made friends and it was…a safe place to me. My parents thought the Davis thing was over and wanted me to come home, but it's never been over for me. I couldn't stand the thought of living in Texas—too many painful memories. Dad actually agreed with my decision. I came back to the States and Dad helped me get a job with a magazine in New York.

Within a few months, I was transferred to their London office. I know Dad pulled a lot of strings, but I didn't care. It was where I wanted to be. I had met a Reverend Gillis. He helped me through a lot of my problems. He runs a special boarding school for delinquent youths, and after work and on the weekends I help at the school. I counsel fourteen- and fifteen-year-old kids, trying to keep them off drugs.''

Lucas was impressed, but he needed to know something else. "How long have you been off drugs?"

"Since Bonnie Davis died. I sobered up that night and I haven't looked back."

"Time's up, Counselor," the guard called.

As Lucas walked out of the cell, down the hall and to his car, he knew with certainty that he'd made the right decision. Blake needed someone to fight for him because he'd decided he deserved to be punished. But Lucas was determined not to let that happen. He hadn't seen the evidence, but in his heart he knew that Blake and Blair had paid enough. Blair...

In less than two days, she'd begun to dominate his life...his thoughts. All he could see was Blair's face. He could see her dancing in her office, smiling and happy. He saw her at her parents', angry and hurt. Then he saw her today, wounded and tearful. He wanted to keep her dancing; that was all he could think. He wasn't sure what it meant and he wasn't going to analyze it. He'd had enough for one day.

WHEN HE FINALLY got to his house, it was four o'clock. He dropped across his bed fully clothed and fell instantly asleep. He didn't need a lot of sleep; Jacob didn't, either. It was something they'd apparently inherited from their father...something neither of them complained about.

Lucas was awake at six and headed for the coffeepot. After a cup to jolt him back to reality, he showered, shaved and dressed. Then he called Jacob. The phone was picked up on the first ring.

"Hello." Jacob's strong voice came down the line.

"Hey, big brother, what're you doing?"

"At the moment I've got one child asleep on my shoulder and another wrapped around my leg."

"Let me guess." Lucas smiled. "Gracie and Lizzie." Every time he said Gracie's name, he got a lump in his throat. Grace had been their mother. Jacob and Miranda had named their new daughter Alicia Grace, after her grandmothers.

"All that schooling's finally paying off," Jacob teased.

"So where's the rest of the gang?"

"The boys are asleep. Gracie's been up most of the night with an earache, so I have her in the kitchen hoping Miranda will sleep in. Now Gracie's sleeping like the sweet baby she is."

"And Lizzie's always up early," Lucas said.

"You know Lizzie." Jacob sighed. "She gets that from someone, but I can't recall who."

Lucas heard something in the background. "Is that Bandit?" Bandit was Jacob's dog and he was never far from him. He had been Jacob's only companion for a lot of years.

"Yes, he's growling because I won't let him wake Miranda."

"Still talking to that dog, are you?" Lucas laughed.

Jacob laughed, too. "Sometimes he's the only one who listens."

"Oh, Jacob, I wish I could be there. I miss the kids and you and Miranda."

There was a pause, then Jacob said, "That sounds like you're not coming."

"No, an unexpected murder trial came up and I promised to take the case. I have to cancel my vacation."

"Well, that happens," Jacob said just like Lucas knew he would.

"You've probably heard about it on the news. It's Sam Logan's son."

There was another noticeable pause. "You know who's kin to them, don't you?"

Lucas frowned. "No, can't say I do."

"They're Howard's family."

"Howard the sheriff?" Lucas asked in an incredulous tone. "The one who arrested you for kidnapping Miranda?"

The daughter of a wealthy oilman, Miranda had been kidnapped and hidden in the Texas Hill Country. Jacob had accidentally found her and kept her safe. But eventually the kidnappers caught them and both were shot and in hospital for weeks. Jacob was arrested for the kidnapping and things weren't resolved until Miranda was able to tell her story.

"Yep, one and the same."

"Good God, I didn't think the man had any family." Lucas and the sheriff had gone head to head more than once when Jacob was arrested. That was years ago, and now Howard and Jacob were friends, but Lucas knew very little about the hard-nosed sheriff.

"Ava Logan is his older sister. Howard left yesterday to be with the family. He's very fond of Blake and Blair."

Lucas swallowed. "Do you know Blair?"

Silence.

"Jacob?"

"What?"

"You didn't answer my question."

"I'm just grappling with the way you said her name."

Lucas closed his eyes. "How did I say her name?"

"Like she meant a helluva lot to you. Are you involved with Blair Logan?"

"Depends what you mean by *involved*."

"Lucas, I've got two cranky little girls on my hands, so I don't have time to nitpick with you. You know exactly what I mean by *involved.*"

"She makes me angrier than anyone I've ever met and she makes me say and do things I said I never would. She's driving me crazy and I can't stop thinking about her. So if that's involved, then I guess I am involved with her. But, believe me, she doesn't know it."

He could practically hear Jacob's grin. "Well, well, looks like you've met your match."

"Maybe. But she's been hurt so bad that all I want to do is protect her and I hardly know her."

"I've had those feelings before."

"Is that the way you felt about Miranda?"

"Yeah, and it was hell not being able to walk away."

"I know." Lucas sighed. "God, I don't know what to do."

"Yes, you do," Jacob told him. "Because you've already taken Blake's case and I have a feeling Blair had a lot to do with that."

"Probably."

"Blake has the best defense attorney in Texas, and I know Howard will be pleased when he finds out you're representing his nephew."

"We'll see and—" A baby's cry interrupted him.

"I've got to go, Lucas. Gracie's awake again and chewing on my shirt. Hang in there and call soon. Let me know how things are going."

"Okay, and kiss the kids for me."

"I will."

Lucas hung up the phone and stared at the clock. Damn, he had to go—it was already six-thirty.

SAM'S OFFICE was in the downtown area, in a modern spindle-shaped glass structure that rose over fifty stories to the Houston skyline. At seven o'clock precisely, Lucas stepped off the elevator onto Sam Logan's floor. The receptionist wasn't at work yet, so Lucas walked down the hall until he found the door with Sam's name on it.

He tapped on the door and opened it. The large room was full of people—Derek, Frank, Theo, Sam, Blair and Howard Tate—Howard the sheriff. He was taken aback. He'd thought the meeting was just between him and Sam. He tried not to look at Blair, but that was harder than he'd imagined. Her hair was loose and she wore a cobalt-blue suit. Even though her eyes were worried, she looked great—to him.

"Lawyer man," Howard Tate said, and came over and shook his hand. Howard was tall and thin with a no-nonsense attitude. "We meet again and I'll be damned if you don't resemble Jacob more every day."

"Thank you," he answered politely, his mind working overtime. He felt as if he'd walked into an ambush; he knew Sam was waiting to take control and tell him how he wanted the case handled. He had to disabuse him of that notion, and fast.

He glanced at everyone in the room, then let his eyes settle on Sam. "I'll make this short and sweet. As you heard last night, I'll take this case, but only if you give me complete control. I make all decisions—no interference from anyone."

Sam sat at his desk and Blair stood beside him. Lucas couldn't look at her. He had to do this his own way.

"Blake is my son," Sam said quietly. "I can't just turn his life over to you."

"That's what this is all about," Lucas said, his voice equally soft. "You have to trust me and I have to trust you."

Sam said nothing, just stared down at his hands.

Lucas inclined his head. "Well, then, I guess you don't need me." He moved toward the door.

"Just a minute." Howard stopped him, then he confronted Sam. "What the hell do you think you're doing?"

"Stay out of this, Howard," Sam warned. It was clear the two men were not on the best of terms.

"The hell I will. I'm not gonna let you sacrifice Blake's life because you can't relinquish control."

"Shut up," Sam growled.

But Howard kept on. "Blake is so confused and mixed up he doesn't know who he is anymore. And look at you. You're a mess. In your state you couldn't even represent a cockroach and win. And these top guns of yours are puppets you control with the flick of a finger." He ignored the rumble of protest from the other men. "Let Lucas represent Blake. It's his only chance. Can't you see that?"

Sam sat as if turned to stone and Blair gently touched his shoulder. "Daddy," she said softly. "Uncle Howard's right. You're the one who wanted Lucas to take the case in the first place."

He patted her hand. "I'm just so worried...."

Lucas took a step closer to Sam. "If it'll make you feel any better, I talked with Blake and I feel he's innocent. I think I can get that across to a jury."

Sam's head jerked up. "You've talked to Blake?"

"Yes."

"When?"

"About three o'clock this morning. Why?"

"Derek saw him for a few minutes yesterday, but that was it."

"Well." Lucas shrugged lightly. "The guards trust me and I got in without too much of a problem."

"See, Sam?" Howard slapped Lucas on the back. "He's a good attorney. He'll get the job done, even if he annoys the hell outta you."

The lighthearted words broke the tension in the room, but everyone was still focused on Sam, and Lucas knew he had to draw the line.

# CHAPTER EIGHT

LUCAS ARRIVED at the courthouse in time to talk to Carl Wright and Evan Holt, and it was clear they weren't willing to budge on their decision to oppose bail. But Lucas had other ideas. He was going to fight to get Blake out and he hoped they had a sympathetic judge. Lucas walked into the courtroom ready for battle.

Blair, Ava, Sam and Howard sat behind him and he realized they were waiting for Blake. They wanted to grab this moment to see him. The side door opened and two guards brought him in. He still had on his prison orange and his hands were cuffed, his feet in shackles.

He heard a choking sound and knew it came from Blair. He had to mentally force himself not to turn toward her. When the guard brought Blake to the defense table, Blair immediately jumped up and threw her arms around him.

"I'm sorry, sis, I'm sorry," Blake cried. "I couldn't tell you. I just couldn't."

"It's all right," Blair told him, wiping away a tear.

"Lucas will get you out of this," Howard added, patting him on the shoulder.

Sam and Ava embraced their son. "Don't worry, I—"

The arrival of the judge cut Sam short and they resumed their seats. The guard uncuffed Blake and he took his place beside Lucas.

Lucas was pleased to see Judge Higgins. She was tough but fair, and Lucas felt they stood a good chance with her.

"Mr. Wright, what have you got?" the judge asked.

Carrying a folder, Carl walked to the bench. "Murder in the first degree and rape, Your Honor," he replied. "A sixteen-year-old crime." He set the folder in front of her. "Bonnie Davis was murdered and raped on May tenth. Todd Easton was convicted of that crime, but there was skin tissue from two different people under her fingernails and we were never able to identify the other assailant—until now. Through new DNA testing, we were able to identify Blake Logan."

"I'm impressed," the judge said, paging through the folder.

"We also have eyewitnesses who saw Blake Logan with Todd Easton and Bonnie Davis that night, and we also have a witness who saw him get into a car with them."

The judge closed the folder. "What's the bottom line, Mr. Wright?"

"Mr. Logan lives in London and has done so for the past sixteen years. We consider him a high flight risk and we ask that you deny bail."

The judge glanced at Lucas. "Well, Mr. Culver, it's nice to see you."

Lucas smiled. "It's always a pleasure to see you, too, Judge."

Blair listened to this interchange; she used to hate it when Lucas used his charm on the judges, but she wasn't hating it now. She was glad Lucas had a good rapport with Judge Higgins. It could only help.

"How do you plead, Mr. Logan?" the judge asked.

Blake's back was straight and his voice firm. "Not guilty, Your Honor."

"So, Mr. Culver, give me a reason not to deny bail."

"Your Honor, this crime is sixteen years old and now the state says they have evidence that proves my client's guilt, but until everything's proven conclusively in a court of law, I see no reason to keep Blake Logan locked up. He is not a threat to society."

"DNA is pretty conclusive, Mr. Culver," the judge remarked, and Blair felt her stomach tighten.

Lucas shoved his hands into the pockets of his slacks. "Your Honor, my client will turn in his passport and—"

"Your Honor, please," Carl implored. "This is ridiculous. Mr. Culver is grasping at straws. The fact is that Blake Logan's a flight risk. If you grant bail, his father will get him out of the country and we'll never see him again."

"Calm down, Mr. Wright," the judge said, and looked at Lucas. "Mr. Culver, what I need is a guarantee that Mr. Logan will not flee this country."

Lucas knew he had to pull out all the stops. It was going to take nothing less than a miracle to make this happen. He took a step closer to the bench. "How well do you know me, Your Honor?"

"Too well, Mr. Culver. Too well."

Lucas inhaled deeply. "I give you my word that Blake Logan will be here when the trial starts. If he isn't, you can have my license."

"This is hogwash, even for Mr. Culver, Your Honor," Carl shouted. "We can't let criminals go because some attorney gives his word. That's absurd."

"You never cease to amaze me, Mr. Culver," the judge said.

"I keep trying," Lucas remarked charmingly.

The judge addressed Carl. "Normally I would agree with you, Mr. Wright, but I know Mr. Culver and he means every word he's saying."

"Your Honor," Carl protested.

The judge peered at Blake through narrowed eyes. "Mr. Logan, I hope Mr. Culver's faith in you is justified. Don't let him down. Bail is set at five hundred thousand dollars."

OhmyGod. OhmyGod. *Lucas did it* was all Blair could think. She gave her father and mother a quick hug, and as Lucas came back to the table she threw her arms around his neck and kissed his cheek. "Thank you, Lucas. Thank you," she whispered.

Lucas was still reeling from the judge's decision, but when Blair touched him, his emotions went in a completely different direction. His face felt hot—his whole body felt on fire—and all he wanted to do was hold her. However, she'd already turned to Blake and was hugging him. Lucas was surprised by his own reaction. He'd been kissed before, plenty of times, but he'd never felt this alive—and it was only a peck, a touch. He began to see that he was more involved with Blair than he'd ever thought possible. And he wasn't sure how that had happened.

When Lucas left the courtroom, he saw Blair talking to Roger Collins. Suddenly she hugged him and then ran out, following her parents. An alien emotion ran through him but he knew exactly what it was—plain old jealousy. He wondered how involved Blair and Roger were; he intended to find out for his own peace of mind.

He caught up with Roger and shook hands.

"Hey, Lucas, you pulled it off." Roger smiled his congratulations.

"Yeah." Lucas smiled back. "I think Judge Higgins has a soft spot for me."

"I just hope this wasn't a mistake."

Lucas frowned. "What do you mean?"

"Sam Logan isn't going to let his son be sent to prison and he'll prevent that from happening by whatever means necessary. I hope your career doesn't get destroyed in the process."

In that moment, Lucas knew that Roger didn't love Blair. If he did, he would be wholeheartedly behind her family—the way *he* was. The thought hit him out of the blue and he pushed it from his mind. He couldn't think about it right now; too many other things needed his attention.

"Don't worry about my career," he said cryptically. "I'll survive."

"I'm sure you will," Roger commented, then glanced at his watch. "I've got to run. I promised Blair I'd get her car back to her."

"Roger?" Lucas called as he walked away.

"Yes?" Roger turned to face him.

"Did you find anything on Blair's car?"

Roger looked surprised. "She told you?"

"About the message? Yes."

Roger shook his head. "I can't believe it. Blair was so adamant that you not find out. She didn't want you involved."

"A lot of things have changed in the last forty-eight hours," Lucas told him.

"I know, but still, Blair doesn't share things easily."

"This isn't about sharing. It's about her life," Lucas said shortly.

"That's what I tried to tell her, but she wouldn't listen to me."

"She didn't listen to me, either, but I'm concerned about her. We have to find out who's doing this."

"We found nothing on the car. I'm still questioning Raye's gang, though."

"And I'll talk to Raye."

Roger's eyes narrowed. "You sound more than concerned."

*I am, so stay away from Blair.*

"I am because she won't tell her parents," Lucas replied instead. "And I know Holt isn't going to pursue the incident."

"But I will," Roger asserted. "I'll get it sorted out."

*I'll bet you will,* Lucas thought as Roger walked off.

"WHAT THE HELL IS IT with Culver and women?" Evan roared as Carl entered his office.

Before Carl could respond, Evan raved on, "Higgins has to be sixty if she's a day and Culver smiles at her and she gives him exactly what he wants and all because she *believes* him. This is unprecedented garbage."

"Are you going to speak with Judge Higgins?" Carl asked.

"Hell, no," Evan growled. "The last thing I need to do is to antagonize a judge. It's hard enough getting a conviction these days. Judge Higgins had better pray that Blake Logan doesn't skip bail. If that happens, then I'll have more than a word with the judge."

Evan picked up a golf ball from his desk and leaned back, squeezing it repeatedly. "I underestimated Sam. He knew exactly what he was doing. None of those hotshots in his firm could've done what Culver did today. I just wonder how Sam got him to change his mind."

"The detective we have following Sam said he didn't leave his house until this morning when he came to court," Carl told him.

"Tell the detective to concentrate on Blake Logan. If he heads for an airport, I want to be informed immediately."

"Yes, sir."

Evan gripped the ball. "Blair talked Culver into taking the case," he said thoughtfully. "That's the only explanation."

"But she hates Lucas."

Evan gave a gruff laugh. "Yeah, but now her brother needs him and she's smart enough not to let her pride stand in the way." He threw the ball onto the putting green. "Damn, she's going to be a great asset to Culver."

"Yeah," Carl admitted.

Evan leaned forward. "Let's get this case on the docket as soon as possible. Meanwhile, you keep a close eye on Culver—and make damn sure we get a conviction."

"Yes, sir."

LUCAS WALKED into his office at noon and found Joan in a tizzy. She'd heard on the news that he was representing Blake Logan, and she wanted to know what was going on. He explained, then went to talk to Clive and George. They, too, had heard he'd taken the case. Although they weren't pleased that Lucas had taken such a high-profile case without discussing it with them first, they were delighted with the publicity it would generate for the firm. That, as always, was the selling point.

Later, in the afternoon, he introduced his team to Derek, Frank and Theo. He told everyone what he expected. Discovery motions were the top priority. He wanted transcripts from the first trial and fast; he also wanted all the evidence the D.A. had now. He was very curious about how the DNA evidence had been obtained, and he intended to discuss it with Blake again as soon as possible. He put Derek in charge. Everything went smoothly, although Brad, a young lawyer who'd worked for him a number of years, was disappointed that he wouldn't be second chair. Lucas didn't have time for petty grievances and made it clear that he wouldn't tolerate personal gripes.

In the evening he headed to the jail to talk to Raye during regular visiting hours. He didn't want to annoy the jail personnel any more than he had to.

Hector Raye was shown into the small room where Lucas waited for him. Hector was of medium height with long dark greasy hair and tattoos that covered most of his body. Hector greeted him contemptuously. "Well, if it ain't my esteemed attorney who couldn't do crap in the courtroom."

"Sit down, Hector," he ordered quietly, ignoring the nasty remark.

"Ain't nobody tells me what to do, man," Hector spit out.

Lucas got to his feet, towering over Hector by a good

three inches. With one hand Lucas pushed him into a chair. "Sit down, shut up and listen."

"You can't manhandle me," Hector said belligerently.

Lucas leaned closer and stared him in the eye. "Listen, and listen well. *Stop harassing Ms. Logan.*"

Hector shrank back. "Whaddaya mean, man?"

"Exactly what I said. Stop harassing Ms. Logan."

"I ain't doing nothing to that bitch. Hell, ain't I locked up?"

"But your gang isn't."

"My gang." Hector laughed. "They washed their hands of me the day I got convicted. Big Joe was just waitin' to take over."

Lucas straightened, shaking his head. "You know, Hector, I can never tell whether you're lying or telling the truth."

"Like I care, man."

Lucas bent down again. "Do you care about dying?"

Hector's eyebrows knotted together. "Whaddaya mean?"

"I mean your sentencing is coming up soon. It's either life in prison or a lethal injection. Jim Tenney is back at work, so he'll be handling the sentencing. I might just tell him not to plead for leniency—life in prison would be too easy for you." It was a bluff. Lucas wouldn't do such a thing, but he was counting on Hector's not knowing that.

His reaction confirmed it. "No, man, you can't do that!"

"Then tell me the truth."

"I ain't harassing Ms. Logan," he shouted. "Man, you gotta talk 'em out of giving me a lethal injection. You gotta."

Lucas's instincts told him Hector was telling the truth. He was more concerned with saving his own life than getting even with Blair.

It was late, but Lucas drove over to Blair's anyway. He

wanted to tell her about Hector, although he didn't know if that was good news or bad. If Hector wasn't harassing her, who was?

BLAIR HAD SPENT the evening with her family. She and Blake had talked and talked—just like old times—and he'd told her everything. She couldn't believe she'd been so blind about what was going on with her brother...before *and* after the murder. She had known he was on drugs but hadn't realized it was that bad. She'd known he ran around with a wild crowd but had thought he'd outgrow them. She'd never dreamed his life was such a mess, and neither had her parents, until after the attack.

When Todd had almost killed her, she hadn't understood why her parents wouldn't let Blake come home. Then later she'd wondered why Blake didn't come home on his own. He always gave convincing excuses, but somehow they never satisfied her. Now she understood. Ever since the attack, she'd been so absorbed in her own life, her own pain, that she'd overlooked the needs of her family. She wouldn't do that again.

She thought of Lucas all day. She even called his house later that evening, but he wasn't home. She wondered if he was out with Jennifer. That didn't matter, she told herself, but she couldn't quite believe it.

Today she had kissed him in the courtroom without even thinking. When she realized what she'd done, she'd quickly turned to Blake. Lucas had become rigid, as though he was in shock or something, and she knew it was because she'd let her true emotions show. Lucas wasn't used to that. He was used to her deriding or ridiculing him every chance she got. Things had changed so much in the past couple of days. Now her every other thought was of Lucas. Funny how your attitudes could reverse themselves so completely....

Her outlook on life had been so narrow, determined

solely by what had happened to her. She could see that now. Her goal had been to put criminals behind bars. She'd refused to even consider that there could be another side. Now she had to look at so many things differently. Blake was innocent. Would she believe that if Blake wasn't her brother, though? No, she probably wouldn't, she had to admit. Maybe she'd been unfair in her assessment of other cases.

Lucas had told her everyone deserved a fair trial—even people like Hector Raye. As a lawyer, she knew that and had sworn to uphold justice. Yet her cynicism about Raye and his kind, plus her single-minded dedication to her goal meant that she'd never questioned the guilt of those she'd prosecuted. At the thought of Raye, an old fear ran along her skin, but she couldn't give in to it.

She'd gone back to her apartment, but now she wished she'd stayed at her parents'. The hum of the refrigerator, the tick of the clock, every sound seemed magnified. It was a silly reaction; she was well aware of that, which was the only thing that reassured her.

She put on a silky blue nightgown with tiny straps. It came about six inches above her knees, as did the matching robe she slipped on. She curled up on the sofa, going through case histories—cases that had been tried when the murder was several years in the past. She was hoping to find something Lucas could use.

She almost jumped out of her skin when the intercom buzzed. She immediately pressed the button and found that Lucas was waiting to see her. Her heart started to race and she dashed to her room to change, but again, she knew she didn't have time. She ran back, turned off the alarm system and opened the door.

Lucas stood there, but a different Lucas from the one she'd seen this morning. He still wore his brown suit pants and cream shirt, but his tie and jacket were gone. His hair was rumpled, as were his clothes, and he looked tired. Still, he made her feel breathless.

"Hi," he said in an exhausted voice.

"Come in," she invited.

He walked past her into the living room. He was drained, but the sight of Blair in that blue skimpy thing shot his blood pressure up a few notches. Pushing law books aside, he sank down on the sofa.

"Doing some light reading?" he asked in a teasing tone.

She said something in reply, but she didn't know what. All she could do was stare at his dark stubble and wonder what it would feel like under her fingers. She had to remind herself to concentrate and she realized he could be here only for one reason—Blake's trial.

"Did you learn something?" she asked eagerly.

"You mean about Blake? No," he answered, his eyes slowly traveling over her. Her dark hair was loose around her shoulders the way he liked it, and that blue nightie left little to the imagination.

"Oh," she said in a disappointed voice.

"But I did find out something about Raye," he told her.

Fear entered her blue eyes and she couldn't hide it, not from him. He didn't want to tell her, but she had a right to know.

She sat in the Queen Anne chair and folded her hands in her lap. "What did you find out?"

Lucas took a breath. "He said he's not harassing you."

"And you believe him?"

Lucas shrugged. "It's hard to tell. Raye's a habitual liar, but in my gut I feel he's telling the truth."

"Then who would've done such a thing?"

Lucas shrugged again. "I don't know, but you have to be very careful. It would probably be best if you moved in with your parents."

"I'm not doing that," she snapped, getting up and grabbing law books and placing them on the coffee table.

"They'd watch my every move and worry themselves sick about me. I'm not putting them or myself through that again."

He saw how adamant she was, but he was concerned about her being here alone. "You could use the excuse of spending time with Blake."

"Blake has a lot of fences to mend with my parents, and I don't need to be around for that. Since I don't have a job anymore, I can visit with Blake during the day."

While she was talking, she stacked all the books on the table, then picked up several and carried them to a built-in bookcase. When she came back for more, Lucas grabbed her hand and pulled her onto the sofa. "Stop fussing and listen to me."

Blair was winded for a moment when she looked into Lucas's dark eyes, and all breath left her as she experienced sensual, delightful things that had nothing to do with fear.

"You have to be very careful," he repeated. "We don't know who's doing this, so you have to be on the alert."

She gulped in some desperately needed oxygen. "I *am* careful, but I'm not letting some lunatic dictate how I live my life."

Lucas groaned. "You're so damn independent, so damn stubborn."

"Maybe," she said.

"And you know what I'm thinking."

"No," she whispered.

"I'm thinking you make me angrier than anyone I've ever met. You make me say and do things I normally wouldn't. And all I'm thinking right now is how much I'd like to kiss you."

His smoldering eyes focused on her lips, and her breath was trapped in her throat. "You would?" The words came out low and husky.

"Yeah," he murmured, and his forefinger touched her full lower lip.

Unconsciously her tongue licked the sensitive spot. He watched the tantalizing movement as his hand moved slowly across her cheek, brushed hair behind her ear and came to rest on the nape of her neck. His eyes were riveted on her, and Blair sensed that she was being swept away by something stronger than herself, stronger than her fear. *Lucas.* He was stilling her fears with his gentleness and she wanted him to go on touching her. Oh yes, she wanted more.

Her desire darkened her eyes and Lucas didn't miss it. Slowly he eased her toward him and his lips tentatively touched hers, then covered them. She felt an aching need, felt it all the way to her soul. Lucas deepened the kiss, and then Blair was kissing him back with an intensity that shocked her.

At her capitulation, Lucas groaned and pulled her tight against him. "God, you smell good and you feel even better." His hand roamed freely across her back. "Just like I always thought you would."

"You've thought of me?" she asked in a small voice.

"Sure," was the quick answer. "When you were spitting fire at me in the courtroom, I used to wonder what you'd do if I kissed you. Would all that fire turn into passion?"

"And?" she prompted, knowing she was fishing for a compliment but unable to help herself.

"Oh, Blair, stop tormenting me," he moaned. "Stop dancing in my dreams."

Blair drew back; Lucas wasn't making any sense. And she knew why. He was half-asleep.

"Lucas, how much sleep have you had?"

"About two hours."

"I think you're punch-drunk."

"I'm definitely drunk on something." He grinned, and his hand lightly touched her breast.

She caught his hand, not because she wanted him to stop, but because she knew he'd have no memory of it in the morning. And she wanted him wide-awake when they did this for real. Somehow she felt it was a foregone conclusion and that didn't frighten her at all—not at all.

"Spoilsport," he mumbled.

"Go to sleep, Lucas," she whispered, and settled her head under his chin. Her body rested on his and she loved the way their contours seemed to fit—so close, so perfectly together.

Soon she heard his deep breathing and knew he was asleep, but she still didn't move. Even with all the crises and problems in her life, she felt safe and at peace in Lucas's arms. Eventually, though, she moved from the security of his embrace.

Blair went into the bedroom and grabbed a pillow and a blanket. She threw the pillow on the sofa, then stooped to take off Lucas's shoes. He didn't wake up. She drew his head down to the pillow and arranged his long legs across the end of the sofa. Finally, she covered him with the blanket and stared down at his face, resisting the urge to steal another kiss.

She didn't know what tomorrow might bring, but she knew that Lucas would be part of it. He had forgiven her rudeness and come to their rescue today. For that, she would be forever grateful.

*What the hell,* she thought, and reached down to give him a quick kiss. He stirred and murmured her name. She smiled. He had definitely said *Blair* and not another woman's name. The smile lingered as she floated into bed.

# CHAPTER NINE

BLAIR SLEPT more soundly and deeply than she had in months. A noise woke her in the early hours of the morning. She sat up as fear charged through her, then relaxed as she remembered Lucas sleeping on the sofa. The noise became louder and she slipped out of bed and headed to the living room. The sofa was empty, and the blanket lay on the floor, as did Lucas's clothes. Her eyes swung toward the noise. Lucas was in the kitchen opening doors and drawers. He had nothing on but a pair of black briefs. Her breath lodged in her throat at the sight of his lean, masculine body. She turned toward the bedroom, thinking it was best if she left Lucas alone, especially after her reaction to him last night. She felt so vulnerable to him and didn't understand why. All she knew was that he was affecting her emotions in ways she hadn't expected.

She heard a curse and decided she could handle a half-naked Lucas. He was obviously searching for something and needed help.

"What are you searching for?" she asked, walking into the kitchen. She purposely avoided looking at his body and the dark swirls of hair on his chest.

"Coffee," came the gruff answer. "I need coffee."

"It's in the canister by the sink," she told him.

"By the sink?" he growled. "Why isn't it by the coffeepot? Coffee should be kept by the coffeepot."

"I keep it in the canister—by the sink," she replied

stiffly, beginning to lose her temper at his arrogant attitude. "And I'd appreciate it if you'd put some clothes on."

His dark eyes bore into her. "And I'd appreciate it if you left me alone."

"Fine," she snapped, and returned to her bedroom.

She straightened her bed and found her robe and pulled it on. She took a couple of deep breaths and smiled. She'd never had a man in her apartment in the morning and if this was what it was like, then she wasn't missing a thing—except maybe seeing Lucas's body. That might just be worth his bad mood.

When she went back to the kitchen, Lucas had his slacks on and he was opening cabinets again. The slacks didn't help all that much. She'd already seen the briefs and knew—

"Where're your mugs?" he asked when he noticed her.

"Mugs?"

"Yeah, you know the round things you put coffee in."

"First door on the right."

He opened the door and groaned. "That's a cup. I need a mug."

"I don't have a mug. I have cups."

He picked up one of the fragile blue-and-white cups and stared at it. "I can't drink out of this dainty thing."

She bit her tongue. "It's all I have."

"Women," he complained, filling the cup to the rim. "They have to have everything just so. Miranda's the same way. With five kids, you'd think she'd learn."

Blair reached for a cup and wondered who Miranda was. The mother of the children she'd seen on Lucas's wall? It was none of her business, she told herself firmly as she poured a cup of coffee. But she was curious—very curious.

Lucas finished one cup and glanced at her. "Do you know how many times I'll have to fill this thing?"

She added milk and sugar to her coffee. "I'm not counting."

"Why do you do that?"

She glanced up. "What?"

"Ruin your coffee like that. You can get the same sweetness from a soda pop."

She put her hands on her hips. "Do you know you're a grouch first thing in the morning?"

He grinned and she could see the charming Lucas emerging. "So I've been told," he remarked, and headed for the living room.

*Told by whom?*

She picked up her cup and followed. He started putting on his shoes while she sat at the end of the sofa, sipping her coffee.

"I'm not human until I have my first cup of coffee," he was saying. "I guess that's why I'm still single. No woman wants to put up with a bad-tempered man that early in the morning."

That wasn't the reason he was single, she thought. A lot of women—a lot—would put up with Lucas any time, day or night and especially mornings. Including herself. She brought her thoughts to a screeching halt. She was getting in over her head.

As Lucas bent down for his shirt, he caught the look on Blair's face. Her cheeks were flushed and her lips were wet with coffee. Her tongue touched her bottom lip and it triggered something in his head—something pleasurable. He felt as if he'd kissed those lips and felt her tongue against his, which was absurd. He had never kissed Blair like that.

"Sorry about last night," he said, buttoning his shirt. "I came over here to tell you about Raye, but I don't remember much after that."

She'd suspected that. He didn't remember a thing about kissing and holding her. But she did and she would for a very long time.

"You were wiped out from lack of sleep," she replied.

"Normally I need very little sleep. I must be getting older."

"Ancient," she murmured.

"You're not supposed to agree with me."

"I'm afraid not to." She smiled. "You might turn back into Mr. Grouch."

"Naw," he said, smiling back. "Once I've had my coffee, I'm as sweet as a teddy bear for the rest of the day...and night."

She carefully placed her cup on the end table. "I don't believe I thanked you for taking Blake's case."

"Sure you did," he remarked absently. "Where the hell did I put my car keys?"

"Still, I want you to know how much I appreciate it."

Lucas was shoving his hand into various pockets. "Better save those thank yous until the end of the trial. Because it isn't going to be easy. Now, I have a mound of work to sort through today and I need to get going. Ah," he said with a sigh, pulling keys from his pants pocket. "Thanks for letting me crash on your couch," he added as he hurried to the door.

"Is there anything I can do to help?" she asked.

"Yeah." He turned to her. "Could you have Blake at my office by ten o'clock? I need to talk to him about the DNA."

"Sure, no problem," she replied, then added, "I asked Evan about the DNA and he wouldn't tell me, but he said it was all legal."

"We'll see about that," he said, checking the gold watch on his wrist. "I have to run. Be careful, and keep an eye over your shoulder."

"I will," she promised as fear skittered along her nerves.

Lucas noticed the change in her expression and mistook

it for something else. "Blair, I didn't do anything stupid last night, did I?"

She lifted an eyebrow. "Like what?"

He shrugged. "I don't know, but every time I look at you there's something on the edge of my memory."

"Maybe it'll come to you," she said, not wanting to tell him what had happened. She wanted him to remember on his own.

"Maybe," he muttered, wondering why he had the strong urge to kiss her and feeling as if he'd already done that and enjoyed every minute of it.

He shook off the odd sensation. "Keep the door locked," he ordered as he left.

She bolted the door and leaned against it. She let the warmth wash over her—a sense of new discoveries and tantalizing moments. She allowed herself that brief time, then dashed into the living room and folded the blanket. She had to shower and dress and go to her parents' place. Her mind focused once again on what was important—Blake's trial.

LUCAS WAS in his office by seven. He wanted to be prepared for whatever Evan and Carl threw at him. Since Blake was a minor at the time of the murder, he figured Carl would file a motion to have Blake certified as an adult. He didn't have a problem with that. He just needed to go through the evidence to find out where he stood and what kind of chance Blake had.

Derek was handling the new evidence and Frank the old. Theo had volunteered to go to London to get information on Blake's life. Lucas wanted to know all about him, from people he came in contact with every day. He felt the facts would be positive, but he had to be sure.

The DNA match still bothered him and he wanted to talk to Blake. He glanced at the clock, hoping Blair would get him here soon.

BLAIR ENTERED her parents' home through the kitchen, as always. Her mother was at the stove, wearing a long pink robe.

"Hi, Mom," she said, hugging her.

Her mother enveloped her in a tight hold. "Oh, darling, I'm so afraid."

"Lucas will handle everything," she replied in a reassuring voice.

"I suppose," Ava mumbled.

"Where are Dad, Blake and Uncle Howard?"

"Your father's in his study, Howard left early to see some friends and Blake's upstairs."

As Blair moved toward the door, her mother said, "Tell Blake his breakfast is ready. I made his favorite—cheese omelette, biscuits and maple syrup. And tell him not to be long or it'll get cold."

A smile touched Blair's face as she ran upstairs. Her mother was spoiling Blake, but then she'd always done that. Ava had been the buffer between Sam and Blake during those terrible years. Blair had to admit she had, too. She and her mother had lied for her brother and hidden things from Sam so Blake wouldn't get into trouble. They'd been wrong to do that. They should've made Blake face the consequences of his actions. Now she feared that he would—consequences that might be far graver than his actions deserved.

She opened his door and saw him sitting on the window seat, staring off into space.

"Hi," she said and sat beside him. He was neatly dressed in khaki slacks and a blue shirt that matched his eyes. The expression on his face was solemn and brooding.

"Did Mom send you?" he asked quietly.

"Yes, your breakfast's ready."

"I'm not hungry," he said gloomily.

"Blake, it's not—"

He broke in. "Stop it," he shouted, jumping to his feet.

"I can't take all this love and support. It's getting to me. I don't deserve it."

She frowned. "What do you mean you don't deserve it?"

He whirled to face her, his eyes filled with pain. "Bonnie Davis died because I was a weak, sniveling coward."

"That's not true!"

"It is," he insisted.

She got up and put her arm around him. She didn't want to say the next words, but she had to.

"You said you didn't kill Bonnie Davis and I believe you, but you're *acting* guilty."

"I didn't kill her, but her death is always with me and I can't live like this anymore."

"Oh, Blake," she cried, feeling his hurt and pain.

"I have to make this right."

"What are you talking about?"

Blake started for the door. "I have to talk to Mr. Culver."

"Oh." Blair ran after him. "Lucas wants to see you before ten o'clock. He wants to talk to you about the DNA evidence."

"Good, because I have to tell him something."

Blair didn't know what that meant, but it didn't sound good and she was going to make sure she was there for the meeting.

LUCAS'S MIND was reeling from so much information that he was ready for a break when Blair, Blake and Sam entered his office. He noticed that Blair was wearing her stern business apparel—a hunter-green pants suit that covered every inch of her body. So different from the feminine woman he had seen last night.

"Good morning, Mr. Culver," Blake said politely.

"Call me Lucas," he invited, eyeing the three solemn

faces. Blake looked dejected and Blair seemed tense. Lucas knew something was up.

As they took their seats, Blake said, "I need to talk to you."

Lucas nodded. "I need to talk to you, too."

"What about?"

"The DNA evidence."

Blake's face colored slightly. "What about it?"

"I asked you once before if you had any idea how the district attorney got your DNA." Lucas paused. "I'm asking again."

Blake glanced nervously at Sam, then back at Lucas. "I gave it to them."

"What?" Sam leaped out of his chair. "Are you stupid?"

Lucas could see Blake cringing. Blair got up and touched Sam's arm. "Daddy, please."

"No," he shook off her hand and addressed Blake. "Tell me you didn't do something that stupid?"

"Yes, I did," Blake flared in a spurt of anger. "Your stupid, ignorant son screwed up again, but this time I did it because I wanted to. That's the reason I came home. Mr. Ramsey, the private investigator who found me in London, asked if I'd give a DNA sample and I said yes. I came back to the States and went to the lab Mr. Ramsey told me about. I had some blood taken, and then he informed the D.A." Blake paused, shaking his head. "I knew what was going to happen. I knew my DNA would match. I can't live with the guilt anymore. I wish you'd try and understand that."

That was it, Blair thought. That was what Blake had to tell Lucas. He had voluntarily provided his DNA and had come home to accept his punishment, but now he had to face the rage of his father—once again.

Lucas recognized that he was rapidly losing control of the situation. "Sam, I need to talk to Blake alone."

"What the hell for?" he roared. "He just handed Holt the case on a platter and he doesn't even realize what he's done. Out of some obscure sense of guilt, he's willing to sacrifice both our lives."

Lucas motioned for Blair to get Sam out of the room. This open hostility wasn't helping anyone, especially Blake.

Blair caught Lucas's eye and led her father from the room. He didn't object. "What's wrong with him, Blair? What's wrong with him?" Sam kept saying.

That scene gave Lucas a view into Blake Logan's life and it wasn't pretty. As much as Lucas hated what his father had done to his mother, he had to admit that his father had never called him stupid. He'd always called him his brilliant son and Jacob his dependable, responsible son. He'd brag about his fine boys. Funny how he'd suddenly remembered that. It had somehow slipped his mind.

Blake was noticeably shaken and Lucas walked into the small kitchen attached to his office and poured a glass of water. He handed it to Blake, who grabbed it like a lifeline.

Lucas leaned back against his desk, allowing Blake a few minutes to recover. He thought about Sam's behavior. Yesterday he'd been heartbroken, unable to tolerate the thought of his son in jail. Today he was like a madman—berating and belittling his son in front of others. This must have been a pattern all of Blake's life and probably the reason for many of his problems.

He wondered if Sam treated Blair the same way. If so, she'd handled it better than Blake. She was fiercely independent and had a strong sense of self. She was coping with a lot—her brother's trial, the loss of her job, anonymous threats—and he wondered how much more she could stand.

"I wanted to tell you when you came to see me in jail, but I lost my courage," Blake finally said.

"You can't keep things from me. You have to be honest with me," Lucas said.

"I know and I'm sorry, but I knew how Dad would react." He shrugged. "I didn't mean for him to get caught in the middle. I just want this to be over."

Lucas folded his arms across his chest. "You were saying similar things the other night. It's very clear that guilt is what's driving you. So you have to make a decision right here, right now. Do you want to fight this thing or do you want to go to prison?"

"God." He shakily put the glass on a table. "One night in jail's more than I can bear. I don't know how I'd survive prison, but…"

His voice trailed off and Lucas watched him. "Okay, Blake, talk to me. Tell me what you're feeling."

"If I hadn't been so high on drugs and booze that it made me physically ill, I might've been able to stop Todd. And later, I should've told the police the truth, but I was scared—scared for my own stinking life. If I hadn't been such a coward, Todd wouldn't have beaten Blair practically to death. And now her life is messed up. She has a hard time with intimacy, avoids any kind of serious relationship. And it's all my fault."

Blake's words triggered something in Lucas's head. He could feel Blair's tender, yielding lips under his. Last night came back to him in a rush. He tried to remember if Blair had resisted his kiss. If she was repulsed. But, no, she was soft, pliable and— Oh, God. He straightened and walked around his desk. Had he done such a male, selfish thing? Oh, God, he had.

He'd have to think about it later. First he had to deal with Blake. "Listen to me, Blake. You couldn't have stopped Todd. He probably would've killed you, too. And you couldn't help what happened to Blair. She's not blaming you, so stop blaming yourself. She's fighting for your freedom—your life. Quit wallowing in self-pity and show me some backbone. I can't win this case without your help. If you can't do it for yourself, then do it for Blair. She deserves that much.''

Blake buried his face in his hands. "I'd do anything for her.''

Lucas gave him a moment. "I know you're filled with guilt, remorse and so many other feelings I can barely imagine. You've been punishing yourself for sixteen years. You said Blair didn't have much of a life. I'm guessing you don't, either.''

He looked up. "How can I? Every time I get close to someone, I remember my past and I put an end to the relationship. I just can't hurt anyone else.''

Such a nightmare, Lucas thought, and he wondered if his skills were equal to the task. He could only try because he knew that Blake needed someone, besides his sister, to believe in him. And he also knew the only way to reach Blake was through Blair.

"A minute ago you said you'd do anything for Blair," Lucas reminded him.

"Yes, and I meant it.''

"You and Blair have been living in your own self-imposed prisons. It's time to set both of you free.''

Blake frowned uncertainly. "How?''

"By not letting guilt overshadow the fact that you were an innocent bystander.''

Blake didn't say anything, just stared at him as if he couldn't comprehend the statement.

Lucas continued. "And by keeping a picture of Blair in your head—the way she used to be and will be again. A happy, smiling Blair.''

"And dancing?'' Blake added with a touch of excitement.

Lucas's eyes widened. "Dancing?'' He remembered Blair dancing in her office. Did she do that often?

"Yeah. When we were small, Blair took ballet lessons.

She was very good at it. Sometimes she'd line up her dolls on the sofa in the living room and she'd dance for them. I caught her one day and I laughed and she chased me around the sofa. We tumbled on the floor, laughing and laughing. After that, she danced all over the house. Whenever she was happy, she'd dance. God, I wish I could see her like that again.''

Lucas felt a lump in his throat. He'd seen Blair like that and it was definitely something to behold. He felt a twinge of jealousy that someone else had witnessed the transformation, which was ridiculous. He was becoming too involved with thoughts of Blair.

Lucas walked around and leaned against the desk again. ''Well, Blake, let's make that our goal.''

''What?'' Blake looked confused.

''That at the end of this trial Blair will be happy and dancing again.''

''You think it can happen?'' Blake seemed more confused than ever.

''I'm going to put everything I've got into getting you out of this mess,'' Lucas promised.

A tiny smile lifted his lips. ''I don't know why Blair disliked you so much. You're really very nice.''

''Blair and I have a bit of...history.''

''Defense attorney history?''

''Yeah.'' Lucas sighed regretfully.

''That's all because of the attack,'' Blake said. ''Nothing against you personally.''

Lucas cocked his head to one side. ''Maybe, but I think she and I are on the same wavelength now.''

Blake looked down at his hands. ''Because of me, Blair has done a ninety-degree turn.''

''Yes, she's looking at things differently and personally, I don't think that's all bad.''

Blake glanced up, that tiny smile returning to his face. ''I think you could be good for her.''

Lucas imagined Blair's lips against his and for a moment he was completely lost in the feeling. He quickly jolted himself back to reality. "Maybe," he said again, and pushed a button on his desk. "Now I want you to go with one of my assistants. I want you to tell him everything that happened on May tenth—from the moment you woke up to the time you went to bed. Then I want you to do the same thing tomorrow and the day after, and once I get all the evidence, we'll go over it again and again until I'm clear about every single detail."

Blake frowned. "Why so many times?"

"Because the only way to bring it all back is to talk about it, and the more you talk about it, the more you'll remember."

"Oh God," Blake groaned. "I don't *want* to remember."

"I know it's hard," Lucas told him, "but it might bring back some fact that can help your case."

At Blake's silence, he added, "Just keep seeing Blair's happy, smiling face… Imagine her dancing again."

Blake nodded and got slowly to his feet, the thought of Blair's happiness obviously working wonders with his attitude.

There was a tap at the door and Greg, his assistant, stepped in. Lucas introduced them and they left for the first round of questioning.

Lucas threw himself down in his chair and rubbed his face in a weary gesture. This case was going to be the hardest he'd ever tried. There were so many things working against Blake—the DNA evidence, Sam Logan's attitude and Blake's own guilt. He had to find a way to resolve all three. But through all of that, Blair was uppermost in his mind.

He was trying to remember what had happened last night. He recalled looking at her shining face and saying he wanted to kiss her. She'd caught her breath and he'd taken that as a sign of permission or agreement, but maybe it had been something else. Maybe she'd dreaded his touch, his kiss. Surely he would have known that. He was exhausted, but even in his tired state he wouldn't have kissed her unless she'd wanted him to. Would he? No, he'd never done anything like that in his life and he knew that if she'd resisted he wouldn't have touched her.

He shouldn't even be in this position, he told himself. He knew her past, so he shouldn't have been thinking about doing anything with Blair. Until a few days ago, she was just a woman who infuriated the hell out of him. Now she was a woman who intrigued him in so many ways—professionally and personally, and he was having a hard time separating the two.

# CHAPTER TEN

LUCAS HEARD A KNOCK at the door and Blair poked her head around. "Can I talk to you for a minute?" she asked.

He stood up. "Sure," he replied, knowing he had to talk to her, too. He couldn't get emotionally involved with her while working on Blake's case. Too much was at stake and she would understand that. But how did he tell her? How did he explain last night? Easy, he told himself. Blair wasn't a teenager, and she knew that something was happening between them. But did she? She was so naive when it came to relationships although that was strictly an assumption based on her past and what Blake had said. Hell, how did he handle this?

*Tell the truth, even if it hurts*—that was what Jacob had always told him. But how was he going to do that when he didn't even know what the truth was? All he knew was that he had to apologize for last night, then he'd take it from there.

"I know you were surprised by Dad's outburst," she was saying, and Lucas glanced at her face. She had taken the chair Blake had vacated and her dark hair was up and he didn't like it that way, but it didn't keep the beauty of her eyes from shining through. Eyes that were filled with worry and pain. He knew Blair wasn't focused on anything but her family and this tragic situation. Whatever had happened last night she'd either forgotten or chosen to ignore. He wasn't happy with either of those possibilities. "But he's terribly upset and emotions are running high."

Lucas walked around the desk and sat on the corner facing her, trying to understand what she was really saying. "Are you excusing his rude behavior?" he asked.

She twisted her purse strap. "No, of course not, and I told him that if he ever did that again I'd never forgive him. Besides, he knows as well as I do that Evan could have gotten a court order to get Blake's DNA. It would've taken longer, but the results would have been the same. Dad hates it that Blake is making this easy for Evan."

"I don't condone the way Sam talked to Blake. Blake is carrying enough guilt without Sam adding to it." Blair didn't say anything, merely sat there with her head bowed. "And I can't help wondering if he treats you in the same manner."

She raised her head, those blue eyes defensive. "Dad's not a bad person. He just loves his kids too much."

Lucas clasped one knee with both hands. "Cut the crap, Blair. If you can't be honest with me, then we're in big trouble."

Blair looked down at her lap again. She had a difficult time talking about her childhood. It hadn't been unhappy, just fraught with tension. How did she explain that to Lucas?

Seeing she was having a hard time, Lucas said, "I can guess at your childhood. As early as you can remember, you probably knew that the very best was expected of you because you were Sam Logan's daughter. Being the stronger, more intelligent twin, you made sure you never disappointed your parents. Blake, on the other hand, probably found out at an early age that his sister outshined him in everything and, having a rebellious streak, he refused to give in to Sam's wishes. I imagine there was a great deal of tension in your household, with you always protecting your brother and making excuses for Sam—like now."

Her eyes met his. She wanted to deny what he'd said, but it was as near to the truth as he could get. "I'm not making excuses,'' she muttered, conscious of how feeble that sounded.

"Oh, yes, you are," he replied quickly. "Excuses for Sam and Blake. You've probably done that all your life. But now you have to let Blake tell Sam that he can't treat him like a child. Blake has to stand up to him without your help."

Lucas was right, but it was so hard to stop protecting Blake. It seemed to be second nature to her. "Why are we talking about this?" she asked shortly. "That's not why I came in here."

*To avoid talking about other things, Blair—like you and me.*

"Why *did* you come in here?"

Blair swallowed. "To ask if you'd also handle Dad's case. You'd be the best lawyer to represent him since you're familiar with everything."

Lucas didn't know why he resented her words, but he did. He swung his leg off the desk. "I am not your family's salvation nor am I a miracle worker," he said in a burst of temper.

Her eyes darkened. "I didn't say you were."

"Until a few days ago you hated my guts and now I'm expected…expected to redeem your family."

Standing, she slipped the strap of her purse over her shoulder in a quick movement. "I'm sorry if I'm expecting too much of you."

Oh God, she was hurt and he knew that tears weren't far away. *Don't cry, Blair. I can't stand it when you cry.* The truth hit him square between the eyes—and not for the first time. His emotions were already involved and Blair controlled him with a glance, a look, a tear.

"Don't do that," he said more sharply than he'd intended.

She frowned. "What?"

"Don't look at me like I'm the most important person in the world to you."

*You are,* her heart answered. She wondered how that had happened—and so quickly. But as Lucas had said, he wasn't her salvation. He was just an attorney she didn't like all that much. And that was probably the biggest lie she'd ever told herself. At least she recognized it. For once.

A flustered look came over her face. "I'd better go before we get into an argument."

"Now, that would be a first," he said sarcastically.

She started for the door and he knew he couldn't leave things like this. He was acting irrational again. But at the core of his disquiet was the fact that he might not be able to give her the miracle she wanted. That shook him. He *wanted* to help the Logan family—for her.

"Blair…"

She turned as the door burst open and a man charged in. He was of medium height with graying brown hair and grayish-green eyes. And he was angry—that was very clear from his red face to the veins bulging in his neck.

He pointed a finger at Lucas. "You won't get Logan's boy off. They're going to put him away like they should've done sixteen years ago and there's nothing you can do about it. Sam's money can't save him now."

Joan stood behind the man and Lucas nodded to her and she got the message. She went to call the police.

A gasp left Blair's throat and the man whirled in her direction. "You," he shouted angrily. "You're the reason my boy's dead."

Lucas jumped across his desk and got between Blair and the insane man. "Get out of my office or I'll throw you out," Lucas warned.

The man's feverish eyes took in Lucas's bigger frame. "You won't get him off, Culver. You won't," he sneered as he disappeared through the door.

Lucas followed him to make sure he was gone.

"The police are on their way," Joan whispered. "That was Lloyd Easton, Todd Easton's father."

"I figured," Lucas muttered, and hurried back to Blair.

His heart constricted at the sight of her. Her face was white and she was trembling badly. She was locked in her own inner fear and he wasn't sure how to reach her.

"Blair." He touched her arm gently.

She jerked away. "No, don't touch me," she whimpered in a strangled voice that tied his heart into such a tight knot he could scarcely breathe. The man had opened a window into the past—a past she couldn't deal with.

He was at a complete loss as to how to help her but he had to. He remembered when Miranda had been so afraid and how Jacob had always been able to calm her with his soothing voice. He and Blair didn't have the bond that Jacob and Miranda had, but he was hoping against hope that his voice would reach her.

He bent to look directly into her dazed eyes. "Blair, it's Lucas. He's gone. He can't hurt you. I won't let anyone hurt you. Blair, can you hear me? It's Lucas."

She felt a blow to her face, to her chest, to her stomach—the butt of the gun digging deeper and deeper into her flesh. The pain ripped through her body as real as it had been sixteen years ago. The wild grayish-green eyes were the same, as were the anger and rage, and all of it was centered on her. She couldn't breathe and she felt herself sinking farther and farther into the abyss of oblivion where nothing could touch her ever again.

Then she heard it.

*Blair. Blair. Blair.*

Someone was calling her name in a loving, caring, reassuring way. She tried to shut her ears to the sound and let the fear control her—she was tired of fighting it—but the voice wouldn't let her.

"Blair, look at me. Blair." The voice became demanding, pulling her back. She didn't want to go, but the voice was relentless.

"Blair. Blair."

Against everything in her, she focused her eyes and stared into Lucas's worried face.

"Lucas?" she whispered.

"Yes, yes, it's me," he answered gratefully, wanting to touch her, to hold her, but he knew she wasn't ready.

"Todd's father was here," she said plaintively as the events came rushing back. "He has the same eyes, the same rage—and all of a sudden it all came back—the fear, the pain, the agony." She reached down and grabbed her purse, which she had dropped on the floor. "I've got to go." She didn't know where, but she had to get away.

Without thinking, Lucas caught her arm and she didn't pull away. She didn't do anything but stare into his dark eyes, letting their warmth and comfort soothe her.

"You're not going anywhere until Easton's in custody," he told her. "Here—" he led her to a chair "—sit until I can talk with the police, then I'll take you home."

"I'm fine now," she protested.

"No, you're not," he replied. "So stay there and I'll be right back."

Blair sat staring off into space, wondering what had just happened to her. It was almost like an out-of-body experience, and for the first time she'd seen herself giving up— letting the fear claim her. If it hadn't been for Lucas.... She shuddered, not wanting to think that after all these years the fear could still destroy her sanity. Oh God, would she ever be free?

Lucas met one of the policemen in Joan's office. They had apprehended Easton in the lobby; they were going to take him to the station and let him cool off. The officer told Lucas there wasn't a lot they could hold him on, and Lucas knew he was right. However, Lucas asked them to make it very plain that Easton was to stay away from Blair. The officer agreed.

Lucas made a quick decision. "Joan, I'll be gone for the rest of the day."

"Lucas," Joan said irritably, "how can you even think such a thing with all this chaos? Remember, I'm supposed to be on vacation."

"I know and I appreciate your helping out, but this is important and I know you'll understand."

She lifted an eyebrow, showing him that she didn't understand at all, but it didn't change Lucas's mind.

"If anything comes up, either Derek or Brad can take care of it. We're only dealing with preliminary issues right now, but if anything needs my attention you can reach me on my cell phone."

"Yeah, yeah, yeah." She accepted his decision with her usual good nature. "I suppose this has to do with Blair Logan?"

"It does," he admitted, walking toward his office. Then he stopped. "When Greg finishes with Blake, could you get someone to drive him to his parents' house?"

"And I could also do your laundry in my spare time," she said with a touch of sarcasm.

"Come on, Joan," he coaxed. "Do me this little favor."

She shook her head. "Someday, Lucas, a woman is going to say no to you. Unfortunately it's not me, so go and I'll handle this bedlam."

"You're a doll," he said with a grin.

"Yeah, yeah, yeah." She brushed him off.

He hurried back to his office, glancing at Blair to make sure she was still with him and not in that dark place where he couldn't reach her. He patted his slacks, then shoved his hands into his jacket pockets.

"What are you looking for?" Blair asked, but she'd already guessed. He was searching for his keys again. Apparently, Lucas had a hard time keeping track of them.

"Keys," he answered as he fished them out of his trousers. "Now, let's get the hell out of here."

"I can't," she objected. "I have to wait for Blake—to drive him back to my parents' house."

"Joan will make sure he gets a ride home," he told her.

"Still…" She hesitated. "I need to be here for him."

Lucas walked over to her. "Blair, listen to me. Blake doesn't need a second mother and he doesn't need a baby-sitter. He has to come to terms with his own life, his own problems, without pressure from anyone."

She didn't say anything, but she acknowledged that Lucas was right. She had to stop protecting Blake, and her father had to stop pressuring him. They had to let him make decisions on his own.

"You have to start thinking about yourself," she heard Lucas say. "You wanted to get away and I'm offering you that opportunity." He strolled to the side door and opened it. "You coming?"

She still sat in the chair unmoving, her emotions scattering in all directions, but one thing was very clear. She *did* want to get away—just for a little while—to clear her head. She needed that above everything else.

Without another thought, she stood up and followed Lucas out the door, down the hall to the elevators. They walked to the parking garage in silence. When they came to his blue Expedition, he pressed the button on his key ring to unlock the doors. Blair went around to the passenger side and got in. As she did, she noticed two children's car seats in the back; they reminded her of the small bicycles she'd seen at his house. What did Lucas need children's seats—or bicycles—for? She'd ask him later. She wasn't in the mood for asking questions.

Lucas drove out of the garage and toward the highway. She didn't know where they were going and she really didn't care. She leaned her head against the headrest and let Lucas take her away.

After a while, Lucas slowed down, and pulled into a McDonald's. She glanced at him.

"We haven't had lunch and I'm starving," he said.

She never ate fast food, but she didn't tell him that. She had a feeling Lucas ate anything he wanted without worry, and today she would try to do the same thing.

He ordered two Big Macs with fries and drinks, and soon they were on their way. Lucas exited the freeway onto a feeder road, then turned down a gravel road that led to a small pond hidden among tall oak tress. In early June, the place was peaceful and serene. Ducks and geese swam freely and an old man fished at one end. There were several park benches and picnic tables around the area.

"Time for lunch," Lucas said, slipping out of his suit jacket and removing his tie. He threw them into the back seat, grabbed the bag of burgers and climbed out of the vehicle. Blair followed more slowly. Lucas sat at one end of a park bench and she sat at the other; he spread the food between them and handed her a burger. She accepted it although she doubted she could eat the food. But the tantalizing smell and her empty stomach persuaded her and she took a bite, then another. Before she knew it, she was dipping fries into ketchup and actually enjoying the treat. They ate without speaking. Soon Lucas wadded up the empty papers and carried them to one of the large trash cans. They held on to their drinks, and Blair was idly sipping hers, trying to keep the memories at bay.

Lucas settled beside her, gazing across the water, giving her time. He'd brought her here so she could talk. He felt she probably needed that more than anything. The silence grew.

"How did you find this place?" she finally asked.

"My dad used to bring my brother and me fishing here. Of course, I wasn't interested in fishing, but my brother was. I was completely satisfied to lie under one of these big old oaks and read. I wasn't much of an outdoor person back then.''

''But you are now?''

''Yeah.'' He looked at her. ''Life changes everyone, I suppose.''

He said the words with a touch of regret. ''You say that like you're sorry about it.''

''No, I'm not sorry,'' he told her. ''I'm just sorry about the way it happened.''

''Oh?'' She turned on the seat to face him, wanting to hear his story more than she would ever have thought possible.

He twisted the paper cup in his hand. ''My parents both died when I was fifteen. My brother was five years older, and he was my strength, my support. He worked two jobs to put me through law school. He made sure I had everything I wanted. He's that type of person—strong, selfless, dedicated. He didn't deserve what happened to him.''

*Oh God, please don't let him be dead,* she prayed. She didn't want Lucas to have experienced that kind of pain. The thought confused her, and she knew she was beginning to care about him in all sorts of ways. She wasn't sure how to cope with that so she returned her thoughts to his brother. She remembered his mentioning a brother the night of the dinner—something about needing his approval. His brother meant a lot to him. She knew that from the sound of his voice.

''What happened?'' she asked quietly.

''He was a detective on a homicide squad here in Houston, and he was accused of murdering his wife and small son.''

''Oh, no!''

''Yeah, that's how I felt.'' He crushed the cup in his hand in an angry movement. Ice spilled to the grass, but he didn't seem to notice. ''Instead of believing in him, the man I knew him to be, I offered my services as an attorney.''

Even now, the words had the power to hurt and Lucas jerked to his feet and threw his cup in the trash. He had wanted Blair to talk. He had not intended to air his own past.

Lucas resumed his seat and Blair held her breath as she waited for his next words.

"He couldn't deal with the pain, the loss of his son, and he disappeared before a warrant for his arrest could be issued. Soon after he left, his best friend confessed to the murders, but my brother was gone and I didn't know when he was coming back—if ever. I used to come and sit here, hoping I'd see him again. Months turned into years, but I never gave up. I knew he'd return someday. I just wasn't prepared for the way it came about.''

He took a breath and stared up at the sky. "I got a call that he was in an Austin hospital and they didn't expect him to make it through the night. He tried to save a girl from her kidnappers and he was shot seven times.''

Blair gasped; she couldn't help it. There was such pain in his voice.

He glanced at her. "Don't worry.'' Lucas smiled, and her heart did funny things. "He survived, forgave me, which I didn't deserve, and actually married the woman he rescued.''

"Then he's happy?''

Lucas nodded. "Oh yeah, he's very happy.''

"I'm glad he forgave you,'' she couldn't help saying.

"Me, too.'' He smiled again. "And I'm grateful for the relationship we have now.''

"Does he live in Houston?''

Lucas leaned back and rested his arms along the bench. "No, he owns a ranch outside of Austin.''

"Is this where the outdoor stuff comes in?'' she asked with a hint of humor.

"Yeah. I can't wait to visit and get into boots and jeans and muck around in the fields, go fishing and hunting. When I was younger, I didn't enjoy it because I was forced to do it. Now I do it because I want to, and because it's a chance to spend time with Jacob."

"Is that your brother's name?"

"Yes, Jacob, and his wife's name is Miranda and they have five gorgeous kids—three boys and two girls."

That answered a lot of questions—the bicycles, the pictures in his house and the car seats. "And you baby-sit a lot?" she guessed.

His eyes positively glowed at the question. "Don't get me started on the kids. I'll never shut up. You'll have to ask your uncle Howard about them."

"Uncle Howard knows them?" she echoed in disbelief.

"Sure, he has dinner with them about once a month."

"Small world," she said, a little shocked, making a mental note to talk to Uncle Howard as soon as possible. Howard Tate knew so many people and it was hard to keep track of them all. She'd realized from the way he'd greeted Lucas that they'd met before. She remembered now that he'd mentioned something about a man called Jacob. She could also remember Uncle Howard talking at various times about a Jacob and his family and how much he liked them.

"Life is strange," she added quietly. "Uncle Howard is a big part of my life. My maternal grandparents had this farm outside of Houston. After their deaths, Uncle Howard used to take Blake and me there. He knew how much we missed Grandma and Grandpa. I loved the outdoors, but Blake wasn't too keen on it. Uncle Howard took me there after the attack."

There was silence for a while, and Lucas knew this was what she needed to talk about. She couldn't keep everything hidden inside, the way she'd been doing for years.

"Sometimes it helps to speak about painful situations," he said into the silence.

She ran her finger along the edge of the bench. "Is that what you did when your brother was missing?"

"Yep, I talked to all my friends. Without their help and support, I would never have survived."

She looked across the pond. "After the attack, my mother wanted me to talk to her about it, but I couldn't. Then she wanted me to see a psychiatrist, but I couldn't do that, either. I didn't want to dredge it all up. I just wanted to forget it had ever happened."

"But you haven't forgotten," he said into the stillness.

"What?" She glanced at him with a perplexed frown.

"You haven't forgotten," he said again.

"You don't know that," she replied shortly.

"Yes, I do. It's with you every minute of every hour of every day."

She turned away from him. "I don't want to discuss this."

"You have to. It's the only way you can deal with it."

"I deal with it fine."

"No, you don't. Look how you reacted today."

"No, no, no," she cried, and closed her eyes tight. No one was going to make her relive that awful day—no one.

# CHAPTER ELEVEN

"BLAIR."

She heard Lucas's voice soothing and calming her. She didn't want to hear it, but it felt good to have someone understand what she was feeling. And she was certain that Lucas did. He'd been through so much himself. He knew about pain and private anguish.

"Talk to me," he pleaded, and she felt him reaching into her heart the way he'd done before. Something was unfurling inside her, letting go, letting go....

Lucas could see she was struggling with her emotions and he didn't want to force her, but he couldn't stop. "I know Todd Easton broke into your house and he had a gun. He was looking for your father, but he decided to vent his anger on you."

She stifled a sob in her throat, then the words came tumbling out. "I tried to run from him, but he caught me, beating me with the butt of the gun. Over and over he drove it into my body, and he was laughing all the time. I could hear my bones cracking and feel my skin tearing apart, and then he started to rip off my clothes and I knew what he was going to do. I began to fight. He only laughed that much harder. I thought I'd black out, then I heard the sirens, and the police burst in and ordered him to drop his weapon. He turned the gun on them and they fired. They killed him and he fell across my body. I tried to scream, but I couldn't. My throat was full of blood." She gulped in some air. "Sometimes at night I feel his weight on me and I wake up screaming."

Lucas was frozen in pain and shock. He had wanted her to talk, but he wasn't prepared for his own reaction. He wanted to murder Todd Easton, to break some of his bones and put him through the kind of hell he'd put her through.

"When I saw those same eyes today filled with rage, I lost it. I thought I could control the fear, but the truth is that it's controlling me." There, she'd admitted it and it wasn't hard, not at all. Talking to Lucas was easy because he was such a compassionate listener.

Lucas was quiet and she glanced at him. He was leaning forward, his elbows on his knees, hands clasped. She sensed that he was deeply upset at what she'd told him.

"Lucas."

"Hmm." He looked at her with black, tortured eyes.

"I'm fine, really."

He shook his head. "No, you're not. You'll never be fine until this thing is resolved."

He was right. Sixteen years had finally come full circle, and it was time to resolve this whole situation—including Blake and her father's involvement—everything.

"How do you feel about Blake's part in this?" he asked softly.

"Shocked, and I still can't believe he was there and he never said a word to anyone. I guess he was just scared, but I do believe his story and I also believe Dad didn't know about it until after I was beaten up."

"I believe them, too," he said.

"Then you'll represent Dad?" Her voice held a hint of excitement.

His eyes held hers. "Yes, I'll represent him."

"Thank you. We're in very good hands."

Her faith in him disconcerted him, overwhelmed him, and he was tired of trying to fight it. He and Blair were bound together for a while, and he no longer saw that as something negative. In fact, he saw it as very positive, indeed.

He wasn't even angry that she expected him to be a miracle worker. There was only so much he could do—exposing the truth was at the top of the list. He'd already decided what his defense was going to be. He only hoped it was going to work.

Lucas still planned to offer her an apology, and he needed to do it before they went any further. "I'd like to talk to you about something else."

"What?"

"Last night."

"What about last night?"

"You said I didn't do anything stupid."

She arched an eyebrow. "I don't recall anything stupid."

"I kissed you," he reminded her in an aggrieved tone. She raised her shoulders. "So?"

"I know how you feel about intimacy and I shouldn't have done that. I must have frightened the hell out of you."

"Did I seem frightened?"

"I can only remember bits and pieces, but no, you didn't appear to be…"

"I wasn't," she informed him, "so please don't treat me like a child because of what happened to me in the past."

*And you can kiss me anytime you want,* she was tempted to say but she didn't have that much nerve.

An enormous weight was lifted from his shoulders. "Okay," he said with a relieved smile. "I won't treat you like a child. I'll treat you like an adult, a beautiful woman."

The way he said *beautiful* made her feel suddenly breathless.

"I think it's time Blair Logan had some fun." His smile

was so bright now that it was blinding. "We're going wading in the pond," he said. "I'd suggest skinny-dipping, but I don't think my blood pressure could take it. Besides, that old man would have us arrested." As he was talking, he removed his shoes and socks, then glanced at her. "Don't just sit there. Take off your shoes."

"Lucas, you're not serious!"

"Woman, I've never been so serious in my life." Before this day was over he was going to hear her laugh. "Off with those shoes."

She raised her feet. "But I've got panty hose on." She'd put them on that morning, before deciding what to wear. Afterward, she hadn't bothered to remove them. Now she wished she had.

He rubbed his chin in thought. "That does present a problem." He snapped his fingers. "You can take them off in the car."

Without another thought, she ran to the car. In minutes, she was out of the panty hose. She slipped on her slacks and hurried back to Lucas. He was waiting for her with his trousers rolled up to his knees. He pointed to her legs and she immediately rolled hers up, too.

They stood staring at each other, then Lucas said, "One more thing."

"What?"

"Your hair," he told her. "Take down your hair. I don't like it that way."

Her eyes opened wide at that remark. "Lucas!"

"Blair."

"Okay, okay." She gave in. "But you're not getting any more favors."

She quickly pulled out the pins, and dark hair tumbled around her shoulders.

"Perfect," he sighed, then ran to the water. He didn't even stop at the water's edge; he just plunged right in and turned to wave at her. "Come on," he called.

She removed her jacket and let it drop to the grass, revealing the sleeveless green shell beneath. She walked slowly to the water and stuck her toes in and immediately jerked them back. "It's *cold*," she shouted.

"Chicken!" he said, laughing.

"I'll show you chicken." She marched into the water, grimacing. The mud squished between her toes and she felt something touch her leg, but she didn't have time to worry about it. Lucas was splashing toward her—and she laughed.

That sound was everything Lucas knew it would be. Infectious, appealing, heartwarming, and her face reflected those emotions. The transformation from the grave Blair to the laughing Blair was magical and he had to look into those gorgeous eyes.

As he drew near, she reached down with her hand and threw water at him. He laughed and retaliated, and the antics began. Their laughter and shrieks of joy filled the air as they tried to avoid each other and at the same time get the other one wet.

The man across the pond picked up his chair and fishing gear and left. They didn't notice.

Finally Blair ran from the water and sank to the grass on her knees. Lucas fell down beside her, unable to take his eyes off her. Her eyes were bright and her cheeks were glowing with an inner fire that went all the way to her heart. She had finally released some of the pain; he was sure of it.

She was wet from head to toe, as was he, and to him, she'd never looked more beautiful. Her slacks molded her shapely hips and the green top clung provocatively to her breasts. He could see the outline of her lacy bra. Desire swept through him and all he could think about was lowering her to the grass and making slow, sweet love to her. He lay back with a groan, using his hands as a pillow, trying to curb the longing inside him. He knew she wasn't ready.

She ran her hands through her damp hair. "Look at me. I'm all wet," she cried, laughter in every word.

Lucas closed his eyes. He *couldn't* look. He was in too deep already. One peek, and he'd be lost. He was forty-two years old and Blair Logan had the power to make him act and feel seventeen. It was more than overwhelming. It was downright sinful.

"I'm not exactly dry," he muttered.

"It's your fault. You deserve to be wet."

His eyes popped open. "Excuse me? I wasn't the one who splashed water first."

"I know." She smiled. "You should've seen your face." She raised a hand to her mouth to stop a bout of laughter, then her expression changed—drastically.

Lucas immediately sat up. "Blair, what is it?"

Her eyes widened in alarm. "I...ah...I forgot everything. Blake, my father, that awful Easton man, my fears—everything. I just let it go...for the moment. Now..."

"That's okay."

"Is it?"

"Yes," he assured her. "You've been keeping everything inside you, and you were getting close to the edge. I think you almost reached it today in my office. You have to have some fun—laugh a little more—or you're not going to make it through this."

She sat back on her heels, letting his voice bolster her. She tilted her head to one side. "I'm wondering how I ever thought you were a terrible person."

He grinned and wrapped his arms around his knees. "Me, too, especially when I've been told I'm such a charming man."

"You are," she whispered breathlessly as primal, fundamental emotions engulfed her. His wet dark hair curled against his face and his eyes were smoldering with a need that was answered deep inside her. She ached with that need and she desperately wanted him to kiss her, but he wouldn't unless....

"Would you kiss me, please?" she asked in that same breathless voice.

Lucas's breath solidified in his throat and he realized he was in trouble, because he couldn't say no to her. "Blair," he murmured in anguish.

She leaned over and gently touched his cheek with her lips and he turned his head, unable to stop himself from taking her lips in a gentle kiss. He wouldn't allow himself anything else.

"That's not how you kissed me last night," she murmured.

"Blair." His resistance was growing weaker.

"You said you weren't going to treat me like a child," she whispered against his skin.

Somewhere between her voice and her touch, he gave up. He held her face in his hands, his lips covering hers. She moaned softly and he deepened the kiss to the intensity he craved. Her lips, her tongue, melted under his and he knew she was with him every step of the way. But he also knew that things couldn't go any further. She was too vulnerable.

Lucas's kiss was everything she remembered and more. Under his touch everything vanished—her fears, her uncertainties—and all she wanted to do was lose herself in Lucas. It was a feeling she'd never experienced, never expected, and she let it take her away.

Reluctantly Lucas broke the kiss and rested his forehead against hers. Without a word, she curled into his side and he wrapped an arm around her as they watched the sun sinking slowly in the west.

"Oh," Blair breathed as the sunset bathed the trees in an orange glow. The brilliant color reflected off the pond in a dazzling display of color. "How beautiful."

"Yes," Lucas agreed, but he wasn't thinking about the sunset.

As it grew dark, they stood and made their way to the car. Lucas told her he'd drop her off at her apartment. He didn't want her driving alone at night. She didn't protest. They barely talked on the drive to Blair's apartment; there was no need. They both knew that what had just happened was special, but because of everything else in their lives, they accepted that their feelings had to be put aside—for now.

WHEN LUCAS DROVE UP to the gated entrance, Roger was waiting for them. Blair pushed the button to roll down her window.

"Thank God you're okay," Roger said. "I was so worried."

"Why?" Blair asked.

"Because I heard what happened with Easton."

Blair finally understood what Roger's visit was all about. "I'm fine."

A car honked behind them. "I'll tell the guard to let you in," Blair said hurriedly.

Roger ran back to his car with an expectant look on his face and Lucas felt a jab of jealousy. If Blair wanted to talk to Roger, that was her business, but he didn't like it—not one bit.

Blair knew she had to talk to Roger. He was becoming too protective, too worried about her, and it was her own fault. Roger was a nice person and she had leaned on him for her own selfish reasons. Now she had to tell him she couldn't return his feelings. She didn't feel for him the way he felt for her. Not the way she felt for....

Lucas pulled into the parking space by her apartment.

"I hope you understand that I have to see Roger," she said.

"Sure," Lucas replied, and she could hear the disappointment in his voice. "I'll pick you up in the morning so you can get your car."

"You don't have to do that."

"Fine, I won't do it then," he snapped, and she groaned inwardly. This wasn't how she wanted the evening to end. She had so many visions of their being together, of enjoying new and delightful experiences. Now it was all ruined.

Lucas couldn't believe how testy he sounded. Jealousy was turning him into someone he didn't much like. Roger was worried about Blair; he cared for her. Lucas was familiar with that feeling, but he hated the thought of her turning to another man for help, for support, for anything. The green-eyed monster was about to eat him alive and he knew he had to leave.

Roger pulled up beside them. "I'd better go," Lucas said quickly. "I'm feeling rather grubby."

She couldn't let him leave like this. She reached out and touched his arm. "Thank you for a wonderful afternoon."

Her touch weakened his control. Her slim fingers felt like silk against his bare arm and suddenly all the negative feelings evaporated and all he wanted was to spend the rest of the evening holding her, kissing her and doing all the other sensual things he'd be dreaming about later.

"You're welcome." He forced himself to smile, still annoyed that Roger was waiting for her.

Without another word, she got out and joined Roger on the pavement. As Lucas drove away, he wondered how Blair would explain her scruffy appearance.

BLAIR OPENED THE DOOR, flipped on lights and turned off the alarm system. She tried not to think about Lucas, but that was difficult. She just wanted to immerse herself in his touch, his smile, his kiss. She shook her head, forcing such thoughts away. She had to talk to Roger.

She faced him in the living room and he was staring at her with a strange expression.

"What happened to you?" he asked suspiciously, eyeing her appearance.

She glanced down at herself. She held her shoes and purse, and carried her jacket draped over one arm. Her feet were bare and dirty, her slacks still rolled up to her knees. Her clothes were somewhat dry and her hair hung in rattails around her face. She looked a mess and she was trying to find a way to explain. *Tell the truth—that's what Lucas would do.*

"Lucas decided to cheer me up and got me completely wet in the process."

"Really?" His voice held derision. "A few days ago you didn't want anything to do with him. Now you're...what? Friends?"

She sank onto the sofa, still clutching her purse, jacket and shoes. "It's a long story," she answered, not sure how to answer, but feeling it was none of Roger's business. Still, he was her friend. "I'm sorry you were worried about me."

"No problem," Roger said with a shrug. "I'm just glad Lucas was there for you."

"Yes, he's been a big help." She couldn't keep the pleasure out of her voice. "With Blake and all," she added, and didn't know why she said that. Maybe it was the look on Roger's face. As if he suspected something was going on between Lucas and her and he was hurt. God, how did she handle this? She had no idea. But she had to take *some* kind of action, and she had to do it now.

She placed her things on the sofa, searching for the right words. "I need to talk to you."

"Sure, anything," he said, and sat across from her.

She took a moment to compose her thoughts. "I've taken advantage of your good nature," she began.

His eyes narrowed. "What do you mean?"

"I've leaned on you and used your help without realizing how that was affecting you."

"I'm still not following you."

She inhaled slowly. "You have feelings for me that I can't return."

"Oh, that. Don't worry about it." He shifted nervously in his chair. "I'm aware of your past and I'm not expecting anything from you that you're not willing to give."

"Roger," she said uneasily. "You're not listening to me."

"I can wait, Blair."

She bit her lip, hating to say the next words, but she had to. "I'm never going to have those feelings for you."

After a second, the words sank in, then he asked coolly, "Does this have anything to do with Lucas?"

"No, it doesn't," she answered truthfully. She'd known she felt only friendship for Roger long before Lucas had opened her heart.

Roger wasn't convinced. "I like Lucas, but he has a reputation with the ladies. There're so many broken hearts at the courthouse it's like a battle zone."

Blair was well aware of Lucas's reputation and she'd never heard any woman bad-mouth him. They all seemed crazy about him, even after he broke up with them. For the first time she wondered if she'd be one in a line of many. Her relationship with Lucas was very fragile, very new, and she refused to let Roger make her think like that.

"This isn't about Lucas," she said forcefully.

He rose to his feet. "I just don't want to see you get hurt."

"I'm not," she assured him, rising, too.

"I'm still working on this Raye thing and I'll also keep an eye on Easton."

"Roger," she sighed. "You're too nice for your own good."

"I just want you to be happy and safe."

She grimaced. "You're making me feel bad."

"Don't," he said, and headed for the door. "I'll talk to you tomorrow. Be sure to lock this door."

Blair stood there for a moment, feeling so many reactions she didn't understand. Why did Roger have to be so considerate? Why had Lucas, of all men, touched her heart in a way no one ever had? Unable to find any answers, she quickly locked the door and set the alarm, then went to the sofa, picked up her things and walked into the bedroom.

She shook out her jacket and looked in her purse. She couldn't find her panty hose. Heavens, she'd left them in Lucas's car. Oh, well... She shrugged it off. Lucas was probably used to women leaving things in his car, but she wasn't keen on that idea—not at all.

Was she crazy for putting her heart in the hands of a man like Lucas? She dropped onto the bed. Was that what she'd done? Yes, she answered her question, she had. And she didn't even know if he wanted it.

She ordered herself to stop thinking about Lucas. She had other problems to worry about—like Blake's trial. She hurried toward the bathroom. A quick shower and then she'd call her brother and explain why she'd disappeared today.

LUCAS DROVE into his garage, still wearing a somber expression. He couldn't get Blair and Roger out of his mind. Was he still at her place? Would he spend the evening? "Okay," he spoke aloud. "That's enough." This jealousy was getting to him and he intended to stop it right now. Roger would *not* be spending the night. There was no way that his jealous mind was going to convince him otherwise.

With that firmly decided, he got out and noticed something on the floor. He reached down and scooped it up, smiling. Blair's panty hose. He wondered if she'd missed them yet. He knew she didn't need them because women had lots of these things.

The smile lingered around his mouth, and he thought of attaching them to his radio antenna and letting them flap in the wind to tease her. The young Lucas would have done exactly that. But now he tucked them into his console, planning to give them to her in a quiet moment. He certainly hoped there'd be one of those in the near future.

# CHAPTER TWELVE

LUCAS SPENT the weekend at his office, reading through transcripts, familiarizing himself with the first trial. Frank would sort through them later, but Lucas wanted to know what had happened back then, and get some idea of what might happen now. He was absorbed in his work when the door opened and Roger walked in, breaking his concentration. Lucas wasn't surprised to see him.

"Hey, Roger," he said, leaning back in his chair.

"Stay away from her, Lucas," he warned. "She doesn't deserve to be hurt."

Lucas frowned. "What are you talking about?" he asked, but he knew. He'd have to be stupid not to.

"Don't play dumb," Roger snapped. "Blair's emotions are very fragile, so don't toy with her."

"Whoa." Lucas put up a hand, resenting Roger's tone of voice. "Blair's in charge of her own life."

"Are you serious?" Roger shouted. "After everything she's been through—the beating, Raye's harassment, Blake's arrest and now Easton showing up—she needs someone to care for her."

"That someone being you," Lucas murmured.

Roger clenched his hands, and Lucas saw the bulging muscles in his arms. Clearly, Roger worked out. Lucas had never noticed that before. "Lucas, you knew how I felt about her, so why'd you go after her? I thought you were a better man than that."

"I didn't go after her," Lucas answered in a wooden

voice as he shoved his chair back and stood. "Easton confronted her in my office and I could see she was close to a nervous breakdown. I did what I would've done for anyone—I helped her deal with it. I don't really see this as any of your business."

They eyed each other in silent combat. Lucas was taller, but Roger had the asset of built muscles. Still, Lucas didn't back down. He never did, and Roger got the message.

"Hell, man, I don't want to fight," Roger said.

"Neither do I," Lucas responded. "I think we both need to focus on keeping Blair safe."

"That's always been my goal."

Lucas took a deep breath. "I talked with Raye and I don't think his gang is involved in the harassment. He said Big Joe's taken over and he wasn't interested in avenging anything."

"He lied to you."

"What?"

"Big Joe hasn't taken over. There's a war going on between Big Joe and Raye's followers. Nothing's been settled. Most of them are waiting for the sentencing, to see who they'll follow."

"Damn, I would've sworn Raye wasn't lying."

"You're losing it, Lucas, if you're starting to believe criminals like Raye."

Lucas objected to the tone of that and it showed in the darkening of his eyes. "If you came here to warn me off Blair, consider it done."

Roger nodded and walked to the door. "And Roger…" Lucas stopped him. "Don't warn me again. If Blair and I decide to take our relationship a step further, that has nothing to do with you."

Roger gritted his teeth and swept through the door.

Lucas resumed his seat with a grim expression. He liked Roger—always had—but when it came to Blair, no one was going to tell him what to do. No one but Blair.

He glanced at the telephone, feeling a need to hear her voice, but he didn't call. She was with her family, he felt sure—which was where she should be.

BLAIR SPENT Sunday with her parents. They'd heard about Easton and they were worried. Her father had arranged for her car to be brought over, so at least she had her transportation.

They had a family dinner with Natalie, Calvin, Tiff and Uncle Howard. It was what Blake needed—his family's support. Her father had apologized to him for the outburst in Lucas's office and that seemed to make a world of difference. Slowly, surely, this tragedy was pulling them together in a way Blair had never expected.

Uncle Howard had left after dinner and she never got a chance to talk to him about the Culver family, but she decided she'd rather hear it all from Lucas. She enjoyed her visit with Blake, talking about old times and sharing fears—and dreams—about the future. They were bound together by a single birth, but sometimes she felt she didn't know him at all. At other times, she felt as if she knew him as well as she knew herself. These contradictory emotions were disturbing, but they were twins and nothing would ever change that.

She did wonder whether things would have turned out differently if she'd been more considerate of his feelings when they were small, if she hadn't stolen the spotlight with her grades and achievements. They were such big ifs and she didn't have any answers. All she knew was that she couldn't change history. She could only help Blake now and make sure the future was brighter than the past. She hoped that was possible.

She and Blake played tennis on Sunday afternoon. She had to practically twist his arm. But in a matter of minutes she had him laughing as she danced across the court and bowed gracefully at his feet. Lucas had taught her that they had to laugh or they weren't going to make it through this.

Afterward, they had one of their mother's mouthwatering suppers. They sat around the kitchen table talking and trying to avoid the horror that was hanging over them, but it was never very far from either one.

Blake and her parents tried to persuade her to spend the night, but she wanted to go back home—in case Lucas called. She'd waited for him to call yesterday, but he hadn't. And he didn't call this morning, either. Roger had phoned, but it wasn't the voice she'd wanted to hear—the voice that teased, cajoled and revitalized her. The voice that made her feel safe and secure in herself and her emotions.

*Why hadn't Lucas called?*

Did men kiss with such passion and then never call? She was beginning to wonder if she'd exaggerated it, made it something more than it was. Lucas had been put out with her when they parted and she wasn't sure why. Because of Roger?

Then it hit her. It was the weekend and Lucas surely had a date. She suspected he didn't spend his weekends alone. He was probably with Jennifer. *Was she stupid, or what?* Lucas would much rather spend his off time with someone who was gorgeous and carefree instead of someone whose life was crumbling around her. *She was so stupid.* But it didn't matter. Lucas had touched her heart. He had reached through the pain, anguish and fear and she had opened up to him like a thirsty flower to the misty rain. He had encouraged her to talk, to laugh and enjoy herself in spite of all the terrible things. Through that, she'd found an inner strength she hadn't even realized she possessed and now she could face the future—no matter what. And that wasn't stupid at all.

In the end, she decided to spend the night. She didn't see any reason to go home and wait for the phone to ring.

If Lucas was going to call, he would have called by now. She had enough sense to know that.

ON MONDAY Lucas was at work before seven. The offices were dark and quiet and he needed this solitary hour to gather his thoughts for the week ahead. But when he tried to concentrate on Blake Logan, Blair kept intruding. He'd have to do something about that. She was controlling his mind and his heart. No woman had ever had this effect on him before, and he wasn't comfortable with the feeling. But all he could think about was Blair, warm and tantalizing and… Oh, he was in deep—too deep. Now what? He was forty-two years old and he wasn't sure what he should do. That was so ironic.

He thought about Roger's feelings for Blair. He'd never moved in on another man's woman—never intended to sink to that level. But then, the woman had never been Blair. He wondered how she felt about Roger. She'd seemed genuinely glad to see him the other night, even asked him to come in when— Okay, that had bothered him and he'd been jealous. Now he could look at things more clearly.

How did Blair feel? That was the big question—but not really. She was so consumed with fear and with the uncertainties in her life that she was struggling just to stay afloat. She needed time and support from the people around her.

He could feel himself backing off. For her sake, he was willing to take it slow. He had to put all his effort into this trial and set his personal feelings aside—somehow. And if Roger was the man she wanted, then he'd make damn sure Roger was good enough for her. Oh yeah, he'd just keep telling himself that and maybe he'd believe it—someday.

An hour later, Sam walked into his office. "Good morning, Lucas."

Lucas raised his head. "Morning."

Sam took a seat and crossed his legs. "I brought Blake in. He's with Greg now."

"Good, good," Lucas replied, flexing his tired shoulder muscles.

Sam watched him closely. "How long have you been working?"

"Nonstop all weekend," Lucas admitted.

"Damn, you're going to get burned out before the trial even starts." His tone wasn't accusing but concerned.

Lucas shook his head. "Don't worry, I need very little sleep and I have lots of energy. Besides, I've learned how to pace myself."

"Still..." Sam hesitated, then threw up his hands. "What the hell do I know? I seem to have made a mess of everything." He got up and shoved his hands into his tailored slacks. "Thank God Howard's gone back to wherever the hell he hibernates. He says I'm controlling and manipulative and I've destroyed my kids' lives. He doesn't have kids, so he doesn't know what the hell he's talking about."

Lucas leaned back, realizing that Sam needed to talk.

"When Blair was beaten up, I couldn't stand to look at her. I went into the bathroom and cried my heart out. But Ava didn't. She sat by her bed, holding her hand, talking to her. I was filled with a murderous rage—I couldn't take it. I guess that's why Blake told Ava first instead of me."

"Told her what?" Lucas asked, although he already knew. He was giving Sam a springboard.

"That he was there the night Bonnie Davis was murdered. He told his mother because he was afraid of my temper. When I heard, I wanted to strangle my own son, but Ava has a calming effect on me. She always has. After my anger subsided, my goal was to keep Blake safe. Blair was struggling to live and I was desperate not to lose both my children.'' He took a breath. "Howard says I don't love my kids, but everything I've done, I've done because I love them. I got Blake out of the country as fast as I could. I wasn't certain what kind of evidence Holt had on the second boy, and I couldn't take any chances. Then Ava and I spent all our time with our daughter, hoping and praying she'd make it.''

Sam returned to his chair, staring down at the floor. "She survived, but it wasn't easy. She has a lot of inner strength—like Ava. But we lost our beautiful, lively teenage daughter that night. She used to laugh and dance around the house, but I haven't heard her laugh or seen her dance in years. These days, she's content to put criminals behind bars. That's her whole life, and Howard says it's my fault. Howard says everything is my fault.'' He groaned. "I'm so afraid Ava believes him.''

"Have you asked her?'' Lucas inquired. Sam was wrestling with a lot of turbulent emotions, but most of all he was trying to keep his family intact. Lucas couldn't fault him for that.

"Yes, and she says she loves me and doesn't blame me for anything, but she thinks that Howard hung the moon and she listens to him. My kids do, too.''

Lucas wasn't quite sure how he got caught in the middle of the Logan family disputes, but he knew one thing. "Pay attention to your wife, Sam,'' he said confidently. "Howard's a good man and he won't do anything to hurt his sister or his niece or nephew.''

Sam dragged both hands over his face. "God, I'm so tired of hearing that Howard's a good man. I just wish he'd stay the hell out of my life.''

Lucas recognized those words for what they were—jealousy. He'd been feeling some of that himself.

The silence stretched.

"Good Lord," Sam finally said. "How did I get so completely sidetracked?"

Lucas shrugged. "You needed to talk."

"My family's doing a lot of that these days. Blair and Blake talked all weekend. It was good seeing them together again. Blair seemed different though. I couldn't put my finger on it. Ava couldn't, either. We thought she'd be so upset about Lloyd Easton's threats, but she's holding up very well."

Lucas felt a moment of relief. Those were the words he wanted to hear. Blair was doing fine—and she hadn't spent the weekend with Roger.

Sam looked up. "Hell, I almost forgot why I came in here. I wanted to thank you for helping her the other day."

Lucas blew out a long breath. "No problem."

"And I wanted to apologize for my inexcusable behavior."

Lucas picked up a pencil and studied it. He didn't have a pat answer this time. He couldn't condone what Sam had done. It *was* inexcusable and, as always, Lucas had to speak his mind.

Before he could say a word, Sam spoke up. "I can see you're having a problem with it, too. Blair gave me an earful over the weekend. I wish I could explain my reaction in rational terms, but I can't. There's just so much history between Blake and me. When he was small I had so many dreams, so many hopes for him, and I pushed him and drove him until—" he raised his hands "—until he rebelled. That was my fault—Howard's right. I can see that now. I expected too much from my son, and I wasn't willing to settle for anything less. When he said he'd given the DNA willingly, I lost it...again. I promised Ava I wouldn't, but I did. It's hard to change years of bad habits, but I'm trying. For my kids, I have to keep trying."

Lucas felt sorry for him. Life had dealt Sam a difficult

blow. But they had to find some common ground, all of them, to survive the months ahead.

"I can't excuse your behavior, but I know you love your son. You have to curb your temper, especially in front of him. He needs encouragement, not ridicule. When he walks into that courtroom, I want him to have a deep sense of remorse and a deep sense of family support."

"He will," Sam assured him, then asked, "Have you come up with a defense strategy?"

"Not yet," Lucas answered. He definitely had an idea, but he wasn't ready to talk about it.

"Blair said she asked you to take my case."

Lucas twisted the pencil, feeling a catch in his throat at the mention of Blair. "Yes, she did."

"I told her Derek would do fine, but she insists you'd do a better job."

So it was Blair's idea, not Sam's. She was putting too much faith in him and he wished it didn't make him feel so good.

"I want you to concentrate totally on Blake's case," Sam was saying. "My hearing will come later, and I'll worry about it then. If I lose my license, so be it. It's a small price to pay for my son's freedom."

Lucas glanced at him. "You'd be content to lose your license?"

"Hell, no," Sam growled. "But I want my son free. I want him out of this mess."

"I'll do everything I can to make that happen," Lucas promised.

"I know you will. That's why I was so determined to get you on our side."

"It's early yet, so let's take this one step at a time," Lucas told him. "There'll be plenty of twists and turns before this is over, but if you want me to represent you, I'd be glad to."

"I don't think I have any choice," Sam smiled. "My daughter would have a fit if I retained anyone else."

The door suddenly opened and Blair stepped in. Lucas felt muscles, traitorous muscles, tighten in response. God, she looked wonderful. She wore navy-blue slacks and a short-sleeved navy jacket that came to her waist. The jacket was open and he saw a blue-and-white-striped navy T-shirt was underneath. Her hair hung loose around her shoulders, and she seemed *different,* just as Sam had said. Staring at her, he knew what it was. Her jacket wasn't buttoned up to her throat and her hair wasn't screwed into a tight knot. She wasn't hiding her femininity the way she had in the past. She was slowly letting go of the fear. Was that possible? he wondered. Considering everything she was facing, could she really continue this process of healing? Could she maintain control of all those overwhelming anxieties, those fears? He didn't know, but he hoped so. God, he sure hoped so.

"Am I interrupting?" she asked courteously. "Joan said I could come in."

Sam stood up and hugged her. "No, sweetie, you're not interrupting. I've got to go, anyway," he said. "Will you be here a while?"

"I'm not sure. Why?" She'd been restless all morning, wanting to see Lucas. It was clear he wasn't going to seek her out, so she'd taken the initiative and decided to see him.

"I need to check on some things at the office and I was hoping you'd give Blake a ride home when he's through."

"Sure, go ahead," she said, grateful for the excuse her father had just provided.

As Sam left, Lucas wondered why they didn't let Blake find his own way home. They were treating him like a ten-year-old. Then it occurred to him that they were keeping tabs on Blake because they feared he might flee the country if they left him alone. Lucas had been acquainted with him only a short while, but he knew Blake wasn't going anywhere—that was why he'd staked his career on it.

Blair took her father's seat and stared at Lucas. He wore a dark gray shirt with his sleeves rolled up to the elbows. His tie was undone and he looked as if he'd been working for some time. His hair practically stood on end from all the times he'd raked his hand through it. But his eyes were warm and doing funny things to her insides. She felt a thump in her chest, and a strange feeling gripped her stomach.

"Did you have a good weekend?" she asked in a rush, needing to say *something*.

"I worked all weekend," was his quick reply.

"You didn't go out with Jennifer Walker?" She bit her tongue, wanting to snatch the words back, but suddenly she had to know.

"I'm not seeing Jennifer anymore," he said, and waited for her reaction.

"Oh," she murmured. She had no idea what else to say. She felt like a fool…a happy, embarrassed fool.

As he watched the color fluctuate in her cheeks, he felt elated. She was curious about the women in his life. That meant she recognized that something was happening between them. She obviously wasn't ready to talk about it, though, so he wouldn't. But he couldn't take his eyes from her face, the pink in her cheeks, the glow in her eyes, and…

Lucas stood up. He had to. Blair was gazing at him with those gorgeous eyes and didn't even realize what that look was doing to him. He walked around the desk and leaned against it.

"Does Blake have a driver's license?" he asked, forcing his thoughts in another direction.

She didn't mind the quick change of subject; in fact, she was grateful. "Yes," she answered slowly.

"Then why don't you let him drive himself around Houston? He'll be here a while."

"Because it's different driving here than it is in London. He's not used to it."

Lucas raised an eyebrow. "Blair."

"What?"

"Tell me the truth."

"That is the truth."

He folded his arms across his chest. "The truth is you and Sam are dogging his every move because you're afraid he'll flee the country."

She gasped. "That's not…not…" she sputtered, unable to finish the sentence because in her heart she knew he was right. Unconsciously, they were all keeping an eye on Blake, unsure of what he was going to do—unwilling to trust him. Until that moment, she'd believed that she did, that she trusted him fully, and it was a blow to realize that a small part of her was waiting for the old Blake to emerge and disappoint them once again. But Lucas believed in her brother, trusted him, had even put his career on the line for him. That degree of faith was unheard of, but it showed her the kind of man Lucas was and her heart swelled with so many new emotions.

She brushed hair away from her face. "I didn't even realize we were doing that."

He understood that. He also understood it was natural for her to protect Blake. She'd been doing it all her life. "Give him some freedom, that's all he needs. Freedom to find himself."

A smile spread across her face. A smile blinding in its intensity, warmth, and oh God, its need—a need that was echoed in the tightening of his loins.

"Lucas Culver, I have misjudged you so badly."

He grinned and walked around to his chair and sat down, desperately needing to put some distance between

them. He was good at controlling his emotions, but around
her they were running riot.

"All the women say that," he countered flippantly.

"They don't, either. They're all crazy about you."

*And you, Blair. How do you feel?*

Of course, the words never left his mouth. He was already so involved he could hardly breathe, let alone concentrate. Any encouragement from her and he'd be lost.

"Rumors, that's all," he said in the same flippant tone.
"And now, Ms. Logan, if you're through disturbing me,
I've got a lot of work to do on your brother's behalf."

The way he said *disturbing* made her feel warm all over
and she knew he meant it in a very nice way. She walked
to his desk. "Let me help, please."

She stood so close he could smell the delicate fragrance
of her perfume and he knew he couldn't have her around.
She was too big a distraction.

"Blair," he sighed.

"But I can help," she pleaded. "I won't interfere and
I'll do exactly what you tell me."

That conjured up many other images in his head, none
of which had anything to do with Blake's trial. Despite all
his admonishments, he couldn't say no to her. The sad fact
was that he'd never be able to say no to her. She had him
wrapped around her little finger and she hadn't even noticed.

"Okay." He gave in gracefully. "There's a pile of stuff
from the first trial. Frank's handling it, but you can help
him. I need something that will corroborate Blake's
story."

"I can do that," she said brightly.

"Blair..." He hesitated.

"What?"

"Some of it's gruesome. I just want you to be prepared." She'd be seeing pictures of the crime scene and

what Todd Easton had done to Bonnie Davis. On second thought, this probably wasn't such a good idea.

"I can cope," she said strongly. "I've dealt with heinous crimes before."

"But this is Todd Easton we're talking about," he reminded her, and he saw her fighting to win the battle of fear.

"I can do this, Lucas," she stated again. "I *need* to do this...for Blake. For myself."

He still hesitated.

She didn't give him time to reconsider. "I'll get with Frank and talk to you later."

"Blair?"

She turned, her hand on the doorknob.

"Be careful."

She lifted an eyebrow. "I'm always careful." She guessed he was referring to the harassment.

"You know what I mean."

She shifted her purse strap onto her shoulder. "I know exactly what you mean, but don't worry. I have a friend who takes very good care of me."

*Who the hell was that? Roger, of course.*

Jealousy ripped through him again. He hated it but knew the situation was only going to get worse unless he did something about it. He had to stay away from Blair. How did he do that? He'd just agreed to let her work with him. He'd see her every day, hear her voice, her... Okay, he could do this. He wasn't an overeager teenager with raging hormones. But he sure felt like one.

Later, Lucas thought. Later he'd feel differently. He always did. Later he'd be able to walk away. He always did.

*Later he'd still be lying to himself.*

## CHAPTER THIRTEEN

THE NEXT COUPLE OF WEEKS passed quickly. Carl filed a motion to have Blake certified as an adult, as Lucas knew he would. Lucas met with Carl and managed to get the rape charge reduced to attempted rape because only Todd Easton's semen had been found on Bonnie Davis. The grand jury met and Carl got the indictment he wanted. Lucas was waiting for a trial date and he was hoping for an early one; the Logan family needed some relief. Everyone was working very hard to secure Blake's freedom. Lucas was surprised that Sam stayed out of his way, letting him handle things. Even Blair stuck to her word. He saw her every day, but just in passing. She was busy with Frank, and he was busy building a defense.

Lucas had thought it would be hard seeing so much of her but, in fact, it was easy. He knew where she was and he knew she was safe. Roger hadn't turned up anything on Raye or Easton, and things seemed to be settling down.

Jim Tenney stopped by his office to talk about the Raye sentencing. He and Jim had gone to law school together and they had remained friends. Jim's wife, Stacey, and Lucas had been more than friends. Years ago Stacey had been ready for marriage and family, but Lucas wasn't. Looking back, Lucas could see they'd made the right decision in parting company. Jim and Stacey were happy and now had two children. And he…he was still searching for the perfect woman.

Jim didn't look good and Lucas questioned his friend's

judgment in going back to work so soon after the surgery, but he didn't say anything. Jim could take care of his own business and he was sure Stacey was keeping a close eye on him.

BLAIR MADE A TRIP to the D.A.'s offices to discuss the Raye sentencing with Gwen, the A.D.A. who'd taken over Blair's caseload. It felt strange—a little disorienting—to be in the building where she'd spent so much time the past six years. She knew why. She was now an outsider, but everyone treated her cordially, especially Gwen. They'd been friends for a long time and Blair was sure that wouldn't change.

They went over the case and Blair didn't push for the death penalty. She now understood that there were two sides to every story. Hector Raye was a victim of gangs and violence, and killing him would serve no purpose. She tried not to let external forces influence her decision. Besides, it really *wasn't* her decision. The jury would have the final say.

As she left the building, she realized it would be her last visit. She felt a moment of sadness for all the years she'd fought for justice wearing blinders. Things were so different now and she wondered if she would ever look at justice in the same way again.

RAYE HAD HIS SENTENCING and got life without parole. Jim Tenney called Lucas and said Hector took it relatively well. Lucas still felt Raye had nothing to do with harassing Blair. Jim agreed.

Roger was keeping an eye on Easton, which was a relief to Lucas. Roger and Blair he didn't think about. He didn't have time to wallow in those destructive emotions. Besides, Blair was just as consumed as he was with the trial.

The frustrating part was the reporters. They staked out his home, his office, the Logan house, each desperate to get a story. But he wasn't ready to talk to the press, so they hounded him constantly.

He took the Fourth of July weekend off and went to see Jacob and the family. It was what he needed—the serenity and support of his loved ones. He played with the kids, teased Miranda and talked with Jacob, but Blair occupied his thoughts. He couldn't wait to get home, and that shocked him. In the past, whenever he'd left the ranch, he'd felt sad and harbored ideas of moving to Austin. But now all he felt was an eagerness to see Blair.

LATER THAT WEEK, the reporters became more aggressive, trying to get into his office. He was at his wits' end and finally issued a press release for Frank to read, hoping that would satisfy them.

That afternoon, Blair slipped into his office and laid some papers on his desk. She wore a multicolored dress that buttoned up the front, showing off her slim hips and breasts. She wore her hair down these days, and he wondered if he had anything to do with that.

She jabbed a finger at the papers. "Look at these."

There were several photos from the crime scene. Blair was so eager—so lovely—that it required every bit of discipline he possessed to concentrate on what she was saying.

"The photographer was very thorough. He took photos of the crime scene and everything around it." She pointed to the photo on top. "What does that look like to you?"

He picked up the photo and studied it, then turned the picture over. On the back was written, "Located outside the perimeter of the crime scene, about fifty feet away. Pungent smell—appears to be disgorged stomach matter."

He glanced up and smiled. "This is where Blake threw up."

"Yes." She smiled back. "This picture was mixed in with all the other ones, and I'm sure no one knew what it was, but we do. It proves Blake threw up, just like he said he did.''

"This is going to help," he told her. "Now let's hope the photographer's still around."

"I'll track him down tomorrow," she said excitedly. Despite her desire to help Blake, Lucas had an investigator who could do that much more easily than she could.

"Blair…"

A knock at the door stopped him. Blake walked in. "Ready to go, sis?" he asked.

"I…I…" She hesitated. She wasn't ready. She needed to talk to Lucas. Remembering an earlier comment of Lucas's, she made a sudden decision. "The keys are in my purse in the library. You can drive yourself home."

Blake's eyes opened wide. "You're joking, right?"

"No, I'm not joking. It's time you learned your way around Houston again."

"Dad's not going to like this," he said slowly. "I mean, he's had someone with me ever since I've been home. I know he's afraid…"

The unfinished sentence hung between them. Lucas was right. Blake knew no one trusted him.

Blair walked over and threw her arms around him and rested her head on his chest. "I trust you," she said simply. "You came home to rectify this horrible situation, and that took a lot of courage."

Blake blinked back tears. He cupped Blair's face in his hand and kissed her forehead. "I love you."

She pushed out of his arms. "I know." She smiled, playfully tapping his shoulder. "Just don't wreck my car."

"I won't," Blake assured her, and glanced at Lucas. "If you don't need anything else, I'll head home."

"I want to talk to you in the morning," Lucas told him.

"Sure," Blake replied. "Has something happened?"

"Just some details we need to discuss."

Blake groaned exaggeratedly. "Why is it necessary to go over this so many times?"

"I'm sorry, it just is," Lucas said.

"Well, then, I guess I'll keep talking," he responded stoically. "Because I know you're doing everything you can to help me, and I appreciate that. I don't mean to sound ungrateful."

"Don't worry about it. Just be here in the morning."

"I will." Blake made his way to the door, then turned back. "How are you getting home, sis?"

"I'm hoping a tall, handsome man will give me a lift," she said cheekily.

Blake's eyebrows knotted together in disapproval. "That's not funny, Blair."

"I think she's talking about me," Lucas broke in. "At least I hope she is."

Blair put her hands on her hips. "Will you two lighten up?"

"I'll get her home safely," Lucas said to Blake.

"Good." His gaze swung to Blair. "Please don't take any chances."

"Stop worrying about me."

"I will, if you'll stop worrying about me," Blake countered shrewdly. They embraced affectionately, and Lucas could feel the bond between them.

After Blake left, Lucas leaned back in his chair with a mischievous expression on his face. "So I'm supposed to give you a ride home?"

"Yes." Her blue eyes twinkled. "It was your idea to give Blake some freedom, so now you have to be my taxi."

*I'll be anything you want.*

"But first let's talk about the photo. I realize you didn't want to mention it to Blake until we were sure, but it looks conclusive to me." She was back to business quicker than his arousal could subside.

"Blair," he said tiredly. "It's been a long day, and I'm exhausted and hungry. Right now I just want to go home, grab a burger and a beer and just relax. We can talk about the photo tomorrow."

"Do you live on burgers?" she asked critically.

He cocked an eyebrow. "Sometimes, and sometimes a pretty woman offers to cook for me."

"Is that a hint?"

"Can you cook?"

"Of course," she retorted. "My mother made sure of that."

"Then it's a hint." He grinned, his lighthearted mood returning. "You want a taxi and I want food."

*And a whole lot more.*

"I'll just grab my purse and be right with you," she said, dashing through Joan's office. In a minute she was back.

"Let me guess," she said as they walked through the door. "You're a meat-and-potatoes guy."

"Yep, and don't you forget it."

Blair smiled all the way to his car. It felt so good to be with him again—to talk, to laugh. She didn't know what this evening was going to bring, but she intended to make the most of it.

On the drive, they discussed the trial, and Lucas talked about his visit with his brother. She wondered if he'd ever take her to meet Jacob and his family. She sincerely hoped so.

As they drove up to the entrance, she waved to the guard who opened the gate for them. Lucas parked in her spot and they got out and began to walk to her apartment. Suddenly they came to a complete stop.

"No, no, no," she cried as she stared at her front door. In slashing red letters were the words, *I'll get you, bitch.*

Lucas was in shock for a second, then he grabbed her and hauled her shaking body to the car. "Get inside,

Blair,'' he ordered, glancing around quickly to make sure no one was still lurking in the vicinity.

"Lucas, what's happening?'' she asked in a voice that twisted his insides.

"I don't know,'' he answered. "What's the guard number?''

She gave it to him, surprised she could actually remember it in her dazed state.

Lucas reached across her for the cell phone. "Get over to apartment twenty-four now,'' he shouted into the phone.

The guard must have said something, because Lucas shouted again, "I said now!''

In a moment they could see the guard running through the darkness toward them. "What's going on? I can't leave my post,'' he said, panting.

Lucas pointed to the door. "How in hell did that happen?''

"Oh my God,'' the guard gasped. "I have to call for backup. Someone has to stay at the gate.''

In a matter of minutes, the place was overrun with people and uniformed police. Lucas was pacing, demanding answers. Blair sat in the car with her hands locked tightly in her lap. She could no longer feel her fingers but still didn't release her grip. She lived in a gated, secure complex. *No one could get in here.* She'd told herself that so many times, especially when fear threatened her fragile emotions. *No one could get in here.* The words always calmed her, made her feel safe. But now…now all that security was blown to hell. She didn't know what to do. She wanted to cry, but she didn't. She wanted to run, but she didn't do that, either. She kept her eyes on Lucas, counting on him to keep her safe. That frightened her, too. She shouldn't rely on him so much. But she did.

She heard a siren, saw Roger pull up behind them. He jumped out and ran to her side. "Are you all right?'' he asked through the car window.

She nodded, unable to speak.

He frowned at the door. "Goddamn bastard. Don't worry, I'll get whoever did this."

Blair nodded again, unable to speak, but feeling the urge to flee—with Lucas.

"Sit tight," Roger said. "I'll check things out, and after that I'll take you to your parents'."

Blair started to protest, then stopped. Her brain was on overload, but one thing was clear: She wasn't going anywhere with Roger.

The apartment manager joined the group just as Roger did. Raised voices went over her head as her eyes traveled to the door. *I'll get you, bitch. I'll get you, bitch.* The fear tried to capture her mind, her emotions, but she fought back. She wasn't giving in; she wasn't letting it control her. But she had to leave, and soon. *Lucas, please!*

As her eyes found Lucas, she saw that he and Roger were confronting each other a few yards away. Their voices were loud, but she couldn't make out the words.

"What are you doing here?" Roger wanted to know.

"What am I doing here?" Lucas repeated sarcastically. "This is a secure apartment complex and someone came right up to her door and spray-painted a welcoming message and you're worried what *I'm* doing here."

"Cool it, Lucas," Roger said in a forbidding tone.

"I thought you were watching Easton! I thought you had this damn thing under control."

"It isn't Easton. He's out of town." Roger gestured at the door. "This looks like the work of Raye's gang."

"Raye's going away for the rest of his life. How the hell would his gang benefit from frightening Blair?"

"Don't worry, I'll find out."

"When you do, give me a call," Lucas muttered. "Right now I'm getting Blair the hell out of here."

"Where are you taking her?"

"Somewhere safe."

"I'll take care of her. You just worry about the trial. Leave her alone."

Lucas moved close to Roger's face, dark eyes boring into him. "I told you before—don't warn me again, Roger."

"Calm down and look at this realistically."

"Yeah, right." Lucas swung away. "You catch this creep and then I'll look at it realistically." Lucas walked toward his car.

"Lucas," Roger called, but Lucas ignored him.

He got into the car and drove away from the apartment complex, maneuvering around various police vehicles. He stopped when he arrived at the street, then turned toward Blair. She was staring down at her hands, her hair hiding her face.

"Blair," he whispered, gently touching her cheek. "It's all right."

Her hands shook, and he reached down and caught them, prying her fingers apart. "It's all right," he said again, wanting to ease her pain but knowing there was very little he could do.

"It's not all right," she whispered. "Someone wants to hurt me, and I…" She glanced at him with tear-filled eyes. "I'm so afraid."

He rubbed her hands. "That's understandable, but Roger will catch the guy. He seems to have a personal stake in this."

"I know," she said, her voice catching. "I've told him I can't—that I don't feel the same way, but he doesn't seem to listen."

Tears ran down her face, and he brushed them away with his thumb. Blair thought of Roger as a friend; that was all Lucas needed to hear.

"Do you have a tissue?" she asked. She'd been determined not to cry, but now she couldn't help it.

He opened the console, rummaged around and pulled

out something. "I don't have a tissue, but I have these." He held up her panty hose.

Through the pain, a gurgle of laughter escaped her and she snatched them out of his hand. "What would your nephews think if they found these in your car?" Her eyes were watery, her emotions still shaky, but laughter was releasing the fear.

"They'd think their uncle was very naughty—and Miranda would have my hide."

She dabbed at her eyes with the panty hose. "Then it's not a common occurrence to find ladies' underthings in your car?"

"Hardly." He raised his eyebrows. "The rumors you've heard about me are highly exaggerated."

"Are they?" she asked, blinking back tears.

"Yes," he assured her. "Now I think its time to get you to your parents'."

She grabbed his arm. "No, Lucas, please."

"Blair," he sighed softly. "You can't stay in your apartment. Someone knows how to get past the guard without being detected. It's too dangerous."

"I know, but I can't go to my parents' just yet. They'll fuss and worry and…and smother me. I can't handle that."

"Okay," Lucas said, trying to understand what she was feeling, what she was asking. "Where do you want to go?"

"I don't…I…" She paused, then lifted her eyes to his. "I know the perfect place."

His eyebrows lifted again. "Do we need airline tickets to get there?" he asked jokingly.

"No, it's about forty minutes out of Houston. Remember I told you about my grandparents' farm?"

"Yes."

"We can go there. It's quiet and out of the way. The place belongs to my mom and Uncle Howard now. They grew up there, so I guess that's why they never sold it.

The house is vacant and Uncle Howard leases the land. I go there a lot just to get away. It's very relaxing. Sometimes Uncle Howard goes with me.''

*Lucky Uncle Howard.*

''Howard grew up on a farm?''

''Yes, he did. Just ask him and he'll tell you all about it.'' She smiled unsteadily. ''He's been like a second father to Blake and me.''

For some reason, Lucas thought of his own father—how alike he feared they were and fervently hoped they weren't. But he couldn't brood about that now. He had to consider Blair and her safety—nothing else. ''Are you sure about this?'' he asked. ''It doesn't sound too safe.''

''But you'll stay with me, won't you?'' There was a note of alarm in her voice.

''Of course,'' he answered immediately. He would do everything he could to make her feel secure. ''But you have to call your parents first.''

''Lucas.'' She closed her eyes.

''As soon as Roger wraps up his investigation, he'll call them,'' he said logically. ''It's better if they hear the story from you.'' He handed her the cell phone.

She eyed him crossly, then took it. She didn't want to talk to anybody, but she had no choice.

Lucas pulled out into traffic. ''How do we get to this farm?''

''Take the 610 Loop, then U.S. 290 north,'' she told him, and poked out her parents' number.

From what Lucas could hear, her parents were upset and asking her to come home, but Blair refused. He could see the strong will Sam had talked about. It had kept her going for the past sixteen years and it was sustaining her now.

As she hung up, she said, ''We have to stop for groceries. There's no food at the house.''

Lucas drove into a supermarket parking lot on the outskirts of town. "I don't know if this is wise. Too many people around."

"You don't think someone's following us, do you?" Her eyes grew enormous.

"Probably not, but I just want to be careful."

"Don't worry," she said, opening her purse. "I have my friend with me."

Lucas stared at the small revolver in shock. "You carry a gun?" It suddenly hit him that *this* was the "friend" she'd been talking about that day in his office—not Roger.

"Yes, Dad got it for me after the attack. I was scared of it for a long time, but I still carried it. A weapon gives me a measure of…reassurance. Uncle Howard taught me how to shoot about ten years ago, and I'm not afraid of the gun anymore. Roger also gave me lessons. But I don't know if I could use it. I hope I never have to find out."

All at once, he realized the fear she lived with every single day of her life. How it controlled her every thought, her every move. He also realized that she couldn't go on like this. The situation had to be resolved and she had to find a life without fear—without a gun. Someway, somehow, he had to make that happen.

"Let's hope we won't need it." He gave a long sigh. "Now, why don't we buy some food and find this farm."

They quickly bought what they needed and drove out of town. Soon Blair directed him to a freeway exit. They took a paved road, then turned onto a gravel road that led to the farm. Cornfields and cotton fields lay on either side, and a small house appeared in the headlights—white frame with black shutters and a picket fence. Just what Lucas had expected.

"Go around to the back," Blair instructed.

As he did, he could make out a garage and several barns. He parked by the gate and turned off the engine.

They sat for a moment, then she asked, "Do you hear it?"

Lucas listened closely, but didn't hear a thing. "What?"

"The silence—the unending silence. No traffic, no people, no offensive noises. Just blissful silence. That's why I love it. The nature, the peace and serenity. I can get my thoughts together here, and somehow I can deal with everything in my life when I've spent time at the farm."

"My brother, Jacob, would love you."

"Why? Does he like the silence, too?"

Lucas nodded. "After his wife and son died, he lived in the Texas Hill Country for five years, completely alone except for his dog. No modern conveniences."

"I couldn't do *that*. I'd have to go shopping at least once." A bubbly laugh left her throat, and he knew this place was magical for her. She was much better than she was an hour ago, and by morning she'd be better still.

Lucas got the groceries out of the car and they walked up the path to the back door. A motion light came on, illuminating the yard. The grass was lushly green and he saw flower beds with roses, shrubs and various flowers. Blair reached for a key above the door and opened it. They entered a long, screened-in porch and walked into a small kitchen. Blair was flipping lights on as she went. The kitchen was white and green, and Lucas set the groceries on the heavy oak table. Blair ran into the living room; Lucas followed. There was a large fireplace on one wall; an area rug occupied the center and various pieces of antique furniture were grouped around the room.

Blair clapped her hands together. "If I close my eyes, I can smell my grandmother's homemade bread. It's the most heavenly scent on earth. I smell it every time I walk into this house." It was clear how much she loved her grandparents and this place. He saw it in her eyes, heard it in her voice, and Lucas knew that coming here had been the right decision.

"Speaking of bread," he said, his eyes on her moist

lips. His thoughts veered in a different direction and he quickly curbed them. "How about some food?"

When Blair said she could cook, she wasn't kidding. Within ten minutes, she'd whipped up a ham-and-cheese omelette and a salad. As Lucas ate, he decided this simple meal was among the best he'd ever tasted.

He sipped his iced tea and realized the kitchen was getting hot. "Where's the air-conditioning control? I'll turn it on."

She glanced up. "There's no air-conditioning."

"What?" He sounded unbelieving.

"There's no air-conditioning," she repeated. "My grandparents didn't believe in it. Uncle Howard and my mom argued with them all the time, but they absolutely refused."

"Blair, it's July in Texas! It's hot."

She shook her head in amusement. "Lucas Culver, I do believe you're a spoiled city man."

He grinned. "You're probably right, but if my brother can endure five years without modern technology, I can surely tolerate one night."

"And you said you liked the outdoors," she teased, and stood up to open the kitchen window. She went into the living room next, opening all the windows. "In a few minutes, it'll be so cool in here, you'll think it's air-conditioned. And you'll be able to hear the crickets and all the soothing night sounds. It's like camping—without the mosquitoes."

Lucas could only stare at her enraptured face. It was such a transformation from the trembling, frightened woman she'd been earlier.

"In the meantime, you can take a shower and—" She stopped, holding a hand to her mouth.

"What?" he prompted.

"We didn't bring any extra clothes, but I can remedy that." She hurried into one of the bedrooms. There were two, separated by a bathroom. A minute later, she returned. "Here's a T-shirt and some shorts. They're either Blake's or Dad's, but they should fit."

"Thanks," he said, accepting them from her. A shower sounded great, exactly what he needed after this dreadful day. He disappeared into the bathroom and smiled as he saw the tub, which was a large antique with four legs and a sloping back. Everything in the house seemed to be antique—except Blair. She was one of a kind and would never go out of style. He was proud of the way she was handling things. She could still laugh and tease, and he hoped she could continue to do that, no matter what happened in the future.

Blair busied herself doing the dishes, keeping her mind a blank. She folded the dish towel and laid it across the sink. She stared out the window into the blackness of the night: crickets chirped and a light breeze cooled her skin. She felt so at peace, so safe here—with Lucas. But that was an illusion; she *wasn't* safe. She had to face the reality of her situation. A chill ran up her spine and she immediately tried to dispel the feeling of foreboding.

She couldn't think about herself. She had to think about Blake and his life—his future. A sob rose in her throat. Why were these awful things happening to her and her family? It was almost more than she could bear.

The sound of running water stopped and she thought of Lucas. He was with her tonight, and for now, that was all she needed. He'd said he wasn't her miracle worker, but he was. He calmed her fears, encouraged her to talk, made her laugh. And he made her feel like a woman....

# CHAPTER FOURTEEN

LUCAS CAME OUT of the bathroom towelling his hair. Blair's heart thumped in her chest with a new awareness. The khaki shorts and white T-shirt seemed to fit his lean frame perfectly. He lowered the towel and stared at her. His tousled hair fell across his forehead and the shadow of a beard darkened his face. His clean manly scent reached out to her and she ached for something that was frightening in its intensity.

At her strange look, he asked, "What's wrong?"

She quickly collected herself. "Nothing. Just waiting for the bathroom." She took the towel from him as she passed him.

Lucas sat on the oversize sofa, his bare feet propped on the coffee table, while Blair took a shower. She was right, he decided; the house was cool and pleasant. He breathed deeply, drawing fresh air into his lungs—no smog, no pollution and the silence was blissful, like she'd said. He noticed a big piano in one corner and he wondered who played it. Blair, of course. It had to be Blair. He could just picture her as a little girl in pigtails, playing for her grandparents.

Lucas rested his head against the sofa. The simplicity of what he experienced here, in this serene house, was appealing, but his complacency couldn't last. Too much needed his attention. He considered calling Roger to get a report, but Roger was so upset with him that he probably wouldn't tell him a thing. Lucas knew their working relationship was on the line, but he didn't care. His main goal, besides winning Blake's case, was to keep Blair safe and to find out who was harassing her. After that, he and Roger would settle this one way or another.

Blair came out of the bathroom and sat beside him, a hairbrush in one hand. She wore a big T-shirt, and he didn't think there was much underneath. She brushed her hair with long, even strokes. Her face was devoid of makeup and she was as fresh as the evening breeze and more exciting than any woman he'd ever known. His chest tightened with unbearable need.

"Who plays the piano?" he asked, forcing his eyes away.

"Blake and me," she answered. "We used to put on shows for our grandparents. But Blake never liked it here as much as I did. He's a lot like you. He prefers the city."

He grinned. "You're not going to let me forget that, are you?"

"Probably not," she said impudently. Then the brush stilled in her hand and her eyes grew serious. "Have you ever been happy?"

His eyes narrowed. "I'm not sure exactly what you mean."

She curled her feet beneath her. "When Blake and I were small, we'd come and spend time with our grandparents. We'd laugh and play, run through the cornfields, ride with Granddad on the tractor and eat Grandma's homemade bread with butter dripping from our chins. We were allowed to be kids and we were happy. That's the only time I remember ever being happy. Then we'd return to the city and become Ava and Sam's kids again. We were expected to be perfect, to excel at everything. That was hard and...and stressful." Her voice wavered on the last word.

"But look at you," he said encouragingly. "You've survived a brutal attack and become a successful, accomplished woman.''

She fiddled with the brush. ''I wish things had been different for Blake. I wish…''

''You're not responsible for what happened to Blake,'' he told her gently.

''I know, but I just keep thinking that if I'd stepped back and let him be the smarter, more skilled twin, then maybe…''

''You can't deny who and what you are.''

''I suppose,'' she admitted reluctantly. Blake had carved out his future with rebellion and defiance; she'd tried to change him, but nothing had worked. Blake was the only one who could have changed his life. And now things just seemed hopeless… Her head was about to explode with so many painful things she couldn't fix and couldn't wipe out. She wanted to talk about something pleasant for a change.

''Lucas, did you have a happy childhood?''

His head jerked up. ''I never really thought about it, but yeah, I guess I did. At least until I was fifteen.''

''That was when you lost your parents, wasn't it?'' she asked quietly.

There was a long pause as Lucas grappled with the past. He never liked to talk about it in any detail—had only done that with Jacob—but now it seemed right to talk to her. She'd been through so much herself that he knew she'd understand his feelings.

''Yes,'' he answered. He stopped for a moment, then went on. ''Before that, when I was younger, my mom and dad were very close. They talked all the time and laughed a lot. There was always laughter in our house. Then my mom started having chest pains. We found out she had a heart condition. The doctor said if she didn't slow down and change her lifestyle—he meant diet and exercise—she would have a heart attack. After that, she got scared and things changed. There was no more laughter. Just silence and arguments. I guess my dad had a rough time dealing with a sick wife.''

He stopped again. ''You see, my dad was a policeman and he often worked late hours. Jacob and I worshipped him, but as it turned out, he had a secret that shattered our lives.''

''A secret?'' she echoed.

''He had a mistress. No,'' he corrected himself, ''he had several mistresses, unbeknownst to my mother, Jacob or me. When he tried to break up with the last one, she shot him with his own gun and he died instantly. My mother couldn't cope with the shame and the devastation of his betrayal. She died a week later of a massive heart attack.''

Her throat constricted with so many emotions, but all she wanted to do was comfort him. ''Oh, Lucas,'' she said, wrapping her arms around him. ''I'm so sorry.''

''It's all right,'' he murmured into her hair. ''It happened a long time ago.''

''That doesn't matter. You still feel the pain.''

He drew back and gazed into her eyes. ''It's not so much the pain, it's…'' He had difficulty finding the right words. ''I'm afraid I'm just like him.''

She was genuinely shocked. ''Why would you say that?''

He raked one hand through his hair and tousled it even more. ''Because I'm forty-two years old and I've never been married and there's a very good reason for that.''

''What?'' she asked, holding her breath.

''I can't stay interested in one woman for any length of time.''

Shakily she let out her breath. ''Maybe you just haven't fallen in love.''

He made a disgruntled sound. ''At my age, that's hardly likely to happen, and I promised myself that I wouldn't marry a woman I couldn't be faithful to. I would never hurt a woman the way my father hurt my mother—never.''

That one sentence explained so much about Lucas—his integrity, his honesty, and his charm with women. He was determined not to be like his father, and she wondered if he even realized that he was nothing like the man he'd described. Lucas wouldn't knowingly hurt anyone. Of that she was sure.

But his words left an ache in her heart. Lucas expected never to fall in love, and it was clear that he avoided it at all costs.

''How'd we get onto this subject?'' He grinned at her.

She raised her head, lost for a moment in her own thoughts. ''We seem to be able to talk about anything.''

''Yeah,'' he murmured, staring into the blue of her eyes.

''You remember that night in my apartment when you kissed me?''

''Sure.'' His breath became thick.

''You said you'd been dreaming about doing it for a long time. Did you mean that?''

''If I said it, I guess I must have.'' He had to joke or he wasn't going to be able to breathe at all.

''Don't tease, Lucas. I'm serious.''

He slowly removed his feet from the coffee table. ''I'm not sure what you want me to say.''

''The truth,'' was her quick reply.

''Okay.'' He glanced at her. ''Even with your hair pulled tightly back and your suit buttoned up to your neck, you can't disguise your beauty.''

''You think I'm beautiful?'' she asked in a winded voice.

He frowned at her, hardly able to believe she had to ask. ''Have you looked in a mirror lately?''

For answer, she reached over and kissed him gently behind the ear. She didn't remove her lips, and his head tilted toward her. ''Blair,'' he said raggedly.

She rained light kisses along his bristly jawline to his mouth. "I've been dreaming about doing that for a long time, too."

"Blair," he groaned, having difficulty breathing under her touch. "We shouldn't be—"

"You promised not to treat me like a child," she reminded him, her tongue licking out the words against his skin.

"Blair," he groaned again. Then he claimed her lips with his own. Their breaths mingled and their bodies melted together. Her response was everything he'd dreamed about—and more. He wanted to taste and feel every inch of her. His tongue explored the sweetness of her mouth and his hands found the hem of the T-shirt and the cool skin beneath.

As he touched her breasts, Blair's world spun completely out of control. She'd had nightmares about being touched in this way, but now she couldn't get enough. She wanted Lucas's hands all over her and she wanted to feel him inside her. She moaned softly and ran her hands around his strong neck, his shoulders and back.

Her softness and her eagerness sent Lucas up in flames. He tried not to rush her. He tried not to frighten her, but when she moaned, the longing in him grew stronger and stronger.

He pressed her into the sofa, their bodies welded together, hip to hip, heart to heart, mouth to mouth. He'd never wanted anyone as much as he wanted her, and his hard body gave credence to that fact.

His hand slid over her hipbone to her narrow waist and full breast. His thumb teased the taut nipple and his mouth soon replaced the erotic movement. Her body grew warm, moist and...

"Lucas." She ran her fingers along the muscles in his back. "Love me, please. Make the nightmare go away."

Her words were like a dash of cold water to his senses.

Suddenly, painfully, he knew he couldn't do this. Much as he wanted her, he had to stop.

"Oh, God, Blair." He buried his face in the sweet hollow of her breasts.

"Lucas?" Her voice was achy, and he knew she wanted answers. He only hoped she'd understand.

"Give me a minute," he begged.

At his tortured tone, she asked, "Are you all right?"

He moved to the side, his back against the sofa. "No, but I will be," he told her, and pulled her T-shirt down to cover her nakedness.

He wasn't going to make love to her, although Blair didn't know why. She couldn't believe it. She'd waited and waited for this moment, and now...now Lucas was rejecting her. All her frustrations welled up inside her.

"Don't you want me?" she asked without shame.

"Can't you feel how much I want you?"

She did; his hardness was pressed into her thigh, which made his actions that much more confusing. "Yes, but I'm not sure if it's you or the hairbrush." She made an attempt at levity because she was about to burst into tears.

It was what Lucas needed to hear. His chest rumbled with laughter and he leaned his face against hers. "When I make love to you," he whispered, "I want it to be slow and easy, with so much passion that nothing else matters."

"But..." She'd thought that was what they were doing...

"Let me finish," he cut in. "Afterward, I want to make love to you again, and the next morning and during the day and the next night. I want us to be alone, just the two of us, lost in each other. I don't want harassment or trials or anything else to interfere. I want it to be special—for you and for me."

Her frustration began to lift...just a little.

He played with a strand of her hair. "We could grab this moment and make the nightmare go away, like you said, but afterward all the ugly things would still be there—the harassment, Blake's trial. Do you understand?''

She smoothed the front of his T-shirt, loving the feel of his tight muscles beneath. ''Yes,'' she breathed weakly. A night of love wasn't going to make their problems disappear. It would only create more. She'd want to be with Lucas every minute, and that would be impossible.

He caught her hand and linked his fingers with hers. ''I have to give this trial everything I've got, and I know that's what you want, too—for Blake.''

''Yes, but it doesn't help this frustration.'' She smiled.

''I know,'' he groaned in answer.

''I just never thought that when I wanted it this much, I'd be rejected.''

He took her chin in his hand and gazed into her eyes. ''Don't you dare think that—not even for a second.''

At his earnest voice, she smiled again. ''You know, Lucas Culver, the more I learn about you, the more I...''

She stopped, unable to finish the sentence out loud. But the truth kept running through her head.

''The more you what?'' he asked at her continued silence.

She inhaled deeply—and lied. ''The more I'm impressed with you.'' She sensed that he wasn't ready to hear she loved him. *She loved him!* When had that happened? She didn't know; all she knew was that she did and probably had for a long time.

''Thanks,'' he said, feeling she was going to say something entirely different. He didn't press her, though.

She snuggled into him, holding her secret to her heart in a moment of pure pleasure.

Silence reigned, and both were consumed with private thoughts.

Finally she asked, ''You don't think it was one of Raye's men who wrote that message on my door, do you?''

"No," he answered honestly. "But I could be wrong. Raye used the same phrase—that's what keeps bothering me. Who'd want to capitalize on that beside Raye and his gang?"

"It doesn't make any sense," she said with a sigh.

"Roger will probably have some kind of answer when we get back."

"I hope so." She sighed again. "Because I can't keep dwelling on it with Blake's trial coming up."

"Then don't," he said. "In the morning I'll take you to your parents', where you'll be safe—and I don't want to hear any protests."

"Yes, sir," she answered glibly, and rested her head against him.

The silence of the night wrapped around them and Blair thought she should get up and turn the lights off, but she didn't want to leave the comfort of his arms. She thought of all the things they'd talked about, and one stood out in her mind.

"Lucas?" she whispered.

"Hmm?"

"You're not like him at all."

"Who?" he murmured sleepily.

"Your father. You're not like him."

Suddenly she had his full attention. "Why do you say that?"

"From what you've said about him, he didn't seem the type of man who'd sacrifice his needs for the feelings of a woman—like you did for me."

He thought about it and had to admit that maybe Blair was right. His father had never cared about anyone but himself. Still, that didn't explain everything; he resembled him in so many other ways that Blair didn't understand. God, he was tired of thinking. He just wanted to go to sleep with Blair in his arms. Tomorrow…tomorrow…

The soothing sounds of the night enveloped them as they drifted off to sleep.

BLAIR WAS THE FIRST to wake. At first she was disoriented; then, as she felt Lucas's strong arms, everything came flooding back. She observed how well their bodies fit together. They were both on their sides, her back against his chest. One of his legs was entwined with hers. This seemed so natural for Lucas—as if he was used to sleeping with a woman in his arms. Jealousy crept through her and she was horrified by it. She'd never considered herself a jealous person, but now she had to admit she was—jealous of all the other women in his life, past, present and future. She quickly brushed those negative thoughts aside. *She* was with Lucas now. So many things stood in the way of their relationship, but she didn't want to think about that, either. Reality would intervene soon enough.

She knew that as soon as Lucas opened his eyes, he'd want coffee. She tried to slip out of his arms to go to the kitchen, but they tightened around her. She turned her head to see if he was awake or if it was just a reflex action. His head swooped and his mouth met hers in a heated, breathless kiss. She moaned, returning the kiss with equal fervor. Then Lucas broke away and crawled over her. "Run, I've got to run," he mumbled in a ragged voice, standing there barefoot and dragging both hands through his hair.

"It's dark outside," she told him, sitting up and glancing at the clock. It was five-thirty in the morning.

"Doesn't matter," he muttered. He looked at her with sleepy eyes. "And you, woman, make coffee." With that, he grabbed his shoes and made a dash for the back door.

Blair shook her head as she slid off the sofa. She'd have to work on Lucas's disposition in the mornings. She filled the coffeepot and peered out the kitchen window to catch sight of him, but it was still dark and she couldn't see a thing.

She sat at the kitchen table; she'd retrieved her brush and slowly, steadily, untangled her hair as the thoughts clamored to be heard. What was she doing? She was weaving a fantasy around Lucas and that was bound to be a mistake. But when Lucas touched her, kissed her or looked at her with those dark eyes, she forgot everything else. Maybe that was a good thing, she told herself. At least then, the fear couldn't control her completely.

LUCAS RAN BLINDLY through the dark until he was exhausted and gasping for breath. He had to. He had to relieve all that sexual frustration. He couldn't go through what he'd endured last night, couldn't do it again. His body still ached with wanting her. God, it felt so good to wake up with her in his arms. He hadn't been able to resist kissing her. A big mistake. All those feelings he'd denied last night came rushing back.

He told himself he was doing the right thing. He just wished he could persuade his body to believe that. He slowly made his way back to the house, clutching his side in agony.

As he opened the gate, he saw Blair sitting on the back steps in a T-shirt and shorts with a cup of coffee in her hand. And not a cup—a big mug.

A smile spread across his face as he plopped down in front of her. She was tying him up in so many knots he was never going to unravel everything he felt for her. He took the mug and sipped the coffee gratefully, trying not to let that last thought weigh him down. There'd been times in the past when he'd questioned his feelings for a woman, but he didn't want to do that with Blair. She deserved so much more than his screwed-up emotions and inconsistent logic. But he couldn't deny that what he felt for her was stronger than anything he'd ever felt before.

"Feel better?" she asked, resting her chin on the top of his head.

"Oh, yeah," he answered, sipping coffee.

She sat on the top step and he sat on the bottom. Her legs enfolded him, and sitting with her in the early hours of the morning, surrounded by her softness and sweetness, was the most sensual experience of his life.

He knew he was in trouble again. But his attention was abruptly diverted when the sun began to play peekaboo with the trees. As it slowly rose, it bathed the trees in a luminescent yellow glow. The earth seemed to sigh and yawn under its brilliance, then quickly gave in to the magnificent awakening.

"Beautiful," he said in a low voice.

"Yes." She echoed his feelings, sliding her arms around his neck.

They were quiet as they enjoyed the early morning. The breeze lightly ruffled the corn, and morning dew glistened invitingly. This time of day was pleasant, but later the hot Texas sun would raise the temperature almost unbearably.

Soon their problems overshadowed the loveliness of morning and Lucas knew he had to talk to her. "You're not going to fight me about staying with your parents, are you?"

"No." She shook her head. "I can't stay in my apartment just yet."

"I don't want you staying there until this maniac is caught," he said emphatically.

"Okay," she replied without even a hint of argument; Lucas realized she was still afraid.

"I want you somewhere safe while I'm working on Blake's trial," he added. "Carl is trying to push the trial date through, so I think it's going to be soon."

Thinking about the trial and what could happen to Blake sent chills racing down her spine. But Lucas would do everything he could for Blake, which meant he needed his total concentration. They would have to put their feelings on hold until this was over.

They continued to sit, both knowing they'd have to leave, and soon. The outside world was waiting, their lives were waiting, but neither made a move—both reluctant to end this special moment, this time out of time.

# CHAPTER FIFTEEN

LUCAS MET with Blake as planned. They went over his story again, and Lucas showed him the photo. For the first time he saw hope in Blake's eyes. He knew there was no way he could prove it was a picture of Blake's vomit, but he would sure as hell try to make a jury believe it. The investigator was busy attempting to locate the photographer and Blair was once again sorting through material from the first trial.

The next weeks were hectic. The trial date was set for September, which was even sooner than Lucas had imagined. He knew Evan's team was ready; now he had to detail his own strategy. Every day he, Derek, Frank, Greg, Brad and Blair were in conference, studying evidence, making sure they hadn't missed a thing. Blair caught problems and inconsistencies the others had overlooked and Lucas saw why she was a good prosecutor. She was doggedly thorough, needing an answer for everything.

Lucas met with Blake several more times, ensuring that there were no holes in his story. Theo had just gotten back from London and his reports looked solid. Everything was running according to schedule and all the team members were doing their jobs.

Roger hadn't found any leads as to who was harassing Blair, but he was keeping a close eye on her. That was good, but it still bothered him, and he knew his feelings were primitive, selfish and purely male.

Sam was waiting to hear his defense, so Lucas scheduled a meeting. He'd wrestled with it for weeks. It was a difficult case, with some damaging evidence—Blake had been there at the time of the murder and his DNA was found under the victim's nails. Lucas was still searching for new evidence. What he counted on to set Blake free was the jury's belief in his innocence. In Lucas's opinion, there was only one way to achieve that. Of course, he expected a lot of opposition, especially from Sam, but he was willing to take his chances.

In the middle of the night, he had the urge to call Blair and talk about his strategy. He picked up the phone, then slowly put it back down. If he told her, she'd tell Blake and encourage him to go along with his plan, and Lucas wanted Blake to make that decision on his own.

He lay staring up at the ceiling, knowing that tomorrow there would be one person behind him a hundred percent—Blair. He fell asleep with that thought on his mind.

THE NEXT MORNING he waited in his office, rehearsing in his head what he was going to say. Joan opened the door and stepped in.

"They're in the conference room," she announced.

Lucas stood with his hands shoved into the pockets of his gray slacks, staring out the window.

"Lucas?" Joan called, seeing his preoccupation.

He turned from the window. "I'm on my way."

"Lucas?"

He glanced at her.

"Smile. It wins them over every time."

Lucas did just that. "Joan," he said, "you're good for my ego."

"Yeah, yeah." She waved him off. "Now, go get this thing settled. Explain your strategy."

Lucas's smile vanished as soon as he entered the boardroom. Raised voices suddenly fell and there was a strained silence as Lucas took his seat at the head of the table.

Everyone was here: Brad and Greg from his own team, and Sam, Blake, Blair, Derek, Frank, Theo and Howard.

Lucas's eyes settled on Blair for a second. She gave a tentative smile, assuring him of her support, which he already knew. He tore his eyes away.

"Well, Lucas." Sam spoke first. "How are we going to win?"

"In this case, there are no clear and obvious answers," Lucas started. "I think that—"

"What do you mean?" Sam broke in. "Go after the girl, prove she was a drug addict and a slut. Let the jury see that."

Lucas took a calming breath. "I'm not going after the girl. Her family's been through enough."

"I'm not worried about her family!" Sam roared. "I'm worried about my son."

He could see that Sam was in one of his black moods, as Lucas was beginning to call them. Still, he stuck to his plan. "I'm not going after the girl," he repeated sternly.

"Then go with Blake's abusive childhood," Howard put in. "That weighs big with a jury."

"Blake did not have an abusive childhood," Sam said angrily.

"What do you call controlling and manipulating him?"

"Shut up, Howard!" Sam shouted. "I don't know what you're doing here, anyway. This is none of your business."

"Blake is my nephew, and I'm not letting you ruin his life any longer." Howard spoke with grit in his voice and Lucas frowned. They were getting off track. This was not the time to air family squabbles.

"Calm down," Lucas ordered. "I'm sure everyone has Blake's best interests at heart."

Silence stretched, then Derek said, "It's not a bad idea to taint Bonnie Davis. We don't have to go after her in a big way—just show the jury she wasn't a saint."

Lucas's gaze swung to Derek. "I'm not going after Bonnie Davis in any way. I've already said that, so let's move on."

"Why don't you tell us what you do have in mind?" Frank asked.

"I've gone over the transcripts from the first trial and the new evidence from start to finish. I've studied the reports Theo brought back from people in London who've known Blake for the past sixteen years. I've read through dozens of case histories." He paused for a second. "We have to cast a shadow of reasonable doubt, and there's only one way to do that."

"What's that?" Sam asked.

"With the truth," Lucas said bluntly.

"The truth?" Sam bellowed. "What the hell are you talking about?"

"I'm talking about telling a jury the truth about what happened that night, and I plan on letting them hear it from Blake in his own words."

"Are you out of your mind?" Sam jumped angrily to his feet. "My son is not testifying under any circumstances!"

Lucas's eyes darkened. "Evan has a strong case and the only thing to weaken it is to have Blake tell his story. Then we support that story with the evidence."

Sam shook his head. "No, no way. I thought you had the guts to go into court and fight to the bitter end, but I can see I was wrong. As of now, you're off the case. Derek and I will take over."

No emotion showed on Lucas's face. He'd been expecting this, but it was hard to walk away. He glanced at Blair; she was staring intently at Blake as if she was willing him to speak out—to do *something*. In his heart, Lucas had been hoping for the same thing. If Blake was going to take control of his life, he had to do it now. Lucas waited an extra second, then stood.

"Fine," he said, and headed for the door. Brad and Greg followed.

Blair continued to stare at Blake—willing him to take a stand instead of allowing their father to manipulate his life. Blake's best chance was with Lucas. Blake's testifying was a great risk, but she trusted Lucas and believed he could make it succeed. Blake had to believe it, too. He had to believe in Lucas as much as she did. If she and Blake had any kind of mental bond, she prayed it was working now.

*Don't let Lucas walk away. Don't let Lucas walk away.*

"No-o-o-o," Blake cried, and leapt to his feet.

Relief swept through Blair and she released the air from her tight lungs.

"Don't go, Lucas," Blake beseeched. "I want you to stay as my attorney. You've believed in me from the start and if you think I need to testify, then I'm with you."

"Son, you don't know what you're saying," Sam put in. "I've been a defense attorney for a long time and I'm telling you this won't work. Carl and Holt will tear you to shreds."

Lucas could see that it was taking everything in Blake to stand up to his father. "It's my life, my decision—and my decision is Lucas," he said shakily.

"Son…"

"You heard him," Howard said as he got up and patted Blake on the back. "It's his decision, so step back and let him control his own life."

"This isn't some game, Howard," Sam snapped. "This is his life—his future."

"Yeah," Howard retorted. "That's the whole point. It's *his,* not yours." He paused, then said, "Why don't you ask Blair how she feels? She loves Blake as much as anyone."

"I'm with Lucas," she replied without even having to think about it.

Those words gave Lucas the incentive he needed. He

walked back to the head of the table. "What's it going to be, Sam?"

Sam glanced at his two children, seeing the same dark hair, same blue eyes and the same determined expressions forcing him to capitulate.

He sank weakly into his chair. "You'd better be right about this, Lucas," he warned. "You'd better be right."

Lucas held his emotions in check because this wasn't over. Blair and Blake were behind him, but he had to have everyone's endorsement before he went a step further.

"I'm not going into court with your warnings hanging over my head," he said. "I either have your wholehearted support, everyone's wholehearted support, or I don't do it at all."

The statement hung in the air as each of them wrestled with its significance. Sam cleared his throat. "You have my support. My kids have spoken."

Lucas wanted more than that, but he took what he could get. Emotions were running high, and he just felt relieved that he was still on the case. He wanted a moment with Blair, but she was hugging Blake and he realized she also had to deal with Sam. Their time together, his and Blair's, seemed to be nonexistent these days. He wondered if that bothered her as much as it bothered him.

LUCAS WAS SO BUSY the next few weeks that he had little time to think about Blair or anything except the trial. Pretrial motions and pretrial hearings kept him on his toes. Carl wasn't willing to give on too many things.

Judge Seton was presiding over the trial. Lucas had tried several cases before him. He was a judge who went by the book, and Lucas knew he had his work cut out for him. Judge Seton didn't allow a lot of leeway in a courtroom, but fortunately Lucas had a good rapport with him, as always, a crucial factor.

Jury selection started in earnest. Lucas was unwilling to

accept anyone who didn't fit his idea of the kind of person capable of judging the truth in this case. He wanted women, as many as he could get, and he didn't mind trading on his looks and his smile to win them over. In his experience, women seemed to recognize the truth more readily than men. He managed to get nine women selected before Carl caught on to his tactics. Lucas then settled for a male college student, a male postal worker and an elderly retired gentleman.

The stage was set, and the showdown began. In his opening statement Carl painted a gruesome picture of a spoiled rich kid who thought he could get away with murder. An out-of-control, rich kid on drugs. Carl went through each chilling detail as the state saw it, from the party to buying drugs to the rape and murder. He said that Blake held Bonnie down, while Todd brutally raped her. When it was his turn, he saw what they'd done to her and chickened out. Carl said witnesses would place Blake with Todd and Bonnie, and his DNA put him at the scene of the murder. He said the state would prove beyond a reasonable doubt that Blake Logan had helped Todd Easton murder Bonnie Davis and would also prove that he'd attempted to rape her.

Lucas stood and walked over to the jury box, staring at the twelve faces. He had to dispel the image of Blake Carl had put into the jurors' minds.

"I'm sure you've heard that there are two sides to every story. Mr. Wright has told you one and now I'm going to tell you the other." He recounted Blake's story just as he'd heard it so many times. He said there was evidence that would show Blake was telling the truth. He mentioned the photo. In the end, he said, "I'm asking you to listen to the evidence and the witnesses with open minds and open hearts. I'm asking you to hear the truth. Thank you."

His preamble was short and to the point, and Lucas could see that it threw Carl. He was expecting Lucas to confuse and distract the jury with a completely different description of Blake, a completely different scenario. Instead, Lucas had enlisted the jurors' help in finding the truth.

It took Carl a moment to recover, then he called three witnesses who'd seen Blake with Todd Easton and Bonnie Davis on the night of the murder.

Lucas let Derek handle the cross-examination. They didn't try to dispute the fact that Blake was with the other two or try to discredit the witnesses. Lucas only wanted them to admit that they saw Blake drinking, smoking pot or buying drugs. Derek got them to say under oath that they saw Blake doing all three. Lucas wanted the jury to hear how much garbage Blake had put into his system that night. Garbage that had made him physically ill, as Blake would testify to later.

Carl then called a DNA expert to conclusively identify the skin tissue under Bonnie's fingernails as Blake's, which he did. Lucas just had a few questions.

"Can you tell us why Blake Logan wasn't identified before now?"

"Because the tissue cells were so minute we couldn't make a match until now. Through new DNA testing we were able to isolate the cells and identify the genetic blueprint of Blake Logan."

"Minute cells?"

"Yes."

"Are you saying there was such a small amount that sixteen years ago it was unidentifiable?"

"We knew it was skin, but as I indicated, we couldn't make the match until now."

"I see." Lucas paused, then said, "No more questions."

Carl then called the police detective who'd handled the case. There wasn't much Lucas could do with his story of the crime. He was one of the first people on the scene and recounted it just as he remembered.

The next day, Carl called the medical examiner, Dr. Lee, to testify how Bonnie Davis died. Carl had a huge photo of Bonnie's murdered body on an easel for the jury to see. Several jurors wouldn't even look at it, and Blake let out a tortured moan. A handful of people got up and left the room. It was one thing to talk about the murder, but it was another to actually see it.

The Davises sat behind Carl, and Bonnie's mother silently wept, refusing to even glance at the photo.

Lloyd Easton sat at the back of the room, as he did each day, listening to every word. His feverish eyes stayed on Sam and his family. Roger was there to keep an eye on him. He worried about Blair, though, with Easton around, but he knew Roger wouldn't let anything happen to her.

Dr. Lee explained in detail how Bonnie was strangled and raped, just the way Carl wanted him to.

Lucas preferred not to dwell on it. He just wanted to get several points across. He picked up several pages of the transcript from the first trial.

Handing them to Dr. Lee, he said, "You're familiar with Todd Easton's trial and the experts who testified?"

"Yes."

"There was a fingernail found embedded in Bonnie's throat. From the transcript, will you please read who the forensic expert matched the nail to?"

Dr. Lee frowned at the paper. "Todd Easton."

"You testified that there were teeth marks on her neck, breasts and right thigh?"

"Yes, some were so deep they broke the skin."

"From the transcript, please read who the forensic dental expert matched the teeth marks to."

Dr. Lee glanced at the papers in his hand. "Todd Easton."

"Also the semen found on Bonnie Davis—who did it match?"

Dr. Lee continued to look at the transcript. "Todd Easton."

"Besides the skin under Bonnie's fingernails—was there any evidence on her body that matched Blake Logan?"

"No."

"Just the skin under her nails?"

"Yes, just the skin under her nails."

"Dr. Lee, please read about the other skin found under Bonnie's nails."

He adjusted his glasses and read, "There were masses of skin under her nails."

"Who did the expert match it to?"

"Todd Easton."

Lucas studied the notes on his desk. "Masses of skin," Lucas repeated.

"Yes."

"In your expert opinion how did that happen?"

"Probably by scratching someone repeatedly."

"I see," Lucas replied thoughtfully. "Would you please read where the minute cells from Blake Logan's skin were found on Bonnie Davis."

Dr. Lee looked through the transcript. "Under her thumb and forefinger on the right hand."

"In your expert opinion, how do you think that happened?"

"Objection," Carl interrupted. "Calls for speculation."

"He's an expert, Your Honor," Lucas said. "He deals with it every day, so he's familiar with the way Blake Logan's skin could have gotten there. Besides, he's already testified how Todd Easton's skin got under her nails."

"I'll allow it," the judge said.

"In your opinion, how could those minute flakes of Blake Logan's skin have gotten under Bonnie Davis's fingers?"

"She caught his arm or touched him in some way."

Lucas thought about that for a minute. "She didn't scratch or claw him," he said slowly and clearly. "She touched Blake Logan."

"Your Honor," Carl objected. "This is ridiculous. It's pure speculation."

"He's your witness, Mr. Wright, so let's move on."

"That's all, Your Honor," Lucas said, then sat down.

Carl had a few more questions.

"If Bonnie Davis was weak and dying, she might not have had any strength left to claw or scratch. Could that be true?"

"Yes, that could be true."

"Thank you," Carl said, and took his seat.

Lucas heard a stir behind him, and he knew that Sam didn't approve of the way this was going. But Lucas had a plan and he was sticking to it. Blair sat directly behind him, next to Sam and Ava, but Lucas purposely kept his eyes off her. Blake deserved his full attention.

He scribbled a note and handed it to Derek. Derek immediately began to go through the files on the desk.

Lucas stood. "Recross, Your Honor."

"Go ahead, Mr. Culver."

Derek quickly passed him a piece of paper. "Dr. Lee, as a matter of record—" he glanced at the paper "—Bonnie Davis was five feet five inches tall and weighed one hundred and twenty-eight pounds at the time of her death. And Todd Easton was five feet eight inches tall and weighed one hundred and sixty pounds." He indicated the notes on his desk. "At sixteen, Blake Logan was six feet tall and weighed one hundred and forty pounds."

"Do you have a question, Mr. Culver?" Judge Seton asked.

"Yes, Your Honor," Lucas replied, walking closer to the witness.

"Would you say that's two pretty good-size sixteen-year-old boys?"

"Yes, I would."

"Then tell me something. If Miss Davis was fighting both boys, as Mr. Wright alleges, why, in your expert opinion, did she repeatedly scratch one boy and get masses of his skin under her nails, yet managed to get only minute cells from the other boy?"

"Your Honor, speculation again," Carl called.

"Overruled," the judge said. "The witness may answer."

Dr. Lee shrugged. "I can't answer that because I don't know."

"Let me see if I can help you," Lucas said. "Could it be possible that Blake Logan, the other boy, wasn't even there when the rape and murder occurred, but was in the bushes vomiting? When he got to her, she reached out to him for help. Is that possible?"

"Yes, but—"

"No further questions," Lucas said, and walked back to his chair.

Carl remained in his seat and Lucas let out a deep breath. Good. He didn't want to confuse the jury. He just wanted them to hear that there was another way the murder could have happened.

They adjourned for the day, but Lucas went back to his office to prepare for tomorrow. Ethan Ramsey was the next witness. He was the private investigator the Davises had hired to find the second killer. Lucas's investigator had done a background check on him, and Lucas was going over every detail—trying to find the best way to cross-examine him. He was a decorated ex-FBI agent who'd been shot in the line of duty. He now ran a ranch outside San Antonio and took special cases like the Davis murder.

Everything Lucas had heard about him was good, so he wasn't going to be able to trip him up. But Lucas knew if he handled it right, Ethan Ramsey could be a crucial witness.

"WHAT THE HELL do you think Lucas is planning?" Carl asked Evan as they went over Ethan Ramsey's testimony.

"I wish I knew," Evan sighed. "Culver isn't disputing anything or trying to discredit witnesses. It's like he's resigned himself to the inevitable, but I know better than that. He's not handing us this case on a platter, so you watch him."

"Well, I know one thing," Carl said. "He won't get anywhere with Ethan Ramsey. He's tough and honest and he'll tell it like it is."

"Don't get cocky," Evan told him. "Just don't leave any doors open for Culver to sneak through. Shut them tight and let's get a conviction."

"Yes, sir," Carl answered, and headed for the door.

"And Carl—" Evan stopped him "—make damn sure your witnesses are rock-solid."

Carl nodded and left.

THAT NIGHT AFTER DINNER, Blake went up to his room. Blair knew something was bothering him and she felt it had to do with the gruesome picture of Bonnie Davis that Carl had shown in court. Blake shouldn't keep this inside, and she intended to make him talk about it.

She hurried upstairs, thinking that Lucas was doing a great job. He was slowly but surely poking holes in the evidence. That was how they could win this case—accumulating enough doubt about the D.A.'s version of events. If anyone could do that, Lucas could.

She missed talking to him. She missed him, period, but she knew there'd be time for them later. There had to be.

She tapped on Blake's door and walked in. He was sitting in the window seat staring out into the darkness. She sat beside him.

Neither spoke for a moment, then she asked, "What's wrong?"

"Nothing. Why?" His eyes swung to her.

"I know you," she replied. "And something's bothering you."

He got up. He had on a pair of baggy shorts and a T-shirt, and he looked so much like the young boy he used to be.

"Leave it alone, Blair," he said crossly as he slumped into a chair.

At his words, apprehension shivered over her skin, and she knew she couldn't leave it alone. He *had* to talk to her.

"I know it was hard seeing Bonnie's picture," she told him. "It was hard for me, too."

He rested his head against the chair. "I've seen it every day for the past sixteen years. All I have to do is close my eyes and I see her—just like that."

She swallowed at the agony in his voice and tried to think of something to reassure him. "Lucas is working wonders and—"

"That's it. That's what—"

He stopped, apparently because he'd realized what he was going to say, and again Blair felt that apprehension.

"What?" she asked.

"Nothing," he said dismissively.

She took a breath. "If it's about Lucas, you have to tell me."

"Leave it alone," he begged. "Just leave it alone." He jumped up and started pacing around the room.

Blair knew that whatever was wrong had to do with Lucas. That could only mean... "Blake, tell me you haven't done something to jeopardize this case."

Blake didn't answer. He just kept pacing.

"Blake?"

He stopped abruptly and stared at her. "Lucas has based this case on me telling him the truth and I...I...haven't told him everything."

"What haven't you told him?" she asked with as much calm as she could muster.

He shook his head and resumed his pacing again. "I shouldn't tell you. Mom said—"

She broke in. "Mom knows about this?"

Blake sank onto the bed and buried his face in his hands. "Yes, she knows," he said feebly.

Blair sat next to him and pulled his hands from his face. "Tell me everything," she said sternly. "Every little detail. Don't leave out a thing."

"That night…that night it happened," he began haltingly. "Todd dropped me off and I was so sick with revulsion…I started throwing up again. Mom heard me and came to check on me. When…when I saw her I burst into tears and crumpled to the floor." He paused and she gave him a moment to regain his composure. "She helped me clean up and I told her everything. I had to tell someone. You were over at your friend's house and—"

One thing kept running through her mind. "All these years, Mom knew you were there at the time of the murder?"

"Yes."

Blair let that sink in, and it prompted another question. "Did she tell Dad?"

Blake shook his head. "No, she never told him. She planned to tell him the next morning, but then he started in on me about my behavior and the drugs, and Mom said it was best just to let things be. But—"

The door opened and Ava walked in. "I wondered where you two had disappeared to. I should've known you were talking and…" Her words trailed off as she saw their stricken faces. "Oh, Blake, darling, you told her."

"Yes, he told me," Blair said angrily. "How could you keep this a secret?"

Before Ava could answer, Blake said, "Tell her the rest, Mom."

Blair's eyes swung to Blake. "There's more?"

"Now, Blake, there's no need to get Blair involved in this," Ava said. "It won't help anyone—especially you."

"I don't care anymore," Blake muttered. "The whole truth has to come out. Lucas has to know."

Ava sat on the other side of Blake and rubbed his arm lightly. "It'll be all right...."

Blair saw what her mother was doing—the same thing she'd done all their lives—protecting them with gentle manipulation. Sam's manipulation was obvious and blatant, but Ava's was subtle and often undetectable. Blair could see it now. She knew her mother's actions were motivated by love, but it had to end.

Blair sprang to her feet and confronted Ava. "Tell me everything," she demanded.

"Darling, don't get so upset. I'm—"

"Tell me." Blair shouted. "And tell me now. Stop trying to placate me. It's not going to work. Just tell me the truth."

Ava watched her, but didn't say a word.

"Tell me!" Blair shouted again.

"Stop shouting," Ava said. "It's so unbecoming."

"Mother." Blair's hands curled into fists.

"All right, all right." Ava gave in. "But as I said, it won't change anything and it certainly won't help Blake."

"Tell me," Blair said in a calmer tone.

Ava sighed deeply. "After Todd Easton was released on bail, he started coming to the house to see Blake. I wouldn't let him in. One day, he became angry, saying his father had cut him off financially and that he had to have money. If he didn't, he said he'd go to the police and tell them that Blake helped him kill Bonnie Davis."

"Oh, God, no," Blair groaned. "Tell me you didn't give him money."

Ava smoothed her dress over her knees and remained silent. That told Blair all she needed to know. Her mother had given Todd Easton money to keep quiet. Oh, God, this couldn't get any worse.

"I can't believe it," Blair muttered. "Lucas is getting the jury to listen to his side of the story, and now your lies have sabotaged everything."

Ava stood and put an arm around her shoulder. "No, it hasn't. Lucas need never know. Blake should never have told you."

Blair stared at her mother as if she were seeing her for the first time. Ava was willing to do anything to keep her son safe—even encourage him to lie. But the lies had to stop.

"Blake should have told Lucas everything," Blair snapped. "Lucas believes in the truth—and I believe in him. I have to tell him."

"No," Ava said, and stood between Blair and the door. "You can't! It's Blake's life we're talking about. Lucas doesn't need to know. Please, Blair, think about your brother. Do you want him to go to prison for the rest of his life for something he didn't do?"

Blair's head began to throb painfully and she knew she had to get away from them. She pushed past her mother and ran to her room, where she flopped onto her bed and tried to sort through the troubling events. Her mother had known all along and had even paid Todd Easton to keep quiet. Lloyd Easton had suspicions about Sam and got Evan to investigate, but it hadn't been Sam—it was Ava. That was where Todd had gotten the money Lloyd and others had seen him with. Blair didn't know her family anymore. One shocking revelation after another....

She had to tell Lucas. But then, what about Blake? Lucas wouldn't keep the information hidden; she knew that about him.

What would this do to Blake's chances? As an attorney she knew the answer. This new information meant a sure prison sentence. For Lucas to recant any part of his story now would be devastating. What should she do? She was caught between her love for Lucas and her love for Blake. What should she do?

She'd call Lucas and tell him. She sat with the phone in her lap. By morning she was still sitting there, no closer to picking up the receiver than she'd been hours ago.

*Lucas, what should I do?*

# CHAPTER SIXTEEN

WHEN LUCAS SAW Blair in court the next morning, she seemed worried and looked as if she hadn't had any sleep. The trial and the harassment were taking their toll on her; he had to get the trial over with as quickly as possible—for her, for the Logan family and for himself.

As people were settling in the courtroom, Lucas caught Blair's arms and pulled her to one side. "You okay?"

"Sure." She tried to smile and failed.

"Has Roger found anything on the harassment?"

She shook her head. "No." She didn't want to think or talk about the harassment. Looking into his eyes, she added, "You're doing a wonderful job."

"Thanks, ma'am." He smiled, and her heart fluttered wildly. "If we weren't in a courtroom, I'd kiss you."

Unable to help herself, she smiled in response—a genuine smile. "If we weren't in a courtroom, I'd let you."

They stared at each other for endless seconds, then Lucas said, "Hold that thought for the next few days."

As Lucas walked to his desk, she felt like the biggest fraud who'd ever lived. She should have told him. She knew that, but the words wouldn't come.

CARL CALLED ETHAN RAMSEY to the stand. He was a tall Texan who wore boots and a Stetson hat. He walked with a slight limp, but with his proud stature it was hardly noticeable.

Carl went over everything with him—from the time the

Davis family had hired him, to getting Blake to submit a blood sample for DNA testing.

Ethan reminded Lucas of Jacob. He was down-to-earth, straightforward and honest to a fault. There was only one way to handle Ethan Ramsey.

"You found four other boys who'd been outside the party with Todd Easton and Bonnie Davis?" Lucas asked, reviewing testimony he'd already given.

"Yes, sir."

"Did you ask for their DNA?"

"Yes, sir."

"What happened?"

"They refused."

"So you flew to London to talk to the fifth boy?"

"Yes, sir."

"Tell the court what happened next," Lucas invited.

"I went to the magazine where Blake Logan worked and I waited for him. When he came out, I asked if I could talk to him. He asked what about and I told him we needed to talk in private. We went to a small courtyard. I told him I was hired by the Davis family to find the other boy involved in their daughter's murder."

"How did my client respond?"

"He just stared off into space with a kind of shattered look."

"What happened then?" Lucas asked.

"I told him he was identified as one of the boys who'd been with Easton and Davis at the party."

"How did my client respond to that?"

"He didn't. He just kept sitting there."

"What happened next?"

"I asked if he'd be willing to give his DNA. He thought about it for a minute, then said yes."

"He said yes?" Lucas repeated.

"Yes, sir. He did."

"He didn't try to run away. He didn't curse or threaten you. He just said yes."

"Yes, sir."

Lucas paused for a second, trying to word the next question just right. "Were you surprised by his answer?"

"Yes, sir, I was."

"Why?"

"Because a guilty person doesn't do that."

A smile endangered Lucas's demeanor, but he quickly curbed it. "Thank you, Mr. Ramsey. Thank you very much."

It was more than Lucas had hoped for, but it was definitely what he needed.

"Your Honor, may I redirect?" Carl asked.

"By all means, Mr. Wright."

"But Mr. Logan is guilty," Carl threw at Ethan.

"Mr. Logan's DNA matched," Ethan countered.

"Your Honor, please instruct the witness to answer the question."

Before the judge could do so, Ethan spoke up, "I don't know if he's guilty. All I know is that his DNA matched."

Carl studied him for a moment, then took another approach. "You've been a lawman for a number of years. You've been with the FBI and now you're a private investigator. We've already established that."

"Yes, sir."

"So you know a great deal about criminals?"

"Yes, sir."

"In your experience, when a defendant's DNA is found on the victim in a murder case, what does that tell you?"

Ethan considered the question for a minute. "Most of the time it tells me he's guilty."

"Thank you, Mr. Ramsey."

Lucas stood up. "Your Honor…"

"Go ahead, Mr. Culver," the judge said in a tired voice.

"Mr. Ramsey, you said *most of the time.* Does that mean sometimes the defendant is not guilty?"

"Yes, sir—sometimes."

"Thank you again, Mr. Ramsey."

Carl got to his feet again. "Your Honor…"

"Enough, Mr. Wright," the judge declared. "This is your witness and he has made perfectly clear how he feels. So let's move on."

*Thank you, Ethan Ramsey,* Lucas thought. Since he was a well-known lawman, the jurors were listening to him and his unwillingness to condemn Blake. They were mulling it over in their minds, thinking, *Maybe the tall Texan's right. Maybe…* That was what Lucas wanted them to think.

Lloyd Easton was next on the prosecution's witness list, as was a friend of Todd's. Lucas and Derek spent most of the evening planning questions, studying details.

BLAIR WAS STILL BATTLING with her conscience. She knew she had to tell Lucas, but things were going so well in court that… She couldn't justify such thoughts. She had to talk to Lucas. She slept with the phone again, trying to gain the courage to do what had to be done.

By dawn, the courage still eluded her.

LLOYD EASTON ENTERED the courtroom, much calmer than the time he'd appeared in Lucas's office. He was dressed in a suit and tie, and his irrational behavior was nowhere in sight. But Lucas knew that could change with the right questions.

Lloyd told a story that portrayed his son as a saint who'd been manipulated by Sam Logan to save his own son. He went on to say that Todd had large sums of money and he didn't know where it was coming from, so he followed him one day and Todd went to the Logan house.

Derek took the first round of questions on cross, and it

didn't take long to get Lloyd rattled and angry. The judge called for a recess and Lucas took the second round. Lloyd had never actually seen Sam give Todd money, and Lucas got him to admit that Todd could have gone to Sam's house simply because Sam was his attorney.

Lloyd's face turned red and the veins in his neck bulged out—just the way Lucas had seen before. When Lucas finished his questioning, Lloyd jumped to his feet and pointed a shaking finger at Sam. "Sam Logan killed my son just as sure as if he personally took a gun and shot him," he screamed. "Now his son will pay. He has to pay." He turned to the jury. "Make him pay. My son is dead. Make him pay."

"Your Honor," Lucas protested, and two guards had to forcibly remove Lloyd from the room. All the while he was screaming curses at Sam.

Judge Seton was instructing the jury, but Blair didn't hear a word. She sat very still, the scene chilling her to the bone. Roger slipped into the seat beside her and patted her arm. "It's all right, Blair. I'm here."

It wasn't, and Blair knew it. Nothing would be right until she'd talked to Lucas. Lloyd Easton knew someone had given his son money and he thought it was Sam. That had fueled his pain and anger for years, and it was clear the man was close to a nervous breakdown. All because of her mother. If her mother hadn't intervened, Sam would've gone with Blake to the police—made him tell the truth, made Blake face the consequences of his actions. That was why her mother hadn't told him about Blake's involvement. Now…Blair had to tell Lucas that money had changed hands—her mother's money. She couldn't keep putting it off because of her fear of what might happen. Fear had controlled her too many times in the past, and it wasn't going to control her now. She loved Lucas and hoped they'd have a future together, but they had nothing until she told him the truth. She knew she was risking so much, but she had no other choice. She finally saw that.

Lucas handled Todd's friend the same way he'd handled Easton. The friend testified that he'd gone with Todd to the Logan mansion and Todd had come out with money, but there was no proof and Lucas was able to discredit his testimony.

LUCAS WAS BUSY after court, so Blair had to wait until he was alone, which would not be until later in the evening. She went home, planning to call him after dinner. The phone rang, startling her. She picked it up and a muffled voice said, "Blair?"

"Yes," she answered, trying to identify the caller.

"Carl has gone through your father's financial records trying to locate the money he'd given Easton. He didn't find a thing. Now he's going after your mother. Thought you should know." The phone went dead in her hand.

She stood frozen in shock. The voice was familiar. A woman's, she decided, and she felt it was someone from her old office—someone giving her a warning. The reality of the words hit her and she quickly went in search of her mother. She and Blake were in the den, and Blair suspected that Ava was applying gentle pressure—pressure Blake wasn't even aware of.

"How much money did you give Todd Easton?" Blair asked her mother.

"Darling."

"How much?" Blair persisted.

Ava shrugged. "About ten thousand, I suppose."

Blair swallowed the retort on her lips. "Where did you get it?"

"I used the money I got from your grandparents' estate."

"Did you write a check or withdraw the money in cash? How did you do it?"

"I withdrew large cash amounts."

"Don't you realize that can be traced?"

"How? It was cash. There's no proof of what I did with the money."

Blair took a deep breath. "All Carl has to do is prove the money was there and that it was withdrawn at the same time Todd had money. The jury can fill in the blanks."

"Oh, no," Ava moaned.

"I just got an anonymous phone call saying that Carl's checking into your financial records."

"Oh, Blair, you can't let this happen," her mother begged.

"This is about to blow up and there's very little I can do to stop it," Blair said. "But I have to tell Lucas. This is going to come down on him like a ton of bricks. He thinks he knows the whole story, and I can't let him go on believing that."

"I'll go with you," Blake said, trailing after her. "This is my fault."

Blair whirled to face him. "Yeah, Blake, this *is* your fault," she said angrily. "So it's time to stop hiding behind Mom and stop hiding behind me and take responsibility for your actions."

Blake paled. She'd never talked to him that way before, but suddenly she'd had enough. "I'm trying, sis," he muttered in a hurt voice.

Blair didn't let it reach her heart. She couldn't be swayed by emotion. She looked at her mother. "Tell Dad as soon as he gets here. Tell him everything."

Ava twisted her hands nervously. "Darling, I…"

"Tell him, because it'll be much better coming from you than from me." With that, she walked out the door and Blake slowly followed.

BLAIR KNEW exactly where to find Lucas—in his office. He was working so hard to win this case she almost didn't have the heart to tell him. But she refused to let Carl hit him with this out of the blue. Lucas had to be prepared.

She had confronted fear in her life, but what she confronted now could completely destroy her. If Lucas hated her... She couldn't even complete the thought. He had to realize she'd never intentionally hurt him.

She drew a deep breath and entered his office. Blake was a step behind her.

Lucas looked up, surprise on his face. The sleeves of his blue shirt were rolled up to his elbows and he was writing on a legal pad. His dark hair was tousled as if he'd been running his hands through it—as she'd often seen before.

He stood up and smiled, and her stomach turned over. She loved him and he was probably never going to know that. As she stared into his dark eyes, she knew that Lucas wouldn't forgive her. He trusted her and her family; he didn't deserve this duplicity. And she didn't deserve Lucas.

"Is anything wrong?" Lucas asked, feeling uneasy at the pained look on Blair's face.

"I need to talk to you," she said in a strained voice.

"I'll tell him." Blake spoke up. "It's like you said. It's time I took responsibility and sorted out my own life."

That uneasiness spread through Lucas's whole body, and he knew he was about to hear something unpleasant. He braced himself.

In his halting fashion, Blake told about the secret he and his mother shared, about the money, and finally that Carl was investigating Ava's financial records.

Lucas sank into his chair. "Oh my God," he murmured as everything began to take shape in his mind. Through the secrets and the lies, he needed to ask one question. He glanced at Blair. "How long have you known about this?"

"I told her a few days ago," Blake answered for her.

"Why didn't you come to me then?" Lucas asked, his eyes never leaving Blair.

She raised her eyes to his. "I wanted to. I—"

"Mom forced her not to," Blake cut in. "Mom thought it was best to forget about this, but Blair couldn't."

"I'll bet not," Lucas said sarcastically. "Especially since Carl's close to uncovering the truth."

"Lucas," Blair appealed, unable to endure that tone of voice.

"No." Lucas shoved out a hand as if to keep her away. "I put my career on the line for you—for your family. God," he said bitterly, "I can't believe this. I can't believe you'd do this to me."

"Don't take it out on Blair," Blake mumbled. "It's my fault."

"Yes, it probably is," Lucas agreed. "And Blair's chosen who she's going to stand by. I said I couldn't work with people I can't trust, and I meant it. You'll have to take your chances with Derek and your father, because I'm off the case."

Lucas was so angry he was about to explode. He swiftly rolled down his sleeves and buttoned the cuffs, then picked up his jacket and walked around the desk.

"Lucas," Blair appealed again, reaching out to catch his arm. "Don't do this." Tears glistened in her eyes, and he tried to ignore them.

But her touch was almost his undoing. Her skin was warm through the fabric of his shirt, and he remembered what it was like to touch her, to hold her—and it had all been a lie.

"I trusted you and you broke that trust," he said with quiet emphasis. "There's nothing left to say." He removed her hand and walked out the door.

Blair's heart shattered into a million pieces. She couldn't breathe with the pain. She sank to the floor and buried her face in her hands. She didn't want to cry, but the tears poured unheeded from her eyes. Blake fell down beside her and wrapped his arms around her. She cried until there were no tears left. Then Blake helped her to her feet and took her home.

LUCAS DROVE straight to his house, his anger consuming him, controlling him. He tore into his house and changed quickly into jogging shorts, then he hit the front door at a run. He ran until he couldn't breathe. He ran until his whole body ached, but he couldn't outrun her face, her memory. He fell onto his sofa, tired, exhausted and hurt beyond anything he'd ever imagined. She had betrayed him in the worst possible way. She hadn't trusted him enough to confide in him and she'd left him hanging.

The look on her face when he'd walked out of the office was still with him. She was hurting, too, but it didn't change anything and it didn't make the pain go away. He'd thought they shared something special, but it was tainted with lies and with secrets.

He got up and paced around the living room, then he did what he always did in a time of crisis—he called Jacob.

"Lucas." Jacob's familiar voice calmed him. "I'm glad you called. I just talked to Howard and he told me what's going on with his sister."

"Howard called you?"

"Yeah, he wanted me to persuade you to stay on the case."

"What did you tell him?"

"I told him you were over twenty-one and made your own decisions, but if you asked for my help, I'd talk to you."

Good old Jacob. Lucas smiled inwardly. No pressure, no control, just love—straight from the heart. How he wished....

"What are you planning to do?" Jacob asked.

"I quit earlier but now I'm not sure," Lucas admitted.

There was a long pause. "Is this more about Blair than about Blake's defense?"

"Maybe," he said reluctantly.

"Don't lose something special because of your pride, and that's all I have to say."

"I'd better go," Lucas said. "I've got a lot of thinking to do."

"Whatever you decide, I'm with you."

"I know that, Jacob, and thanks."

His anger dissipated as quickly as it had come. Lucas was struggling to keep his pride from ruling his emotions, but he was hurting like hell and he couldn't seem to get beyond that.


THE NEXT MORNING Blair sat up in bed, staring at the wall, not seeing anything but feeling so much pain. She wondered how many times you could feel this kind of intense pain before it destroyed you. The last time the wounds had healed, but she knew that these wounds—to her heart— would never heal. And it was her own fault.

She should've gone to Lucas when Blake first told her, but she'd let her mother persuade her otherwise. Now it was too late. Too late for her and Lucas. Too late for Blake and her family. How would they survive this? She didn't know. She only prayed for strength.

The door opened and her mother walked in, dressed in a cream-colored suit. "Darling, you're not up," Ava said as if nothing was wrong. "We have to be in court in a little while."

"How do you do it?" Blair shook her head. "How do you pretend that nothing's wrong?"

Ava paled slightly, unable to completely hide everything. Blair had heard raised voices until the early hours of the morning and she knew her father wasn't pleased with this new revelation. But her mother had gotten around him as she always did, with her subtle manipulation. Blair suddenly remembered all the times Blake had gotten into trouble and her mother had interceded with her father. Sam never disciplined or punished Blake, because her mother wouldn't let him. Blake was now thirty-two and Ava was still doing it. Except that now things had gone beyond even her manipulation.

Ava sank onto the bed and Blair smelled her perfume and it brought back memories of all the times her mother had been there for her, how much love she'd given her and Blake—maybe too much.

"Darling, I wish you'd try to understand."

Blair didn't answer and Ava went on. "I was frantic to keep Blake out of jail. I would have done anything to accomplish that. You won't understand until you have children."

Blair drew her knees up to her chin. "That's not likely to happen now, is it?"

"Oh, darling, I'm so sorry about Lucas. Once he cools off, I'm sure he'll—"

Blair stopped her. "Do you even realize what you've done?"

Ava brushed away a tear and bit her lip. "Yes, I've ruined everything," she muttered. "Your father's upset with me, and you and Blake are, too. I can't take much more. I was only trying to keep Todd from destroying Blake. I went about it the wrong way. I can see that now and…"

Blair said nothing.

Ava glanced up. "What do you think Lucas will do?"

"I don't know," Blair admitted with a catch in her voice. "But promise me something."

"What?"

"Let Blake handle this. Let him make his own decisions. Stop pressuring him."

Ava twisted her hands. "He's always needed me much more than you ever have."

That was probably true, Blair thought. Their personalities were so different. Blair never wanted help with anything and Blake always needed help with everything.

Blair was suddenly seeing things she'd never seen before. Blake's main problem was his mother. Blair wondered if Ava even realized that.

"Mom, do you know that you're the barrier between Blake and Dad?" she said softly. "They don't know each other because you've never let them."

Ava squeezed her lips together tightly, as if to keep from crying out.

"I didn't say that to hurt you," Blair quickly added.

"I know, darling," Ava replied. "Sam always wanted a son and when Blake was born I hoped he'd be everything Sam wanted. I tried to make it happen, but nothing worked. Your father had such a temper, and Blake was a timid, sweet kid who needed lots of love."

"Why couldn't you let Blake be himself? He didn't have to be a clone of Dad."

Ava started to cry, tears rolling down her cheeks into her lap. She made no attempt to brush them away. "Why is this happening to my family?" she cried. "Why does my family have to suffer so much?"

Blair reached over and hugged her mother, loving and forgiving her at the same time. Blake had to face his life and deal with it—without his mother's manipulations. If Lucas bailed on them as he'd said he would, then Blake was going to need all the strength he possessed and then some. And like Blake, Blair had to face the future on her own—without Lucas.

LUCAS FELT BETTER after his talk with Jacob. He'd put a lot of time and hard work into this case and he wasn't going to walk away. He wasn't a quitter and he wasn't starting now. He didn't know exactly what made him change his mind—Jacob, Blair's tears or his own stubborn pride. But the next morning he marched into his office ready for battle. He stopped short as he saw that the room was full—Sam, Blake, Howard, Derek, Frank and Theo were all there.

Lucas walked purposely to his desk and sat down, not saying a word. Blair wasn't here. Why wasn't she here? No, he had to stop thinking about her.

Sam was the first to speak. "I have to apologize for my family," he said. "I didn't know. If I had, I would've done something long ago."

Despite it all, Lucas believed him. That was why Ava had never told her husband. She knew Sam would make his son take responsibility instead of pampering and protecting him.

"Lucas." Howard spoke up. "Please stay on the case. It's Blake's only chance."

"We all want you to stay," Derek said. "This just about blows us out of the water, but I also know you can find a way to rectify things."

Lucas fiddled with a pencil on his desk. He'd already made his decision, but it felt good to finally get this kind of support. His eyes kept straying to the door, waiting for her to walk in. Just as well if she didn't, he told himself. Things were never going to be the same between them.

Blake had been standing toward the back, letting everyone else do the talking as usual, but he suddenly stepped forward, a somber expression on his face.

"I didn't tell you the whole truth," he said gravely, "and for that I'm deeply sorry. Whatever you decide, I'll understand, but please don't blame Blair—that's all I ask."

Absolute silence followed his words and Lucas studied the paperweight on his desk with intense interest. Blake was slowly taking control of his life, his emotions, and Lucas admired that. Lucas wasn't blaming Blair. He was just—God, he no longer knew *what* he was feeling. But he had a knot in his stomach the size of a baseball and it was growing. Somehow, this whole situation had to be corrected. Time for some damage control.

He stared at Blake. "Is there anything else you're not telling me?"

"No, sir," Blake said sincerely.

Lucas took a long breath, then said, "I figured Carl was going to rest his case today, but now I'm thinking he's got a last-minute trick up his sleeve."

His words meant he was still on the case. A sigh of relief echoed around the room. But Lucas didn't waste any time; he got down to business.

"Brad and Greg will continue to prepare Blake to testify, and Frank and Theo, I want you to get Ava ready."

"You want her to testify?" Sam asked cautiously.

"I sure do."

"How do you plan to approach it?" Sam wanted to know. That surprised Lucas. He'd been sure Sam would fight the idea; instead, he'd apparently accepted the necessity of calling Ava to the stand.

"I plan to let her tell the story in her own words."

"If she says she paid Easton to keep quiet, that'll destroy Blake's case."

"We have to trust a jury to hear her testimony for what it is—a mother's misguided attempt to shield her son out of love. We have to hope for a little compassion and understanding from each juror."

"I'm not questioning your judgment," Howard said. "But Ava's pretty distraught and I'm not sure she can handle it."

"She'll handle it," Sam said with force. "She created this mess and now she has to clean it up."

There was a brittle silence, then Howard said, "For once, Sam, I agree with you."

"Let's get to work," Lucas instructed. "Derek and I have to be in court in an hour, and I'm hoping against hope that Carl doesn't have any surprises for us. If he does, we'll have to take it from there.''

Carl didn't, but he asked to speak with the judge. He said he had an important witness his investigator was trying to locate, and he wanted to reserve the right to call him at the appropriate time. Lucas didn't object, because he knew what Carl was trying to do. He was trying to get the goods on Ava, but Lucas planned to unearth the whole mess before that happened.

Carl rested his case, and Lucas began his defense. Three witnesses from London testified to Blake's character. One he went to school with, one he worked with and the other was his neighbor. They all testified that he was a moral, upstanding young man who never showed any signs of violence.

Carl asked a few additional questions and Lucas could see that his mind was somewhere else—on evidence that could secure a conviction. Lucas knew he had to beat him to the punch and he planned on calling Ava first thing in the morning. It was a gamble, but he didn't have many options open to him. The secret was going to come out, and it was better coming from him than from the prosecution.

Lucas didn't sleep much. So many thoughts were clamoring in his head, but one kept overshadowing everything else. Blair hadn't been in court today. He wondered where she was. He had to talk to her. His anger had subsided, and her friendship meant a lot to him. Friendship? Was that all it was? Yes—that was all it could ever be now. And who had made *him* judge and jury of Blair? He was acting irrational, and he was hurting her—something he'd sworn he'd never do. God, he didn't like himself for feeling the way he did. He didn't like himself at all.

BLAIR LAY CURLED in bed, willing the phone to ring, but she knew it wouldn't. Lucas wasn't going to forgive her;

she couldn't forgive herself, so she couldn't expect it from him. She was just glad he was still on the case.

She hadn't been in court today because she couldn't face him. But tomorrow she'd be there to support her mother; so would her father. Ironically, they were pulling together as a family now, the way they should have years ago. However, the price had been too high and she hoped they could survive the final tally.

"WHAT IS THIS?" Evan demanded of Carl. He threw a piece of paper on his desk. "Why is Culver calling Ava Logan as a witness?"

Carl shrugged. "Surprised me, too."

"There's a goddamn leak in this office. I know it! Culver somehow found out you're checking into Ava's finances."

"I don't see how that can possibly help his case. If she gave Easton money, that's going to be very damaging."

Evan took a seat. "How are you coming with her financial records?"

"We found out she has some money left to her by her parents. It's in a personal account, but the records from sixteen years ago aren't on a computer. It's taking a while to dig them out."

"Goddammit, put a rush on it," Evan roared.

"I have, but now it's a waiting game."

Evan shook his head. "We don't have any time left. Culver's up to something. You just be ready."

"Don't worry, I will."

"Yeah, like I wasn't supposed to worry about Ramsey's testimony and look how *that* turned out."

"Evan…"

Evan stopped him. "Just be prepared."

AVA WAS on the witness list and everything was set. Lucas met with Ava and Sam briefly before court started. He looked directly at Ava. "Whatever I ask you today, I want you to answer truthfully. Do you understand?"

"Of course," she said.

"Even if I ask your hair color. Tell me the truth."

Ava glanced worriedly at Sam. "Why would he want to know that?"

"You're not listening to me Ava," Lucas said. "It's not about your hair. It's about the truth. No matter how much you dislike answering, or how distasteful the questions, you *have* to tell the truth."

"Okay," she said slowly.

"Because if you lie, I will know it and the jury will know it and Blake won't have a chance in hell."

"Okay," she said again, and Lucas felt he was finally getting through to her.

As THEY FILED into the courtroom, Carl sent him a dark scowl, and Lucas prayed his plan would work. His attention was diverted for a second when Blair walked into the room, but he quickly got his thoughts under control.

Lucas called Ava to the stand.

After she was sworn in and had stated her name, Lucas asked, "How are you related to Blake Logan?"

"I'm his mother."

"Do you love your son?"

"Yes, very much."

"Your Honor," Carl objected, "where is Mr. Culver going with this?"

"Move on, Counselor."

Lucas asked Ava to tell in her own words what she knew about the Davis murder. In a hesitant fashion, she described finding Blake sick and crying, then talked about Todd coming to the house, his threats, and finally about giving Todd money to stay quiet. She looked directly at the jury and said she'd done everything to keep her son safe, as any mother would. It was wrong, she could see that now, but a mother's love wouldn't allow her to do anything else. Her words were heart-wrenching and sincere, and Lucas could see the jurors were listening to her. That was more than he'd hoped for.

"Now, Mrs. Logan," Lucas said, glancing at his notes, "you said that Blake had vomit all over him and you helped clean him up."

"Yes."

"Did you remove all his clothes."

"All but his underwear."

"Were there scratches on his body?"

"No."

"Was there blood on his clothes?"

"No."

"Was there blood on his body?"

Ava swallowed. "Yes."

"Where?"

"There was a smear of blood on his right forearm."

"A smear of blood?"

"Yes. I asked if he was hurt and he said no."

"Did you ask Blake about it?"

"Yes, he said that Bonnie Davis had caught his arm when he checked her pulse to see if she was...dead."

"And you believed him?"

"Yes. My son's not violent. He never has been."

"Even when he was on drugs?"

"Even then."

Lucas paused for a second. "Mrs. Logan, how long has Blake been off drugs?"

"Since that awful night."

"He stopped cold turkey?"

"Yes, and it wasn't easy. He had tremors, shakes, sweats and severe withdrawal. He had nightmares, and he'd cry. But he endured through all the anguish. I held him and bathed his face, trying to help. I was so afraid he was going to sneak out and get drugs."

"But he didn't?"

"No, he was finally able to break the hold that terrible stuff had on his body."

Lucas paused again. "Did you tell your husband what was happening?"

"No."

"Why not?"

Ava gripped her hands tight. "Because I knew what he'd do. He would've made Blake go to the police and I couldn't stand—" She swallowed. "I couldn't stand the thought of my son in jail. He was just in the wrong place at the wrong time and I—"

After a brief pause, Lucas asked, "Did you eventually tell your husband?"

"Yes. When Todd Easton almost killed our daughter, Blake was beside himself, taking the blame for everything. I told Sam because I couldn't handle it anymore."

"Did you tell him everything?"

Ava twisted her hands. "No, I didn't tell him about giving Todd money."

"Why not?"

"I didn't know what he'd do. We didn't know if our daughter was going to live and I couldn't bear the thought of losing both my children. I couldn't…" She choked, then said, "I'm sorry. I made some really bad decisions, but my son never hurt anyone except…himself."

"Mrs. Logan, are you telling me the truth?"

Ava glanced at the jury. "Yes, finally, I am."

"Thank you."

Blair had to fight back the tears and she ached for what her mother was going through. Out of the corner of her eye, she saw Evan enter the courtroom. That meant only one thing—he wanted Carl to go after Ava. He wanted him to tear her testimony to shreds. And Carl did just that. He went after Ava with a vengeance, but she didn't crack. She kept answering the questions, consistently and truthfully. Carl demeaned Blake, calling him a momma's boy hiding behind her skirts. Ava was teary-eyed, but she still didn't crack. He couldn't get her to admit that she knew Blake had murdered Bonnie Davis. He couldn't get her to admit that Blake had attempted to rape Bonnie Davis. He couldn't get her to admit to anything except shielding Blake and giving Todd money, which was bad enough.

Frustrated, Carl asked, "Mrs. Logan, why are you coming forward now?"

Ava looked directly at him. "To be honest, I wanted to sweep this information under the rug and leave it there. It wasn't going to help my son. It was only going to hurt his defense. But my son told his sister and she said I had to tell Mr. Culver everything." She paused and stared down at her hands for a moment. "I refused because I knew it would hurt Blake. I've been protecting Blake for so long that I couldn't stop. Faced with my stubbornness, Blair finally told Mr. Culver and…and—" she looked back at Carl "—that's why I'm here today. Mr. Culver believes in the truth, and my daughter believes in him."

"That's a bunch of bull and you know it, Mrs. Logan," Carl fired at her. "The only reason you came forward now is that you're afraid of getting caught."

Ava's voice was matter-of-fact. "I've been afraid for sixteen years, so it's time, don't you think?"

"Your Honor," Carl asked irritably, "please instruct the witness not to ask me questions."

Everything after that went right over Lucas's head. It was the first time he'd lost his concentration in a trial, but Ava's words kept tormenting his mind.

*Mr. Culver believes in the truth, and my daughter believes in him.*

God, he'd been a fool. He had messed up the only relationship that had ever meant anything to him. But he couldn't allow himself to dwell on it now. He had to focus on Blake and his defense.

He became aware that Ava was leaving the witness stand. Sam met her and they embraced. "I'm so sorry," she murmured into his shoulder.

"It's all right, darling," Sam assured her, and led her to a seat.

Sam had forgiven Ava for her duplicity. That was very clear. He loved her and forgiveness was part of that love.

*Like it should be. Like it should be.*

The pencil in Lucas's hand snapped in two.

"Lucas?" Blake whispered worriedly.

"It's okay," he said. He returned his attention back to the trial, but he knew his life had been snapped in two, just like the pencil. Now he had to find a way to put it back together—somehow.

# CHAPTER SEVENTEEN

THE NEXT DAY BLAKE was scheduled to take the stand. The moment was tense and dramatic as everyone waited to hear what he had to say. Lucas treated him like he had Ava. He let him tell his story in his own words without bombarding him with questions. He described the sordid events in a quiet, sincere manner. He told of the drugs and liquor, how he, Todd and Bonnie had gone to the park to get high, how he became ill and started throwing up, how he'd heard Bonnie scream, how he found her naked body and pulled her blouse over her bruised breasts. In a steady voice, almost a monotone, he talked about how she reached out and took his arm, then went limp. How he ran to call 911 for help, how he and Todd got into a fight and fled when they heard the sirens, and how his mother had found him later in the bathroom sick and crying.

The room became very quiet when he stopped speaking. The only sound was the weeping of Bonnie Davis's mother.

Lucas picked up a tape that had been entered into evidence—the 911 call from the first trial. The caller had never been identified. He slipped it into the tape recorder and everyone listened.

A voice identified the location, then, "She's hurt bad. She needs help. Hurry."

Lucas switched off the recorder, letting the frantic words ease their way into the jurors' minds.

Then he asked Blake, "Is that your voice, Mr. Logan?"

"Yes, sir, it is."

Lucas reached for a piece of paper that had also been entered into evidence. He handed it to a juror, who passed it around. "That's a sworn statement from Dr. Phillip Smyth. He's a voice expert and he's listened to the tape and matched it conclusively to Blake Logan."

Lucas turned back to Blake. "Mr. Logan, I have a few more questions."

"Okay."

"Did you murder Bonnie Davis?"

"No, sir."

"Did you help Todd Easton murder Bonnie Davis?"

"No, sir."

"Did you attempt to rape Bonnie Davis?"

"No, sir. I did not."

"Thank you," Lucas said, and resumed his seat.

After lunch, Carl took over, and the next four hours were grueling. Carl related a scene that made everyone in the courtroom ill. He said that Blake had held Bonnie down while Todd raped her, then when it was his turn he got scared and couldn't. Once he saw what they'd done to her, he ran for help, but it was too late. On and on Carl tried to break him, but Blake remained steadfast until Carl made him look at the photo of Bonnie. Tears welled up in Blake's eyes and Lucas held his breath. Blake brushed away the tears and said that he'd lived with that picture in his mind for the past sixteen years. The pain in his voice was evident to everyone.

Still Carl didn't let up, and Lucas could see that Blake was tiring under the pressure. Carl got in some good points; he did some damage. Lucas sensed that the jurors were listening and thinking that maybe the murder *had* happened the way Carl was alleging. There was nothing Lucas could do now but wait for Carl to bring his cross-examination to a close.

When he finally did, Lucas was planning his next step.

They'd located the photographer and Lucas intended to call him, but the judge adjourned court for the day.

Later that evening, Lucas kept going through the photos. Something wasn't connecting...but what? Suddenly he knew exactly what it was. He called Derek and told him to get the medical examiner back on the stand. He had a few more questions.

THE NEXT MORNING Lucas called the photographer as a witness. His name was Mel Burke.

"Mr. Burke, did you take the crime-scene photos of the Bonnie Davis murder?"

"Yes, I did."

Lucas handed him the photo Blair had found. "Do you remember this one?"

Mr. Burke looked at it, turned it over. "It's been so long ago and I took so many."

"Take your time."

"Yeah, now I remember. The detective in charge wanted me to get some photos outside the crime area, in case I found something they could use. This was about fifty feet from the body and it smelled awful. I snapped the picture, but the detective never used it."

"What was it?"

"Looked like vomit."

"Was it fresh?"

"Yes, and it had the worst smell."

"Thank you, Mr. Burke."

Carl rose to his feet.

"Mr. Burke, was it animal or human vomit?"

"Don't know. Couldn't tell."

"Did you see Blake Logan throw up?"

"No, of course not."

"So you don't know where this—" Carl tapped the photo "—came from."

"No."

Lucas left it at that. The jury knew it was vomit and they'd have to decide where it came from. Lucas could have called a doctor to testify that the quantity of drugs and liquor Blake had ingested was enough to make him throw up, but he knew that Carl could also get the doctor to admit that with so many intoxicants, a person could be capable of murder. So he didn't take the chance. He didn't want the jury to hear that.

Next he called the medical examiner again.

"Dr. Lee, I want to go over the teeth marks on Bonnie Davis one more time." Lucas looked at the transcript in his hand. "You said that the teeth marks on her breasts and neck were so deep that they broke the skin in places."

"Yes, that's true."

Lucas walked to the evidence table and lifted a plastic bag. "Dr. Lee, can you tell us what this is?"

"It's the blouse Bonnie Davis was wearing the night of the murder."

"Is this all she had on her body?"

"Yes."

Lucas opened the bag and drew out the bright red blouse. It was short-sleeved with a collar and colorful red, yellow and blue buttons. There were grass stains in several places and blood on the collar and a couple of spots on the front.

"All the buttons are still on the blouse—is that correct?"

"Yes."

"So would you say the buttons were not undone in a hasty or violent fashion?"

"Doesn't seem that way."

"Now, Dr. Lee, look at the photo of Bonnie Davis." Dr. Lee turned to stare at the photo that was still on an easel by the jury box. "Her blouse is open, but pulled together across her breasts."

"Yes."

"Are there any teeth marks on the blouse?"

"No, we didn't see any."

Lucas held up the blouse so the jurors could see it. "I don't see any teeth marks or rips, either." Lucas paused, then said, "So tell me how Todd Easton bit Bonnie Davis's breasts through this blouse when clearly there are no teeth marks on the blouse?"

"I don't know."

"Could it be that the blouse was open at the time of the rape and murder?"

"Yes, that would explain it."

"But look at the photo. Bonnie was found *after* the murder with the blouse covering her breasts."

"Yes, that's true."

"So, is it possible that someone pulled the blouse over her breasts afterward?"

"Yes, it's possible."

"Thank you, Dr. Lee."

Carl walked toward the witness.

"Dr. Lee, in the heat of the moment, could the blouse have been pushed aside and then pulled back?"

"Yes, I suppose."

"No further questions."

Lucas stood. "A few more questions, Your Honor."

"Go ahead. Mr. Culver."

Holding pages of transcript, Lucas went to the evidence table and selected another plastic bag. He laid it in front of Dr. Lee. "Dr. Lee, can you tell us what this is?"

"Those are the female clothes found at the crime scene."

"Tell us what clothes are inside the bag."

Dr. Lee peered at the tag attached to the plastic. "A skirt, panties, shoes and a bra."

Lucas handed him the pages. "From the transcript, would you please read where those items were found."

Dr. Lee studied it. "Strewn around her body."

"Specifically where was the bra found?"

"Six feet to the right of her body."

"What kind of bra was it?"

"It was a strapless push-up variety," he read from the transcript.

"Was the bra or any other item of clothing torn or ripped in any way?"

Dr. Lee glanced up. "No."

"Okay," Lucas said. He carried the bag back to the evidence table. "So, in your expert opinion, would you say that these clothes were not removed in a violent way?"

Dr. Lee moved uncomfortably in his seat. "I can't say how they were removed. I can only say they weren't ripped or torn."

"Thank you, Dr. Lee," Lucas answered, letting the jurors deal with his answer in their own way. Lucas suddenly turned back. "One more question, Dr. Lee. Were there any drugs found in Bonnie Davis's system?"

"Yes, the toxicology report showed traces of marijuana and cocaine."

"That's all, Your Honor."

Lucas brought the defense to a close, knowing he'd done everything he could to cast doubts on Blake's guilt.

The judge announced that closing arguments would be heard in the morning.

As Lucas stood, he saw Blair and his heart knocked noisily in his chest. She was hugging her parents. He wanted to talk to her but knew this wasn't the time. She looked up and her eyes caught his. The world seemed to fade away as they gazed at each other. So much hurt, so much pain, yet... Sam said something to her and she turned back to her father.

Lucas took a deep breath. He had to forget about Blair. He had to forget about everything but the closing. The trial was coming down to its final moments and he had to give it everything he had. Derek wanted to help, but Lucas needed to do this alone.

BLAIR COULDN'T SLEEP. She knew that tomorrow it could all be over. The jury would deliberate after the closings. It could take them hours or it could take them days to decide Blake's innocence or guilt. She was hoping for a quick verdict, but she knew the longer they deliberated the better Blake's chances.

She kept seeing Lucas's eyes as he'd looked at her today. He didn't seem angry with her anymore. He almost seemed glad to see her. Of course, that was what she *wanted* to believe. She curled up and closed her eyes, seeing Lucas the way he'd been at the farmhouse that night. A smiling, affectionate Lucas. The man she loved....

THE NEXT MORNING, court convened and Lucas was ready. He'd spent most of the night writing and rehearsing what he was going to say in his closing argument. He'd gone through the evidence and the photos of the crime scene, writing down specific points he wanted to make.

The courtroom was packed. He'd had a hard time escaping reporters to get into the building. The Logan family sat behind him and the Davis family sat behind Carl. Spectators vied for a bird's-eye view. He didn't see Lloyd Easton and wondered why.

Court was called to order and Carl began his closing. He described the gruesome details one more time and brought out the photo of Bonnie. He asked the jurors to take a good look at the photo and try to imagine Bonnie's last minutes of life—to imagine the horror and pain of two boys attacking her. He went over the evidence of Blake's DNA matching, of Blake being high on drugs, of Blake's being at the scene of the crime.

He finished with, "The state has proven its case beyond the shadow of a doubt." He glanced at Lucas. "Lucas

Culver wants you to believe in the truth." He turned back to the jury. "The truth is that Blake Logan's the only one of that threesome still alive and he's twisted the truth to suit his own purposes. The truth is that Blake Logan attempted to rape Bonnie Davis, and helped murder her. He's gotten away with it for sixteen years. It's time for him to pay. It's time to put Blake Logan behind bars where he belongs. I know you'll do that."

Lucas stood up and fastened a button on his dark blue suit jacket. He wore a pristine white shirt and a red tie. It was his red, white and blue outfit—his victory outfit. It gave him the confidence he needed, which would have been a shock to anyone who could have read his mind. He exuded self-confidence and control as he walked over to the photo of Bonnie Davis. He tapped it with his forefinger.

"Mr. Wright is very fond of showing you this picture," he said, speaking to the jury. "I've noticed that some of you have a hard time looking at it. I do, too." He walked closer. "I know you're tired of the evidence, tired of Mr. Wright and me going after each other, tired of the whole thing. But I want you to bear with me once more. Mr. Wright is telling you one story and I'm telling you another. Who's telling the truth?" He turned back to the photo. "I want all of you to look at the photo. It will tell you the truth." Two ladies gazed down at their laps. "Please," Lucas entreated. "Look at the photo." The ladies raised their heads. "Good. Now I'm going to go through this, step by step, and I want you to follow me."

He pointed to the bruises on Bonnie's neck. "Todd Easton squeezed her neck so hard that his thumbnail broke off into her skin. Todd Easton's teeth marks were on her breasts, neck and thigh. Blake Logan's teeth marks are nowhere on her body. It's what the transcripts from the experts told you. *That's* the truth." He paused. "If my client had held her down as the D.A. alleges, it stands to reason there'd be more physical evidence. There were masses of Todd Easton's skin under her nails, remember, but only minute bits from Blake Logan's. Think about it.'' He paused again.

"Now, I want you to look at Bonnie Davis's blouse. See the way it's carefully laid across her breasts to hide them. Blake Logan told you that when he found Bonnie, she was naked and beaten. Her blouse was open and pushed aside. He told you he pulled it together to cover her. Take a good look—that's exactly what you're seeing in this picture. Blake Logan covered her up. That's not the work of someone who murdered her or attempted to rape her. It was the work of someone who wanted to help her. Bonnie sensed this and reached out to Blake and caught his arm. That's how a small amount of his skin got under her nails. She didn't claw or scratch him. She reached out to him for help. It's what the expert told you. *That's* the truth.''

Lucas waited a moment. "You heard the 911 tape. You heard Blake Logan begging for help for Bonnie. *That's* the truth.'' He paused. "So many things have overshadowed the truth—Blake's failure to report the crime, his mother's failure to report the crime and then paying Todd Easton to keep quiet. Colossal mistakes. We have a young, frightened teenager being manipulated by adults into making the wrong decisions. Yes, he's been silent for sixteen years, but when Ethan Ramsey found him, he couldn't stay silent any longer. He gave his DNA willingly and he knew what that meant. He's ready to face his punishment.'' Lucas paused again and looked directly at the jury. "The truth is that he's been punishing himself for sixteen years, blaming himself for not being able to help Bonnie Davis because he was so affected by drugs that he was physically ill.''

He placed his hands on the railing, staring intently at each juror. "Now, I want you to think about Bonnie Davis's clothes. There are no rips or tears on them. If she'd been violently attacked, as the D.A. is alleging, why aren't her clothes torn? Think about it.'' He took a breath. ''Blake Logan told you that Todd and Bonnie were 'going at it pretty heavy.' That's the reason he left the car. He doesn't know what happened after that, but it's not hard to fill in the blanks. Todd became aggressive and violent, hurting Bonnie, and she wanted him to stop. Todd got angry at her for spoiling his fun and he silenced her for good. And all the while, Blake Logan was in the bushes puking his guts out. Blake Logan told you that. You heard the photographer and you saw the photo of the vomit. *That's* the truth.''

Lucas inhaled a long breath. ''I told you that there are two sides to every story—as there are in this case. We're not disputing that Blake was at the party buying drugs. We're not disputing that he was with Todd and Bonnie. We're not disputing that Blake went with them to the park. We're disputing what happened *after* they reached the park. That's where the two stories differ. In the beginning, I asked you to listen to the witnesses and the evidence with open hearts and open minds and hear the truth.'' He walked back to the picture and tapped it. ''This is the truth. Take a last look, ladies and gentlemen. Look at the blouse—how it's carefully laid across her. That tells you so much. It corroborates Blake Logan's story—as do the vomit and Bonnie Davis's clothes. The picture tells you the truth, and the state hasn't proven otherwise.'' He paused for effect. ''Let the truth set Blake Logan free. I trust you to make the right decision. Thank you.''

The room was deathly quiet as Lucas took his seat. No one moved or spoke. Everyone was staring at the photo— even Mrs. Davis.

Blair didn't even realize she was holding her breath until her chest started to burn. She exhaled slowly, realizing she'd just seen a great attorney at work. She also under- stood that was the reason he always got to her when she faced him in a courtroom. She'd never had that rapport with a jury, the charisma and magnetism that made him stand out. Now it was so different; his brilliance didn't intimidate her anymore. It only made her love him more—if that was possible. Her heart ached for all the could-have-beens.

Carl stood, as Blair knew he would. He had to try to taint the image Lucas had just created.

"Rebuttal, Your Honor."

"Go ahead, Mr. Wright."

Carl walked over to the jury box, but every single juror was still staring at the photo. Carl had to step in front of it to get their attention. "Ladies and gentlemen, please don't confuse the truth with fabrication. Mr. Culver is very good at doing that." He pointed to the photo. "As you look at this picture, please remember that this young girl's life was taken by two boys high on drugs. The evidence supports that. Please listen to the evidence. Thank you."

The judge gave final instructions to the jury and they retired to make their decision. Everyone stood.

Blake hugged Lucas, wiping away a tear. "Thanks, Lucas. You did everything you could. Now it's up to the jury."

Derek shook his hand. "Awesome job."

Howard gave him a thumbs-up and Sam and Ava added their thanks. Lucas noticed Howard waving to someone in the back, and he turned to see Jacob strolling down the aisle. The sight of him washed away all Lucas's tension, and they embraced.

No one had to tell Blair who the stranger was. She knew. It was Jacob. Lucas's brother. They had the same dark hair and eyes and build, except that Jacob had a few pounds on Lucas. There was strength and character in every line of Jacob's handsome face, and she had to admit he was definitely a striking man. But he didn't have Lucas's devastating smile, which had reached the coldest part of her heart and warmed her in ways she'd never thought possible. In her eyes, Jacob was nice but he wasn't Lucas.

"What are you doing here?" Lucas asked Jacob.

"Thought I'd come and add my support," Jacob answered in his deep voice. "Glad I didn't miss that closing. Sure made me proud, little brother."

That was all Lucas needed to hear. Jacob's praise made him feel ten feet tall and he needed to feel like that at this particular moment.

Howard came up and introduced Jacob to everyone. When he introduced Blair, Jacob said, "Nice to meet you, ma'am."

"Me, too," she answered politely, and glanced at Lucas. Jacob glanced at him, too, and Lucas knew they were waiting for him to say something. But for once the words stuck in his throat.

Sam broke the silence. "Let's go over to my office and wait. Ava's ordered refreshments. This could be a long day."

"No, thanks," Lucas said. "I haven't seen Jacob in a while and I'd like to talk with him." His eyes caught Blair's, and he could see that she was hurt. Damn, he couldn't explain why he was acting like such an ass. His emotions were tied into such knots that he found it difficult to assimilate what he was doing at times. That didn't explain it and sure as hell didn't make it right.

Blair's heart sank. She'd been holding her breath, and at Lucas's open rejection she knew all her hopes were in vain. Lucas might laugh easily, but he didn't forgive easily. That thought weighed her down, but she couldn't let it affect her visibly. Not now... But it would later when she had nothing except her heartache to keep her company.

"WHERE'S MIRANDA and the kids?" Lucas asked when they reached his office.

Jacob took the chair across from Lucas, stretching his

long legs out in front of him. "They're home," he replied. "Lizzie's got a cold and Gracie's coming down with it, so Miranda didn't want to take them out."

Lucas rubbed his forehead. "I miss them."

"The trial's just about over, so you can come for a long visit."

Lucas nodded. "Yeah, I plan on doing that."

There was silence for a moment, then Jacob said, "She's very beautiful."

Lucas merely frowned.

"Don't give me that look. You know who I'm talking about, and she wanted to spend this time with you, but you blew her off—" he snapped his fingers "—just like that."

"I didn't," Lucas lied. He was now lying to himself. A man who believed in the truth was lying to himself.

Jacob watched him closely. "What the hell's going on with you?"

"Nothing," Lucas said, and got up and walked to the window.

"Well, little brother, you can tell that to some people, but you can't tell it to me."

Silence ensued.

"God, you're not still upset that she didn't tell you immediately about Ava's secret?"

"It's not that." Lucas turned from the window, a tortured look in his eyes. "It's my own reactions. I hurt her and I keep hurting her. I swore I'd never do that, but I can't seem to help myself."

"Can't you see what you're doing?"

"If I could, I wouldn't be going through this."

"Every time a relationship gets serious, you start finding fault. She's too loud, she's too bossy, she's too talkative and on and on. I've lost track of all the excuses. The truth is that you're afraid of getting hurt, and you know Blair has the power to hurt you more than you ever imagined. So you're pushing her away—just like Mom did Dad.''

Lucas's head jerked up. "What are you talking about?"

Jacob saw the fire in Lucas's eyes and knew this conversation was long overdue. "When Mom found out about the heart problem, she had a hard time dealing with it. Dad tried to tell her it didn't matter, that they could still have a full life." Jacob paused, the next words difficult. "She didn't want to be touched anymore. She didn't want sex. She kept pushing him away. That's when she started joining all those clubs—having other interests—anything to keep her away from home when Dad was there. I'd shoved it all to the back of my mind until Miranda made me talk about it. You know how Miranda is about talking. I finally remembered the many arguments and what they were about.''

Lucas didn't say anything. He couldn't.

Jacob continued to watch him. "I know you think you're a lot like Dad. In some ways you are. In others, you're not. Dad wasn't a bad person. If you remember, he was always there for us. I don't condone what he did. Turning to other women wasn't the answer, but I'm not sure what *I'd* do if Miranda didn't want me to touch her anymore. I'd like to think I'd have the guts to give her time and to work it out somehow. You and I both condemned Dad for the way he died. The shame and disgrace got to us and got to Mom, too. She couldn't stand what she'd driven him to.''

Lucas felt himself pale. Scenes from the past flashed through his mind. Arguments in the middle of the night. Words like "I'm tired" or "I don't want to. Why do you keep pressuring me?" or "I don't feel good. Why can't you understand?" Then he could hear the back door slamming, and the screech of tires. His mom crying herself to sleep.

He sank into his chair as if his legs couldn't support him

anymore. He drew both hands down his face in a weary gesture. The truth was there at the edge of his brain, but he didn't want to let it in. He'd hated his father for so long and it was easier to hate him than to believe that his mother wasn't perfect. The truth—he had to admit the truth.

"He hurt her, but she hurt him, too," he uttered in a low incredulous tone. There—he'd admitted it to himself and to Jacob.

"I know it's hard for you to accept that Mom wasn't perfect," Jacob said, "but none of us are—not even Blair."

Lucas raised his head and sucked air into his lungs. "That's the hard part. I don't know if she'll ever forgive me."

"Sure she will," Jacob was quick to say. "If Mom and Dad had been able to talk, maybe things would've been different."

"Why haven't you told me this before?"

Jacob shrugged. "I guess it's because I have a rough time saying anything negative about Mom. It was so much easier blaming Dad, but the fact is she drove him away and his Culver pride wouldn't allow him to bend."

"God, Jacob," he said, resting his head against his chair. "I've blamed and hated him for so long. For years I've fought to be nothing like him."

"I know," Jacob said. "I hated Dad for a long time myself, but we can't let the past keep hurting us. And we need to learn from the past. You have to talk to Blair, sort this out."

Lucas knew that. He'd known it for days, but his pride was holding him back. His Culver pride. She had hurt him and he had hurt her, so he was pushing her away to make sure it didn't happen again. He was afraid of the pain. Jacob was right, but then, Jacob was always right. He wouldn't tell him that, though. But he intended to talk to

Blair as soon as the verdict came in. Oh God, the verdict. For a moment it had slipped his mind.

"How in hell did we get on this subject at a time like this?" Lucas asked in a teasing tone.

"It was your hangdog expression," Jacob told him.

"What?"

"You've got it bad, little brother. I mean bad, and I couldn't let you—"

There was a tap at the door and Joan walked in. "Lucas, the jury's back," she said.

"What!" Lucas's skin turned gray. "They can't be." He looked at his watch. "It's only been an hour and a half. They've barely had time to sit down and discuss it."

"Sorry, Lucas." Joan grimaced. "I just got the call. They're back."

Lucas dragged a hand through his hair. "This isn't good. It's too soon. Much too soon." He shook his head. "I put everything I had into this trial and it wasn't enough… Now Blake will…and Blair…"

"Lucas." Jacob tried to reassure him. "It's not always bad. It sounds like everyone had their minds made up before they went into the jury room."

"Yeah," Lucas admitted, straightening his hair. "Let's get over to the courthouse. I can't take much more of this."

SAM, AVA, HOWARD and the other lawyers were waiting in the corridor. Natalie, Calvin and Tiffany were there, too. Lucas noticed that Blake and Blair were standing to one side talking. It seemed as if Blair was trying to bolster his courage.

"Sorry, Lucas, this doesn't look good," Derek murmured.

Howard patted him on the back and didn't say a word. Lucas expected Sam to go into a tirade about the defense, but he merely nodded, saying, "Ava and I are prepared."

"We can always appeal," Frank put in.

"No, we won't," Blair announced as she walked up with Blake. "We won't have to because we're going to win this thing."

"Darling—" Sam turned to her, but she refused to let him continue.

"No, I don't want to hear it."

Tears stung the back of Lucas's eyes. Her faith in him was almost his undoing. He had hurt her and she still believed in him—in his ability to win this case—and he knew she was trying to convince Blake of that. Everyone was behind him, but it didn't mean a thing compared to her faith in him. What a fool he'd been.

They made their way into the courtroom and Lucas wanted to talk to Blair so badly, he couldn't stand it. But once again this wasn't the time. She gave him a tentative smile and that would sustain him—for now.

Court was called to order and the jurors filed into their seats. Lucas watched their faces, but he couldn't gauge what they were thinking or feeling. They were somber, staring at the judge. His tension grew. Glancing over, he saw that Blake was petrified.

There was nothing to do now except wait.

Carl wore a smug expression, and Lucas knew he was expecting a conviction. And he also knew that Evan Holt was hovering somewhere in the background. They thought they had this one in the bag, but it wouldn't be over till the foreman spoke.

"Have you reached a unanimous verdict?" the judge was asking, and Lucas brought his total concentration to the proceedings.

"Yes, we have," the foreman answered, and handed a piece of paper to the bailiff. The bailiff took it to the judge who looked at it briefly, then the bailiff took it back to the foreman.

The room became deadly quiet as they waited for the judge to speak. "Will the defendant please rise."

Blake got to his feet with Lucas and Derek beside him. Lucas could feel him trembling.

"On the first count of the indictment—murder in the first degree. How do you find?" The judge's words rang out and Blair held her breath until her lungs hurt and everything in her strained to hear the next words.

"We find the defendant—not guilty."

There was absolute, total silence for a second as the words registered. Then happy murmurs and excited whispers. Ava started to cry and Blair bit her lip to keep her emotions in check.

*Not guilty. Not guilty. Not guilty.* It ran through Lucas's mind and he couldn't stop the smile that spread across his face. The jurors had listened and believed him. This was almost more than his heart could take.

Blake slumped into his chair and buried his face into his hands. Ava and Blair whispered something to him.

"Counselor, get your client to his feet," Judge Seton called. "We're not through."

Lucas and Derek helped Blake stand.

"On the second count of the indictment—attempted rape. How do you find?" the judge asked.

"We find the defendant—not guilty."

Cries of joy and jubilation rang out, and reporters rushed from the room to file their stories. Court came to a close and everyone was hugging and kissing and smiling. A sense of exhilaration prevailed. Lucas stood somewhere between joy and shock.

Blair hurried over and threw her arms around his neck and kissed him. His lips met hers with all the emotions he was feeling—shock, joy, satisfaction and desire. He wrapped his arms around her and drew her tight against him, needing her touch more than he'd needed anything in his life. The courtroom—the world—faded away as they renewed a bond that had been damaged but now felt as strong as ever.

Blair wanted this moment to go on forever, but she knew they had to wait—to talk, to sort through what they were feeling. Slowly she stepped back and smiled into his darkened eyes. "Thank you," she whispered.

Those weren't the words Lucas wanted to hear, but they would do for now. Blair moved toward her brother to embrace him.

"It's over, Blair," he muttered. "Thank God it's over."

Suddenly the noise ceased as Mrs. Davis and her husband walked in their direction. Lucas didn't know what to expect so he stepped slightly in front of Blake, as did Blair. Then he saw Mrs. Davis's eyes—they were filled with so much pain and heartache that Lucas moved away. Whatever Mrs. Davis had to say, she had a right to be heard and he could see that Blair had acknowledged it, too. But she held on to Blake's arm to let him know she was there.

Mrs. Davis gazed directly into Blake's eyes. "I've waited sixteen years to hear the truth and I finally heard it in this courtroom. Thank you for trying to help my daughter."

Blake swallowed. "I wish I could have, Mrs. Davis. I really do."

Mrs. Davis didn't answer. She turned to Lucas. "When this trial started, I hated you. I'd heard of your reputation and I knew you'd try to get Sam Logan's son off...but now...now I have to thank you. You've set me free, too, and now maybe I can sleep at nights."

Lucas was touched by her words. Bonnie's parents had suffered so much and endured yet another painful trial. He was grateful he'd given them this closure and shook their hands warmly.

As the couple walked away, Evan came through a side door. Blair knew something was up because Evan wouldn't be here otherwise. He nodded and spoke to Sam. "This must be your lucky day," he said.

"What do you mean?" Sam asked.

"In light of the new evidence, I'm dropping the charges against you."

Blair was stunned. Everyone was. Evan didn't do something like this unless...unless he knew he couldn't win.

"Thanks," was all Sam could say.

"I could prosecute you, Mrs. Logan." He looked sternly at Ava. "But I believe that would be a waste of my time and the taxpayers' money."

That was it, Blair thought. Evan knew Lucas could get the charges dropped against her father now that her mother had confessed. But Evan wanted to display the fact that he was in charge. Blair didn't mind because she knew he could've brought some charges against her mother and made them stick. She was very appreciative of his generosity.

"Thank you, Evan," she said sincerely.

He nodded, spared Lucas a glance and walked away.

Silence lingered for a moment, then Ava spoke up. "This is such wonderful news. We have to celebrate—our house, tonight. Everyone's invited. You, too, Jacob."

"Thanks, ma'am," Jacob replied politely. "But I've got to get back to my family."

Ava's gaze swung to Lucas. "But you'll be there?"

Lucas glanced at Blair. "Yes, I'll be there."

Blair smiled and whispered, "Tonight," as she walked past him. If she'd ever doubted the existence of miracles, she didn't anymore. She saw the future in Lucas's eyes and her heart sang with renewed hope. She couldn't believe she'd gone from the depths of despair to this euphoric state in such a short time. And she vowed to herself that she'd make this a night to remember.

Pure joy reverberated through Lucas and he couldn't

stop smiling. But that smile vanished when Roger walked into the room.

"Congratulations," he said, staring at Blair. "I heard everything worked out."

"Yes," Blair said. "Isn't it wonderful?"

"Hey, Jacob." The two men shook hands. "Damn, it's good to see you."

"How's it going?" Jacob asked.

"Can't complain, and I've got more news." His gaze settled on Blair.

"What?" Blair asked, knowing this must have something to do with the harassment.

"Easton had a nervous breakdown. That's why he wasn't in court today. I found out he *wasn't* out of town when your door was spray-painted, so I stopped by his house and discovered a can of spray paint in his car. I'm on my way over to talk to his wife at the psychiatric unit and I'm hoping she'll tell me everything."

"Oh, Roger." Blair hugged him, and Lucas glanced away. "Thank you. Now all of this is finally over."

"Yeah, it's over," Roger said, and Lucas caught his eye. Lucas didn't believe him although he didn't know why. It probably had a lot to do with the fact that he had his hands on Blair.

## CHAPTER EIGHTEEN

LUCAS SAID his goodbyes to Jacob, finished up at his office and headed home. He showered and put on his black suit and tie. He was feeling good about himself again—and about the future. It had been a long, rigorous trial and tonight he was going to celebrate with Blair. They were going to talk and talk until they'd talked everything out and then…he couldn't allow himself to think beyond that.

He refused to let the past haunt him any longer. He was his father's son and, of course, he would have some of his qualities. He'd thought, after his death, that his father was selfish and unfeeling, but he wasn't and neither was Lucas. He could see that now; he was going to stop being afraid to feel, to love—and to get hurt. He vowed to be himself. Just Lucas Culver. A man of his own making.

He was hurrying out the door when the phone rang. He almost didn't answer but realized it could be Blair. It wasn't. It was a friend letting him know that Jim Tenney had passed away. The news hit him hard. He knew Jim hadn't been feeling well after the surgery, but he'd never dreamed it was this serious. He had to go to Stacey. He picked up the phone and called Blair. She was out; however, Blake said he'd give her the message.

Blair was devastated when she heard the news. Her plans for the evening seemed trivial compared to the tragedy of Jim's death. It no longer mattered that she'd bought a special dress to wear, a black outfit that clung to her body and had a low bodice with tiny straps. She'd never worn anything like it in her life, but now her emotions were free, her fear was gone—all because of Lucas. This was supposed to be their night, although so many things were keeping them apart. She knew Lucas's place tonight was with Jim's wife.

Blair sent food and flowers to the Tenney house. She'd worked with Jim and liked him. She'd never met his wife or family, but her heart went out to them.

Lucas had told Blake that he'd try to make it later. By midnight Blair knew he wasn't coming. When Roger offered to take her home, she accepted gratefully. Blake was driving her car and she didn't want to take it away from him. However, she wanted to return to her apartment because she finally had her life back. She hoped Lucas would come by later; if he did and if the evening ended the way she planned, she wouldn't need her car, anyway.

When Roger asked if he could come in, she couldn't say no. He'd been so nice and he'd solved the harassment problem, and she didn't want to be rude to him. Besides, she wanted to tell him one more time that they were friends and nothing more.

BY THE TIME Lucas left the Tenney house, it was after midnight. Stacey wanted to talk about Jim, their college days, the good times. Lucas knew it was what she needed. He couldn't even imagine what it was like to lose a life partner at such an early age. But Stacey was a survivor and she'd manage.

When her parents arrived from Arizona, Lucas left, assuring Stacey he'd be back tomorrow. He headed straight for River Oaks. He was concerned when Blake told him that Roger had taken Blair home. He didn't understand why she had to go to the apartment and why Roger had to take her. But he intended to find out.

All the way there, Lucas kept thinking about Roger and what he'd said about Easton. Something wasn't right. The first message had been left after the Raye trial ended. Blake hadn't even been arrested then. Still, Easton hated Sam Logan and he could've been watching and waiting for a chance to get even. That didn't ring true, though. It wasn't adding up.

When he drove through the entrance, Lucas noticed the same guard who'd been working the night those ugly words were scribbled on Blair's door.

"Hi, Mr. Culver," he said courteously. "Here to see Ms. Logan?"

"Yes, but could I ask you a question first?"

"Sure." The guard gave a nonchalant shrug.

"The night the message was left on Ms. Logan's door, did you see anyone suspicious?"

"The police already asked me that, and I told them everything I know."

Lucas raised an eyebrow. "Everything?" There was an intonation in the guard's voice when he said *police* that made Lucas think he was holding something back.

The guard sat in a booth with a bulletproof-glass window. The window had a small hole he talked through. The guard fidgeted with papers in front of him and avoided looking at Lucas.

"Ms. Logan's life could be in danger," Lucas said. "If you know anything, you have to tell me."

The guard shrugged again. "I don't. It's just that—"

"What?" Lucas prompted.

The guard leaned closer to the window. "Well, that policeman came over about thirty minutes before you and Ms. Logan discovered it. He asked to see Ms. Logan, and I told him she wasn't in. He wanted to wait for her, but I told him I couldn't let him enter the complex. Another car drove up, and he parked to one side. When I looked over, his car was there, but he wasn't. About fifteen minutes later, I saw him get in and drive away.''

Lucas's pulse began to beat erratically. "Where did he go?"

The guard shook his head. "I don't know. There's no place to go. There's nothing but brick walls around here."

*And shrubs,* Lucas thought. Big shrubs he could hide behind—and then slip through the gate when no one was looking. But Lucas had to be sure.

"Which cop was it?"

"Big tall guy with blond hair and an attitude."

*Roger.*

"Did you tell this to the police?"

"Hell, man, he *is* the police and he was doing the investigating." He paused for a moment, obviously nervous. "The only reason I told you is that he's with her now. He's been there a long time. He usually stays a few minutes and then leaves. It's late and I'm getting a little worried."

It didn't take Lucas more than a second to make up his mind. If he was wrong, he'd deal with it, but if he was right, it could mean Blair was in danger. "Call the police and ask for Tim Mayer." Lucas knew Tim was Roger's captain. "Tell him to get over here as quick as he can. Tell him it's an emergency. Open the gate so I can drive through."

"Sir, I can't do that. I—"

"I'll take full responsibility. Now open it and call the police."

The guard must have sensed the urgency in Lucas's voice because he pushed a button and the gate swung open.

Lucas hoped his emotions weren't running away with him, but Roger's behavior was sounding stranger and stranger. He'd take his chances, he decided, hoping he didn't end up looking like the biggest fool that ever lived.

AS SOON AS THEY ENTERED the apartment, Blair turned to talk to Roger. She didn't ask him to sit because she intended to keep this short.

Before she could find the words, Roger spoke, his eyes traveling over her in the tight-fitting black dress. "You look beautiful. I've never seen you dressed like this."

"Thank you," she murmured.

"I'd like to think it was for my benefit," he went on. "Because you knew I'd be there tonight. But it wasn't, was it, Blair?"

"Roger," she appealed to him, his feverish gaze making her nervous.

"It was for *him*. It was for Lucas, wasn't it?"

"I don't want to hurt you. I—"

"All you ever do is hurt me." He laughed cruelly. "I'm always there for you. I've protected you and busted my butt to solve this harassment thing. Now look at the thanks I get. You're turning to someone else. Someone who'll dump you when he gets tired of you."

"Lucas isn't like that," she snapped, feeling bad that she'd hurt him but angry that he'd disparaged Lucas.

"Now you're defending him." He laughed again, and she backed toward the sofa. Roger was frightening her.

"Do you know that Lucas and Stacey Tenney were an item years ago? She was madly in love with him, but he dumped her and she fell into the arms of his best friend. Instead of being with you, he's consoling *her* right now. Is that the type of man you want? Someone you can't trust?"

"I think you'd better leave," she said coolly. She knew that Lucas and Jim were friends, and if Lucas had once had a thing with Stacey, it was long in the past, something that had happened in his younger days. She knew Lucas and she trusted him.

"I'm not going anywhere," he sneered, yanking off his tie and removing his jacket. "You owe me," he said, advancing on her. "I've treated you with kid gloves for years, just waiting for you to love me the way I love you."

"Oh, Roger, I'm so sorry," she cried.

But he didn't seem to hear her. "I'm tired of being your lapdog and seeing someone else get all the stroking." Before she could respond, he grabbed her around the waist and jerked her to him, his lips covering hers. Fear slammed into her stomach, and she refused to open her mouth. She strained to pull away. He smelled of whiskey and something she couldn't define, but it made her feel sick and she started to struggle. He caught her by the back of her head. "Open your mouth," he hissed.

Blair thought all the old fears would come back and paralyze her, but they didn't. This was a new fear and she knew she had to fight for her sanity, her survival—not as a frightened teenager but as a grown woman who could handle her life. She twisted and turned, trying to break free; he was so much stronger, though. She felt a strap on her dress snap and she knew that tomorrow she'd have bruises. She managed to throw him off balance and they tumbled onto the sofa. His weight was suffocating and when he tried to cover her mouth again, she turned her head. His lips trailed down her neck to her breast and nausea churned in her stomach.

"I did everything for you," he mumbled. "I put my job in jeopardy—everything."

What was he talking about? His job in jeopardy? That didn't make any sense. She had to do something fast.

"Roger, stop, please," she begged, hoping her pleading voice would deter him. It didn't. He slid a hand beneath her dress, caressing her thigh. She tried to think, but fear was fast consuming her.

*Think. Think. Think.*

Then it hit her. Her purse. The gun. She'd brought the bag in, so it had to be somewhere. She glanced on the floor and saw it several feet away. She didn't know if she could reach it. She stretched out her arm and had to strain, but her forefinger touched it. Roger thought she was responding and groaned, a sickening sound. With her finger, she inched the purse closer and closer, then slipped her hand inside and gripped the gun. It was cold and heavy in her hand. She swallowed and brought the weapon to Roger's neck and pressed it against him.

He felt the cold steel and jerked backward. She quickly scrambled from beneath his body and pointed the gun at him. She was trembling inside, but her hand was steady. Roger's eyes dilated with something Blair understood—fear.

LUCAS DROVE UP beside Roger's car and jumped out. He ran to the door and started to ring the doorbell, then tried the knob instead. The door was unlocked. He eased it open and stepped in. His heart stopped when he saw Blair holding the gun on Roger.

Her hair was disheveled and her dress was torn. She didn't look afraid, though. She just looked upset.

Roger lay sprawled on the sofa, his clothes askew and his expression fierce. It didn't take a rocket scientist to figure out exactly what had been going on and a new rage filled Lucas. He wanted to beat Roger to within an inch of his life, but Blair held the gun and he knew she had control of the situation.

Roger sat up and straightened his clothes. "Well, Blair, your Prince Charming has arrived," he said sarcastically.

A deep sense of relief swept through her when she saw Lucas. He was here and she had to tell him what had happened. "He attacked me," she managed to say between gritted teeth.

Lucas clenched and unclenched his fists and had to forcibly suppress his anger. "What the hell's the matter with you?" he yelled at Roger.

Roger clambered to his feet. "Stay out of this, Lucas. I don't want to fight with you."

"Someone needs to knock some sense into you and—"

Their words washed over Blair. Something Roger had said kept niggling at her. "What did you mean when you said you put your job in jeopardy for me?"

"Nothing," Roger muttered, and picked his tie up from the floor. Judging by the look on Roger's face, Lucas knew he was guilty as sin.

"Tell her what you did," Lucas said, knowing that now was the time to get everything out in the open.

"I didn't do anything," Roger spat.

"I don't agree," Lucas said matter-of-factly. "You see, I've been talking to the guard who was on duty the night the message was sprayed on Blair's door. He said you were here earlier and disappeared while he was busy with other people."

"He's lying."

"The Easton story doesn't ring true because Blake wasn't arrested until *after* the Raye trial. And that's what Easton was angry about—angry that Sam Logan's kid was going to get away scot-free."

"What are you saying, Lucas?" Blair asked quietly, still gripping the gun, feeling a need for its security.

"I'm saying Roger wrote those messages—on your windshield and on your door."

"Don't believe him, Blair," Roger said vehemently.

Blair stood completely still. She wasn't breathing. She didn't even think her heart was beating, but through the tortured stillness so many things became clear. She stared at Roger, seeing him as he was—a desperate, unstable man. "It's true, isn't it? You knew I'd call you. You knew I depended on you to... God, it's true!"

The shattered look on her face told its own story.

Roger must have known he couldn't lie anymore. "I did it because I love you," he said defiantly.

"Love?" She gave a pitiful laugh. "And what you tried to do to me a while ago, what do you call that?"

"I had a little too much to drink, that's all."

Blair had reached her limit and didn't know if she could take much more. But anger swiftly chased away that sense of fragility.

"How could you do this to me?" she asked in an agonized tone. "You knew the pain I went through over the attack! You knew how scared I was, how frightened I was of my own shadow, and you traded on that—you..." She raised the gun higher, both hands wrapped tightly around it.

"Put the gun down," Roger begged.

"Why did you do it?" she asked coldly.

"Blair."

"Why?" she screamed.

Roger took a step backward. "All right, all right." He held up a hand. "When Raye hurled those words at you in court, I was worried about you. I went to your office and Lucas was there. Your hair was mussed up and you were looking at him the way I'd been waiting for you to look at me. It made me angry, so I wrote those words on your windshield. I knew you'd call. I wanted to show you that I was the only one who really cared for you."

"Cared?" she shrieked, hardly able to believe what she was hearing.

"But you started turning to Lucas more and more. That wasn't fair. I'd invested years in our relationship." Resentment filled his voice. "I just wanted you to turn to *me* again. I've always been there for you and I wanted you to know I wouldn't let anything happen to you. I wouldn't, Blair. I wouldn't."

"Do you even realize how terrified those messages made me?" she asked.

Roger hung his head.

Blair's hand tightened around the butt of the gun, her

finger on the trigger. "You taught me how to use this gun so I could protect myself. You told me to concentrate, not to lose control, not to let my fear show. Well, Roger, I'm concentrating. I'm not losing control and I'm not afraid." She took a step toward him. "But you should be. I can place a bullet right in the center of your heart. You know I can. You've seen me shoot."

Roger lifted his head. "Blair, please."

Lucas watched that glint in her eyes and saw that she was angry and hurt, but he could also see that she was in control. Just as she'd said....

"What's the matter, Roger? Don't you like being afraid?" Blair asked. "That's how I've felt for the past few months. I couldn't sleep. I couldn't concentrate. I just kept waiting for someone to break into my car, my home, and beat me senseless again. And all the time, it was you. You were putting me through a nightmare because you *loved* me."

"Blair, listen..." Roger backed away from the fire in her blue eyes.

"No, I'm not going to listen."

Roger appealed to Lucas. "For God's sake, man, make her stop."

Lucas just shrugged.

Blair knew she wouldn't shoot him. She just wanted him to feel fear the way she had so many times. Slowly she lowered the gun. "I never want to see you again, Roger— never."

"Blair..."

Tim Mayer entered the room at that moment. Lucas quickly explained what had happened. Roger didn't deny it and he didn't try to fight. He was handcuffed and led away.

Blair sank down on the sofa and laid the gun on the coffee table. Lucas sat beside her.

Silence ensued, then Lucas asked, "Are you okay?"

She looked at him, tears sparkling in her eyes. "I'm fine. I'm better than I've been in a long time. That's ironic, isn't it?"

"Yes," he said, remembering the time Easton had confronted her and she'd almost fallen apart. But she wasn't falling apart now. She was fighting back and winning.

"I wasn't afraid, Lucas. I wasn't afraid."

"Yes, I can see that. You actually had Roger shaking in his shoes."

She frowned at him, her eyes dark and troubled. "How could he do that to me?"

"He's sick and needs help," was the only answer he could give her.

"Part of this is my fault," she murmured sadly.

"What?"

"He was right. I always called him and I leaned on him when I was afraid and he—" She thrust both hands through her hair and held her head. "No, I won't do this," she said with renewed strength. "I'm not taking the blame for other people's actions—not Roger's, not Blake's or my parents'. From now on I'm responsible for my own actions and no one else's." She inhaled deeply, then exhaled a long, shuddering breath.

Lucas could see that something was happening to her. Fear and guilt were vanquished. Right before his eyes, he saw her shake off sixteen years of horror and pain.

In a voice that shook only a little, she admitted what Lucas already knew. "I feel like my emotions have been locked away and suddenly they're free and I can feel again. I can live again. The terrible things are finally over. They're over."

Lucas knew that what he'd wanted for tonight wasn't going to happen. Blair wasn't ready. She was just finding herself and she wasn't even sure what *she* wanted.

Blair felt as if she'd been on a Ferris wheel, going round and round until she was dizzy with all the heartache, but now she'd stepped off that merciless ride and she was standing alone and reveling in feeling.

She glanced at Lucas and saw his worried expression and she remembered Jim and realized she hadn't even offered her condolences. "I'm sorry about Jim. With everything that was happening, I forgot to ask about Jim's wife. How is she?"

"She's coping. Her parents are here. That helps. And she said to thank you for the food and the flowers."

Blair nodded. She didn't even ask about his involvement with Stacey. There was no need. Lucas would always be there for his friends.

She smoothed a wrinkle on her dress. She'd waited all night for Lucas and now that he was here she didn't know what to say. So she decided to tell him the simple truth. "I went out and bought this dress." She lifted the broken strap. "Now it's ruined—like the evening. I had such big plans for us."

"Me, too," he said quietly.

Her eyes met his. "But now things are…different."

"Yes, they're different." They didn't have to say anything else; both knew they had come to an impasse in their relationship. Blair needed time. Lucas needed to understand—and he was trying.

Blair tried to figure out these new feelings she'd begun to experience. "I've been leaning and depending on you like I'd been leaning and depending on Roger. I can't do that anymore. I have to stand on my own and now I can. I have to make it on my own—without guns, without fear, without help."

That didn't diminish what she felt for Lucas. It was as real as anything she'd ever felt. But was it just the result of circumstances they'd found themselves in or was it something more? She didn't know, but she had to find out. And the only way to do that was to… Oh God, did she have the strength to walk away from Lucas?

Sensing her turmoil, he gently tucked her hair behind her ear. "I understand."

She knew he would. That was the kind of man he was.

"I'm sorry if I hurt you that night you told me about Ava's secret." Lucas had to tell her that. He wanted her to know he'd been wrong.

She shook her head. "I should have come to you immediately and—"

"Don't make excuses for my behavior. I have this fault of believing that people in my life should be perfect. But, hell, *I'm* not perfect, so what gives me the right to judge others?"

He *was* perfect, but she wouldn't tell him that. She loved him, but she wouldn't tell him that, either. The time wasn't right and she began to wonder if it ever would be.

"Where do we go from here?" she asked.

Lucas stood up and felt a pain in his chest. "Well, for starters, I'm taking you to your parents' house—just in case Roger makes bail."

She also stood. "My parents are accompanying Blake to London. They want me to go, too."

He took a quick breath. "You should," he said. "Get away from Houston and everything that's happened. It'll do you good."

*Will it?*

As soon as he said the words, he wanted to take them back. But he didn't. Because he wanted what was best for her.

The drive to the Logan mansion was made in silence. Lucas killed the engine in the driveway and turned to her. He didn't know what to say. All he felt was his heart breaking.

"Thank you," she said quietly. "Thanks for all you've done for me and my family."

He tried to swallow the blockage in his throat. "Have a good time in London and enjoy yourself."

*I don't think I can without you.*

"I'll try," was what she said.

"Lucas?"

"Hmm?"

She leaned over and placed her lips gently against his. The moment she touched him, the fire of their emotions took over. He kissed her deeply and for a moment they were lost in each other. Finally he rested his forehead against hers.

*Please don't go,* he wanted to say but didn't. He couldn't. Her emotions were in turmoil and if they were meant to be together, she'd find her way back to him. She slowly got out. Lucas waited until she'd entered the house, then drove away. Love hurt like hell, he decided. Jacob had never told him that. Hell, Jacob didn't *have* to tell him that. He knew. That was why he'd avoided it for so many years. But he also knew, finally, what real love was all about. It was letting go, thinking of the other person more than you thought of yourself, and feeling a selflessness that burned all the way to your heart.

FALL ARRIVED with cooler temperatures, football games and the holidays. Lucas resigned from Harris and Harris. Clive and George talked and talked, trying to get him to change his mind. They raised his salary and his bonus, but still Lucas refused to stay. It wasn't about money. That restlessness he'd felt in the spring was back, and he now realized what it was. Not restlessness. Emptiness. Blair had filled it over the summer and with her gone, it was worse than ever. He had to get away. He had to get out of Houston.

Derek, Frank and Theo came to see him. They said they'd talked to Sam, and the offer was still on the table. Lucas declined. He wasn't making any career decisions in his present mood. He had to clear his head. He had to have peace and quiet. And he knew exactly where to find that.

He packed his clothes and headed off to see Jacob, Miranda and the kids.

Lucas hadn't talked to Blair, but Tim Mayer called and said Blair wouldn't press charges against Roger if he got psychiatric help. That sounded just like her. Compassionate. He knew, too, that she wanted to put all the heartache behind her. Lucas just hoped she didn't leave him behind, as well.

Over the next few weeks, Lucas was up before daylight helping Jacob and the ranch hands. He hauled hay to feed cattle, fixed fence, cleared brush and did every other menial ranch chore known to man. He worked until his hands were callused and his muscles ached.

And Jacob laughed at him. Just like when they were kids, teasing and joking companionably. Jacob had always worked with his muscles and Lucas with his mind. Now Lucas understood why Jacob needed to work hard. It exhausted the body as well as the mind. And Lucas needed that, too. As he needed Jacob and his family.

He and Jacob talked a lot. They talked about Roger; Jacob said that after Roger's wife left him and took their kids to Colorado, Roger hadn't been the same. But he didn't understand how Roger could do something like that to Blair. Lucas didn't, either, and as always his thoughts returned to her.

The times he spent with the kids were his favorite. He wrestled, played ball and rode horses with the boys. He dressed dolls and drank tea from tiny cups with two-and-a-half-year-old Lizzie and he rocked nine-month-old Gracie to sleep when she was fussy. There was so much warmth and love in Jacob's house that he never wanted to leave.

Except when he thought about Blair.

He wondered what she was doing. Was she enjoying herself? Had she finally found that elusive happiness? There were doubts in his mind and he knew why. He wanted her to find that happiness with him. Now all he could do was wait.

THANKSGIVING WAS a big affair in the Culver house. Miranda's whole family came, plus Blackhawk and Maria, the ranch foreman and his wife. Even Howard showed up. The house smelled of pumpkin, cinnamon and apples. Miranda had worked hard to make the day special; Lucas knew these times meant a lot to her. The kids were on their best behavior. Jacob carved the big turkey and everyone was absorbed in conversation.

But Lucas was absorbed in his memories of Blair.

That afternoon Howard told him that he'd heard from Ava, and everyone was having a good time, especially Blair and Blake. Ava said they were like kids again— laughing and plotting with their dark heads together. He added that Blake even got Blair to dance around a fountain in a town square.

That vision stayed with Lucas the rest of the day. Blair was happy. She was dancing—without him.

Later that evening, after everyone had left, Lucas sat in a rocker holding Gracie in one arm and Lizzie in the other. The three boys hovered around his chair and Bandit, now an elderly dog, lay at Jacob's feet. Jacob and Miranda sat on the sofa—close together. Jacob's arm was around her shoulder and he played idly with her hair. Miranda's hand gently caressed Jacob's thigh. Lucas noticed Jacob catching her hand with that "later" look in his eyes. Lucas suddenly recognized that he wanted the same closeness, the same love that Jacob and Miranda shared. He was through nursing his wounded pride. He knew what he had to do.

"Why you look so sad, Uncle Lucas?" six-year-old Jake asked.

"Because he has a broken heart." Jacob smiled at his brother.

"Oh, does it hurt?" five-year-old Daniel wanted to know.

Before Lucas could answer, four-year-old Ben jumped up. "I know, I know," he shouted and ran into the kitchen. They could hear him rummaging in drawers.

"One of us should go see what he's doing," Miranda said to Jacob.

"Let him surprise us," was Jacob's response.

Bandit grunted, got lazily to his feet and trotted into the kitchen. Clearly he was making sure that Ben was all right.

Jacob laughed. "See, we don't have to worry. Bandit's on duty."

In a moment, Ben and Bandit were back. Ben handed Lucas a tube of glue. "Daddy fixes all my broken toys with that. It fixes *everything*."

As Lucas took the glue, he had to suppress a burst of laughter—as did Jacob and Miranda.

"Glue can't fix hearts," little Jake told him indignantly.

"Why not?" Ben demanded.

Jacob reached out and pulled Ben onto his lap. "Son, I was just teasing your uncle. He's fine—just fine. Aren't you?" Jacob glanced at Lucas.

Lucas shot Jacob a sneaky glance, wanting to pay him back, but he knew it would only confuse Ben more. "I'm fine, Ben," he said with a genuine smile.

"Luv yu, Unk 'ucas," Lizzie murmured sleepily against him, and Lucas felt his heart swell with so much love, so much happiness—but it wasn't complete. Not yet.

"Time for baths and bed," Miranda said, getting to her feet.

"Ah, Momma," Jake complained.

"Son," was all Jacob had to say and Jake quickly acquiesced. The three boys gave Lucas and Jacob quick kisses and dashed up the stairs. Bandit followed slowly.

"I'll bring the girls," Jacob said.

Miranda reached down to kiss him. "And don't forget yourself," she murmured wickedly.

Jacob cupped her face and kissed her, too. "You don't have to worry about that."

"You, Jacob Culver, I never worry about," Miranda said. She turned to Lucas and kissed the top of his head. "Good night, Lucas."

Lucas smiled at her. She wore a white cashmere sweater and a long maroon print skirt that whispered around her ankles. She was beautiful—inside and out. "Thanks for the wonderful day," he said. "I'm sorry I was such lousy company."

"And I'm sorry I couldn't give you what you really wanted," she replied, then added, "Don't let your Culver pride keep you from going after what you want."

"She's the one who left," Lucas said more sharply than he'd intended, and he immediately apologized. "I'm sorry, that came out wrong." He understood that Blair had needed time, but he'd been hoping for a postcard, a phone call—something. As each day passed, the gulf between them seemed to grow.

Miranda kissed each of her daughters and gazed into Lucas's hurt eyes. "You Culver men are so stubborn." She kissed his cheek and hurried after her sons.

"She's right," Jacob said.

"I know," Lucas admitted. "I'm through fighting it. I'm leaving in the morning." He'd given Blair time and now he had to see her. He couldn't wait any longer.

"Going to see Blair?"

"Yes."

"Took you long enough."

BLAIR FELT renewed in spirit, body and soul. She was thoroughly enjoying this time with Blake and her parents. The nightmare was finally over. They'd all made mistakes and learned from them. Now they were free—free to live again.

But she missed Lucas.

They stayed in a small hotel not far from Blake's flat. Blake showed them where he worked and lived. Blake and Sam were talking, getting to know each other. Ava didn't interfere and Blair was proud of her for that. While Blake and Sam spent their days together, Ava and Blair went to the theater and the ballet. They visited Buckingham Palace and saw the changing of the guard. They toured castles and all the quaint little places that were steeped in history and tradition.

But she missed Lucas.

Blair found the food atrocious—except for the many Indian restaurants—and the people friendly and reserved, but the city was ageless. The centuries had left their mark and it was awe-inspiring to gaze at the achievements of generations past.

But she missed Lucas.

He was present in every minute of her day, and she looked for him everywhere. She'd see a tall man with dark hair and think it was him. She'd hear a manly laugh and she'd think of him. She'd see a couple embracing and she'd think of him.

She tried to figure out what she was feeling, but she knew. She'd known all along. She loved him, and it wasn't because of circumstance or the trial or what she'd been through. Her feelings were true and they came straight from the heart. It was clear to her now. Even though she missed Lucas, she didn't regret these weeks away. She'd needed this distance from her real life. But now all she needed was Lucas.

She bought a ticket home and no one tried to dissuade her. She was flying back to Lucas. She had to tell him how she felt—had felt for a long time—and she hoped he wanted to hear what she had to say.

She knew all the rumors about Lucas and other women, and the thought crossed her mind that he could be dating someone else by now. But in her heart she knew that he wasn't. She didn't know where she got such confidence, but she knew Lucas. He believed in truth and honesty, and what they had shared was special. That was the truth.

*I'm coming home, Lucas.*

## CHAPTER NINETEEN

THE FIRST THING Lucas did when he got to Houston was buy a ticket to London, but the flight wasn't until the next day, so he collected his mail and went over to his house. Joan had been watching things while he was away. When Lucas resigned from Harris and Harris, Joan retired to stay home with her family. She was a good friend, and Lucas was going to miss her.

Lucas sorted through his mail. He had a letter from Stacey; she and the kids were in Arizona with her family, and she said they were planning to stay. She thanked Lucas for his help and support.

Restless, he started to check his messages, then didn't bother. He didn't want to talk to anyone but Blair. He slipped on a pair of jogging pants and went for a run. The exhaustion didn't help; he still wanted to see Blair. He wanted to see her so badly he ached. Tomorrow seemed so far away.

He took a shower and plopped down on the sofa. Again he noticed the blinking red light on his answering machine and ignored it. Then he thought that one of those calls was probably from Jacob or Miranda, ensuring that he'd made it home okay. They'd put up with his shifting moods for weeks, so the least he could do was call them back.

He got up and pressed the button. A barrage of messages came on, from friends and colleagues. He lay back on the sofa listening, but the last message had him sitting up straight. He knew that voice.

"Lucas, it's Blair—just wanted to let you know I'm back."

Jumping up, he listened for more, but that was it. He grabbed the phone and dialed her apartment—no answer. He called the Logan house. The maid said they were still in London and she hadn't heard from Blair.

"Where are you, Blair?" he asked out loud. "Where are you?"

The room didn't answer.

He changed quickly into jeans, a long-sleeved green shirt and put on his leather jacket. He didn't know where she was, but he was determined to find her. He got into his vehicle, still reflecting. She wasn't at her apartment or at her parents'. So where could she be?

God, Blair, why didn't you say something more—anything? Okay. He calmed down. He could find her. He just had to think. If she wasn't at the two most obvious places, where could she be? Where— Of course! His hand hit the steering wheel. The farm—her favorite place. He backed out of the driveway and headed for the 610 Loop.

Soon he was turning off the freeway onto country roads, relying on memory. Then he found the entrance and his heart started to beat a little faster. When he saw the farmhouse, he drove around back and there was her car. He smiled and felt a sense of relief unlike any he'd ever felt before. *She was here.* Thank God, she was here.

As he opened the back door, he heard classical music. He walked through the kitchen and stopped abruptly when he saw her. She wore black stretch pants and a white long-sleeved sweater. Her hair was longer and fell disheveled to her shoulders. A fire roared in the fireplace, and a quilt and a pillow lay on the floor in front of it.

In a second, he took all of this in, but his eyes were riveted on her. She danced around the living room in sure, graceful movements, her feet bare. Her face was enraptured and his heart pounded so fast he could barely breathe.

She was so beautiful—so everything he wanted in a woman.

She pirouetted and came to a complete stop when she saw him. With a hand to her chest, she breathed, "Lucas."

Blair had waited weeks for this moment, and now that Lucas was here all she could do was stare at him. He looked wonderful. His dark hair curled into the collar of his leather jacket and his jeans molded his long legs, but her eyes were on his face and his smoldering eyes. God, she loved him. How could she ever have thought it was anything else?

Lucas stepped farther into the room and held out his hand. "Can I have this dance?" he asked in a low vibrant voice that made her senses spin wildly.

Blair placed her hand in his and he drew her close, wrapping his other arm around her waist. Cheek to cheek, heart to heart, they moved slowly around the room. The music ended, but they didn't notice. They kept dancing.

Blair thought if she died at this moment, she would die a happy woman. She was in Lucas's arms. That was all she wanted. She lost herself in the moment, in him.

She felt light as a feather in his arms and he breathed in the fragrant scent of her hair and silky skin. He wondered if she knew how much he wanted her—how much....

Her fingers caressed the hair at his neck, beneath the collar of his jacket. When he felt her touch, his movements became slower and slower until they were both standing still.

He gazed into her eyes. "If I don't kiss you soon, I'm going to go out of my mind."

She smiled, stood on tiptoe and met his lips with an urgency that took his breath away. His hands tangled in her silky hair as his mouth opened over hers in a sensuous rhapsody. They both took and gave...until it wasn't enough.

Lucas groaned and rained kisses from her mouth to the hollow of her neck. "God, Blair, I love you," he whispered. "I love you so much it's killing me."

She drew back, wondering if she'd heard him correctly, but she knew she had. There was no mistaking those words.

Her eyes sparkled like diamonds. "I love you, too," she answered in a shaky voice. "That's why I came back. I couldn't stand to be without you another day."

He let out a long breath, not even realizing he'd been holding it in. "I want you so much, but I know that you—"

She knew what he was going to say and she silenced him by placing her finger over his lips. She took his hand, leading him to the rug by the fire. She knelt and pulled him down beside her and slipped his leather jacket off his shoulders. Her eyes were like blue embers and all he could see in them was himself.

She pulled the white sweater over her head and unsnapped her bra in one easy movement. Lucas caught his breath at her beauty and reached out to touch her. He softly kissed one breast, then the other. The fire blazed behind them, but it had nothing to do with the heat that consumed them. In a matter of minutes, their clothes became a hindrance they quickly disposed of. As Lucas urged her down, the firelight made her skin warm and golden, and he couldn't stop touching her.

Blair sighed softly as his hands traveled from her breast to her stomach and lower. His hands were gentle and tantalizing and she wanted more. She pulled his head back to her mouth, needing that sustenance now.

As his mouth took hers, he parted her legs with his knee. He shifted his weight to accommodate her. She felt his arousal against her thigh; it was strong and sure and she wanted him inside her. She wanted to feel everything she knew he could make her feel.

"Lucas," she moaned, and her hands moved over the hard muscles of his chest, reveling in the dark hair that curled to his flat stomach. Tentatively her hands sank lower, and at her touch Lucas groaned. He had waited so long for her and he didn't know if he could hold back any longer.

"Lucas," she moaned again. That sound told him so many things, and he knew the moment was right. He entered her slow and easy. She felt that first stab of discomfort, then so many other pleasurable emotions burst through....

"Lucas, Lucas, Lucas!" she cried out.

Lucas moved inside her with a need that equaled her own and soon joy, pleasure and unbelievable ecstasy welded their bodies into one. The fire flickered around them, and they lay entwined in the afterglow.

Lucas kissed her softly, easing his weight from her. "Okay?" he asked.

She smiled and couldn't seem to stop smiling. With his gentleness, he'd made the experience more than she'd ever dreamed about—just as she'd known he would. And she loved him for it. "What do you think, Counselor?"

He buried his face in the sweet hollow of her neck. "I love you more than I've ever loved anyone in my life and I'm so glad you came home. I couldn't stand it another day."

"Me, neither." She kissed the side of his face. "I was afraid we'd never get to this point. So many other things were standing in the way."

He raised his head. "But not anymore."

"Not anymore," she agreed.

He caressed her arm. "We probably need to talk."

She shook her head. "Not tonight. Tonight is for loving."

"But I need to tell you something."

She took a quick breath and asked, "What?" She felt a

moment of trepidation, but it quickly vanished. She sensed that Lucas wanted her to know everything about him—but she already did. However, she was unprepared for the words that came out of his mouth.

"I'm a jealous man."

Her eyes widened in amusement.

"I never realized it before I met you, but I'm jealous of every man who gets near you—even Blake. That's why I reacted so strongly when you told me about Ava's secret. I was hurt that I wasn't the most important man in your life."

"Oh, Lucas," she cried, entwining her legs with his and running her hand over the hard planes of his chest. "It wasn't about my love for you. It was—"

"You don't have to explain." He caught her hand and kissed her fingers. "I understand now."

She gazed into his dark eyes, knowing that he did and loving him so much her heart ached. "You don't have any reason to be jealous. For me, other men don't exist. I love you and only you." As she said the words, her lips met his in a long, lingering kiss.

Lucas pulled her on top of him, their naked skin fusing warm and invitingly in all the right places. Blair sighed. "Since we're on the subject. I'm jealous, too—jealous of all those other women before me."

Lucas groaned and wished he could change the past. But the past had shaped him into the man he was today and he knew Blair wouldn't want him any other way.

He smoothed her hair away from her face. "I promise you one thing. You are the last—for now and forever. You have my heart, my body...and my soul. That's something I never gave to another woman."

"Oh, Lucas." They kissed passionately, love and need sizzling brightly through their veins. Blair felt his hardness against her and she drew back, a smile of wonder on her face.

"Shameful, isn't it?" He laughed, and urged her onto her back. "But I want you again...and again...and again...."

Some time later, Lucas drew the blanket over them, tucked Blair into his side and wrapped a leg around hers. Two spirits, two souls, merged as one, and the trauma of the past faded into the promise of the future.

# EPILOGUE

*One year later*

"LUCAS," the bloodcurdling cry echoed down the hospital corridors.

The hair on Lucas's arms stood up, and the hand Blair was holding had gone numb. With his free hand, he used a towel to blot the sweat from her forehead. "Breathe, honey. Remember the breathing exercises."

Blair panted and tried to relax, but the pain was too severe—too excruciating. "I can't do this, Lucas. I can't. I don't know anything about babies. What were we thinking?"

Lucas lost his voice for a moment. The labor was long, and he couldn't stand to see her like this, in so much pain, and he didn't think he could take much more. How did Jacob do this five times? More to the point—how did Miranda?

"Mrs. Culver, it's easy," the nurse said. "You just love babies. That's all you have to do. And the pain will ease up as soon as the medication takes effect."

"Deep breaths," Lucas encouraged, and saw that she was beginning to relax. The medicine was helping. Thank God.

"We have to choose names," Blair said between breaths. "Our babies are going to be here any minute." They knew they were having twins—it had been a shock to both of them. They hadn't wanted to know the sex of the babies, so they didn't have firm decisions on names.

"Let's just get them here first, because at the moment my mind is one big mess," Lucas said.

Blair glanced at him and saw his tousled hair and worried expression. He wore a T-shirt and jeans and nothing else. He'd thrown on clothes at the first contraction and had practically flown them to the hospital. Luckily they lived in Lucas's house, which wasn't far away. They were in the process of remodeling the farmhouse, which Uncle Howard and Ava had given them as a wedding present. They had decided to raise their family in sunshine, fresh air and happiness.

"Are you all right?" Blair asked.

"No," Lucas admitted honestly. "But I will be as soon as we bring these babies into the world."

"We're going to be parents, Lucas. *Parents.* I'm not ready. Oh-oh-oh." She bit down on her lip as a sharp contraction gripped her.

"Deep breaths," he coached.

"Okay, okay." She tried to control her breathing and noticed Lucas checking his watch.

She knew he was waiting for Jacob. They'd called Jacob and Miranda as soon as they got to the hospital, but their place was so far away and they had five children. Still, Jacob had been there for every momentous event in Lucas's life, and Lucas wanted him here when his babies were born.

"He'll come," she breathed between gasps. "He'll make it."

Lucas didn't have to ask who she was talking about. He knew. Sometimes they could read each other's minds. "It's one in the morning and I told him just to wait until later when everyone's awake."

"He'll be here," she said, knowing the bond that Lucas and Jacob shared. Nothing was going to keep Jacob away.

She knew exactly how Lucas felt; she wished, too, that Blake could be here.

Reading her mind this time, he said, "Honey, he's in California. He said he'd get here as soon as he could, and your parents are on the way."

"I know," she said weakly. "These babies would have to come early just to confuse everyone." She breathed quick, short breaths. "I'm so proud of Blake and everything he's done with his life, but I thought once he decided to come back to the States we'd see more of him."

"Yeah, I'm proud of him, too. He's doing what he has to do, and I admire him for that," Lucas said, wiping sweat from her forehead.

Blake now worked for a government agency that was fighting drugs in schools. Blake traveled all over the country talking to kids, telling them his story, trying to keep other teenagers from making the mistakes he had.

She touched his face and tried to smile, but the pain seized her. She took a long breath and said, "I'm proud of you, too."

He kissed her hand. It had taken him a while to figure out what he wanted to do with his life. At first he just wanted to spend every moment with Blair, and he had. They'd talked, shared, loved, but he'd known he'd have to make some decisions. Then Sam retired and it helped Lucas make up his mind. He hammered out a deal, and Logan and Associates was now Logan, Culver and Associates. He was able to choose his cases and worked when he wanted to. In the near future, he knew that wasn't going to be very much.

"Oh, God," Blair screamed as her body convulsed with pain.

The nurse checked her. "It's not going to be long now. I'll get the doctor."

"Lucas," Blair gasped. "I can't do this. I can't..."

"Yes, you can." He kissed her trembling lips. "Concentrate and..."

The doctor walked in and examined her. "Okay, Blair, it's showtime," he said. "I want you to push, and push hard."

Blair screamed, pushed and strained until she was exhausted. Lucas felt every pain and every agonizing breath.

"I see a head," the doctor said.

Blair let out another bloodcurdling scream, and Lucas leaned over as their son slipped into the doctor's hands. "Oh my God, Blair, it's a boy. It's a boy." He was bloody, wet, red and wrinkled, but Lucas thought it was the most beautiful sight he'd ever seen.

Lucas took their son from the doctor and laid him in Blair's arms. "Oh, Lucas, he's beautiful—so beautiful," she whispered tiredly. She stared at the tiny miracle, touching his legs, arms, stomach and dark hair. Her breath lodged in her throat and tears welled in her eyes, and she knew it was worth all the agony, all the—

"Oh-oh-oh," she cried as her body jerked in pain.

The nurse immediately took the baby and Lucas groaned as he prepared himself to do this again.

A strong contraction hit Blair and she cried out, gripping Lucas's hand. "Lucas!" she screamed as the pain overtook her. In three minutes flat, their daughter arrived. Lucas placed her in Blair's arms and the nurse brought back their son. Blair held both babies, tired and spent, but it would be a moment neither she nor Lucas would ever forget.

Both babies suckled, which felt strange to Blair, but so right and real at the same time. The nurse took them away to clean and dress them. Blair felt deprived and tears sprang to her eyes again.

Lucas crawled in beside her and put his arms around her. "Lucas," she murmured in wonder. "We have two babies—a boy and a girl. They're so beautiful."

"I know." He kissed her cheek.

Tears spilled from her eyes. "Do you know how much I love you?"

"Do you want me to count the ways?" He grinned.

"No, I want you to kiss me."

His lips met hers tenderly. Just then, the nurse brought their babies back. One was wrapped in a pink blanket and a pink cap, the other in blue.

The nurse arranged the boy in Blair's arms and the girl in Lucas's. For a moment all they could do was gaze at the miracles they'd created. Their babies had dark hair and dark blue eyes.

"I hope they have your eyes," Blair said.

"No way," Lucas disagreed. "I want them to have their momma's gorgeous eyes."

"We'll see," Blair said smugly, knowing the odds were in her favor. "Now we have to give them names. What are we going to call them?"

Lucas thought for a minute, mulling over the names they had talked about. "Since Jacob took all the names on my side of the family, how about Samuel Lucas and Ava Olivia?"

Blair smiled. "That's perfect." Olivia was her grandmother's name and she knew her parents would be pleased.

Lucas kissed the soft cheek of his new daughter. "She'll be strong, independent and feisty like her mom, and we'll probably wind up calling her Livvy." The baby squirmed and threw her fist out in response.

"See, she likes it." Lucas grinned.

Blair touched the face of her son. "We'll call him Luke, and he'll be a happy, well-adjusted young man with integrity and honor like his father."

The nurse returned. "The waiting room is filling up," she said. "There's a handsome man who looks a lot like you." She smiled at Lucas. "He has a beautiful wife and five well-behaved children. He just wanted me to let you know they were here."

"Oh, honey, Jacob's brought the family. I can't wait for him to see these two."

She leaned over, careful not to wake their son, and kissed her husband. "I told you."

"And there's a young man out there who bears a striking resemblance to you." The nurse smiled again, this time at Blair. "Plus two very anxious parents."

"Blake made it." Blair beamed.

"Yeah," Lucas murmured, drowning in the blue of her eyes. "Now everything's perfect—just perfect."

*Two years later*

TWO CHILDREN, a boy and a girl, played on a swing set their father had just installed under a big oak tree. The little girl eyed the big slide and decided to take a chance. She gingerly climbed the ladder, then slid down. She hit the ground with a thud and started to cry. The little boy ran to her and gave her a hug, but she pushed him away saying, "Me not hurt. Me not hurt."

She then marched back to the ladder, determined to try the slide again. The little boy was waiting at the bottom and he caught her as she came down. She didn't want his help and she hit him. He hit her back, and they tumbled onto the grass fighting. Suddenly the little girl kissed the little boy; he ran away rubbing his face in disgust. The little girl chased after him laughing.

Blair watched her children from the kitchen window and smiled. Two strong arms slid around her waist and pulled her against a hard masculine body. Lucas kissed the scented hollow of her neck and asked, "What're you doing?"

"Watching our children," she replied, loving the way his body fit so perfectly against hers.

"And what are they doing?" he asked, glancing out the window.

Blair told him about the incident on the slide and she

laughed. "Livvy's just like you said she'd be—strong, independent and feisty. Luke is strong-willed, dedicated and loyal—just like you. They are so different from Blake and me at that age."

He nuzzled her neck. "Why do you say that?"

She leaned back against him. "If I cried, Blake cried, too. If I pushed him, he never pushed back. Luke is very protective of Livvy, but he doesn't let her take advantage. Luke gives as well as he gets. They both have such strong personalities. I just can't figure out who's the stronger twin."

"Let's not do that, honey," Lucas said softly. "Let's not put labels on them."

"It's hard," she admitted, unable to believe that she was doing exactly what her parents had done to her and Blake. She was comparing her children. Her mother had said she wouldn't understand until she had children of her own. Ava was right; Blair understood now. She wanted Luke to be everything Lucas wanted him to be and she shouldn't do that. She *wouldn't* do that. Luckily, she had Lucas to help her. She and Lucas would not make the mistakes her parents had made. His next words proved it.

"We'll just let them be themselves without control or manipulation. We won't deride or belittle them, we'll just praise and love them—just like my father did…me."

That last word came out on a long sigh and Blair turned in the circle of his arms, her eyes gazing into his with so much love that for a moment all they could do was stare at each other. She gently touched his face. "I'm so happy you finally got through all the bad things about your father."

"Yeah." He kissed her hand. "I carried around that garbage for so long and I let it control my life, but not anymore. My dad was a good father. I can see that now. I just let what happened to him cloud my judgment."

Blair played with a button on his shirt. "Do you remember the first time we came here and you talked about your father?"

"Yes."

"You said you were just like him and you couldn't stay interested in one woman for any length of time." She tilted her head to one side. "It's been over three years now. Has your interest cooled, Counselor?"

He grinned. "You sleep with me every night. What do you think?"

"I think…" Lucas covered her lips with his, ending conversation for several pleasurable minutes. He slipped his arms around her waist and held her tight against him. "Lucas," she whispered into his mouth. "We've got company coming."

"I know," he groaned.

It was the twins' second birthday and they were having a big barbecue, Texas-style, to celebrate. The Culver and Logan families were all coming, and it was going to be a big family day in their home. The farmhouse had now been completely renovated. They'd tried to retain some of the old charm while blending in the new. The result was warm and spacious with a homey atmosphere—just the way they wanted it.

"I can't wait to meet Blake's girlfriend," she murmured. "I'm so glad he's found someone."

"Me, too."

Life was better than Blair had ever thought possible. Blake was happy, while she had found true happiness with the man of her dreams. She was a wife and mother first, but slowly, with Lucas's urging, she'd gone back to work. She worked part-time with her husband, which she thoroughly enjoyed.

Lucas trailed kisses from her mouth to her neck and they slowly began to dance around the kitchen, locked in each other's arms.

Lucas was about to kiss her again when a tiny voice asked from the doorway, "Whatcha doing?"

Lucas and Blair turned to stare at their children. Today

they wore jeans and thick white sweatshirts. It was forty degrees outside, and Blair had a hard time making them keep their jackets on. Olivia's hair was dark like her mother's and in pigtails. Luke's was short. Two sets of dark Culver eyes gazed back at them.

"We're dancing, son," Lucas answered brightly.

Livvy ran and wedged herself between Blair and Lucas, holding her arms up to Lucas. "Me wanna dance. Me wanna dance, Daddy."

Lucas's heart stopped every time he heard that word and he immediately swung her high in his arms. He began to spin her around the room, girlish giggles filling the air.

Blair scooped up her son and began to dance with him. He buried his face in her neck and Blair's heart swelled with motherly love.

Lucas moved close to them and wrapped his free arm around Blair and Luke.

She smiled into his eyes, loving the way his hair had turned gray at the temples, but then she loved everything about this man of hers. She was so happy, so fulfilled, so in love. She had lived in a vacuum of fear for sixteen years, and now...now... Tears stung the back of her eyes.

Lucas saw the tears gathering. "Honey?"

"I was just thinking how happy you've made me."

He grinned. "You were right."

"About what?"

"The reason I hadn't gotten married before was that I'd never fallen in love." His eyes darkened. "I love you with every breath I take." As he said the words, he softly kissed her lips.

Luke and Livvy began to squirm and giggle, and Lucas whirled them around. Love and laughter echoed throughout the Culver house—as it was meant to.

*For now and for always.*

## CREATURE COMFORT

# A heartwarming new series by
# Carolyn McSparren

**Creature Comfort, the largest veterinary clinic in Tennessee, treats animals of all sizes—horses and cattle as well as family pets. Meet the patients—and their owners. And share the laughter and the tears with the men and women who love and care for all creatures great and small.**

#996 THE MONEY MAN
(July 2001)

#1011 THE PAYBACK MAN
(September 2001)

*Look for these Harlequin Superromance titles coming soon to your favorite retail outlet.*

## HARLEQUIN®
*Makes any time special* ®

If you enjoyed what you just read,
then we've got an offer you can't resist!

# Take 2 bestselling love stories FREE!

# Plus get a FREE surprise gift!

# *Harlequin invites you to walk down the aisle...*

To honor our year long celebration of weddings, we are offering an exciting opportunity for you to own the Harlequin Bride Doll. Handcrafted in fine bisque porcelain, the wedding doll is dressed for her wedding day in a cream satin gown accented by lace trim. She carries an exquisite traditional bridal bouquet and wears a cathedral-length dotted Swiss veil. Embroidered flowers cascade down her lace overskirt to the scalloped hemline; underneath all is a multi-layered crinoline.

Join us in our celebration of weddings by sending away for your own Harlequin Bride Doll. This doll regularly retails for $74.95 U.S./approx. $108.68 CDN. One doll per household. Requests must be received no later than December 31, 2001. Offer good while quantities of gifts last. Please allow 6-8 weeks for delivery. Offer good in the U.S. and Canada only. Become part of this exciting offer!

**Simply complete the order form and mail to:**
**"A Walk Down the Aisle"**

| IN U.S.A | IN CANADA |
|---|---|
| P.O. Box 9057 | P.O. Box 622 |
| 3010 Walden Ave. | Fort Erie, Ontario |
| Buffalo, NY 14269-9057 | L2A 5X3 |

**Enclosed are eight (8) proofs of purchase found in the last pages of every specially marked Harlequin series book and $3.75 check or money order (for postage and handling). Please send my Harlequin Bride Doll to:**

Name (PLEASE PRINT)
_____

Address _____ Apt. # _____

City _____ State/Prov. _____ Zip/Postal Code _____

Account # (if applicable) _____ **097 KIK DAEW**

**HARLEQUIN®**
*Makes any time special* ®

*A Walk Down the Aisle*
*Free Bride Doll Offer*
*One Proof-of-Purchase*

Visit us at www.eHarlequin.com

PHWDAPOPR2